STORK RAVING MAD

A Meg Langslow Mystery

Donna Andrews

St. Martin's Paperbacks

This is a work of fiction. All of the characters, organizations, and events portrayed in this novel are either products of the author's imagination or are used fictitiously.

STORK RAVING MAD

For information address St. Martin's Press, 175 Fifth Avenue, New York, NY 10010.

ISBN: 978-0-312-53368-7

Printed in the United States of America

Minotaur hardcover edition / August 2010
St. Martin's Paperbacks edition / July 2011

St. Martin's Paperbacks are published by St. Martin's Press, 175 Fifth Avenue, New York, NY 10010.

10 9 8 7 6 5 4 3 2 1

NO NEST FOR THE WICKET

"Fun, lively, charming."   *—Publishers Weekly*

"Andrews strikes just the right balance between comedy and suspense to keep the reader laughing and on the edge of one's seat . . . Fans of this series will no doubt enjoy this installment, while new readers . . . will be headed to the bookstore for the earlier books."
   —Romantic Times BOOKreviews
   (4 stars)

"Any day when I start reading about Meg is cause for delight. Ending the book makes me yearn for more than one per year. Hint."   *—Deadly Pleasures*

"As usual, Andrews is a reliable source for those who like their murder with plenty of mayhem."
   —Kirkus Reviews

"Andrews's talent for the lovably loony makes this series a winner; to miss it would be a cardinal sin."
   —Richmond Times-Dispatch

OWLS WELL THAT ENDS WELL

"A loony, utterly delightful affair."   *—Booklist*

"It's a hoot . . . a supporting cast of endearingly eccentric characters, perfectly pitched dialogue and a fine sense of humor make this a treat."*—Publishers Weekly*

"Death by yard sale epitomizes the 'everyday people' humor that Andrews does so well . . . for readers who prefer their mysteries light . . . Andrews may be the next best thing to Janet Evanovich."

—*Rocky Mountain News*

"Andrews delivers another wonderfully comic story. . . . This is a fun read, as are all the books in the series. Andrews playfully creates laughable, wacky scenes that are the backdrop for her criminally devious plot. Settle back, dear reader, and enjoy another visit to Meg's anything-but-ordinary world."

—*Romantic Times*
(starred review)

WE'LL ALWAYS HAVE PARROTS

"Laughter, more laughter, we need laughter, so Donna Andrews is giving us *We'll Always Have Parrots* . . . to help us survive February."   —*Washington Times*

"Perfectly showcases Donna Andrews' gift for deadpan comedy."   —*Denver Post*

"Always heavy on the humor, Andrews' most recent Meg Langslow outing is her most over-the-top adventure to date."   —*Booklist*

"I can't say enough good things about this series, and this entry in it."   —*Deadly Pleasures*

"Hilarious . . . another winner . . . keeps you turning pages."   —*Mystery Lovers News*

CROUCHING BUZZARD, LEAPING LOON

"If you long for more 'fun' mysteries, à la Janet Evanovich, you'll love Donna Andrews's Meg Langslow series." —*Charlotte Observer*

"There's a smile on every page, and at least one chuckle per chapter." —*Publishers Weekly*

"This may be the funniest installment of Andrews' wonderfully wacky series yet. It takes a deft hand to make slapstick or physical comedy appealing, yet Andrews masterfully manages it (the climax will have you in stitches.)" —*Romantic Times*

REVENGE OF THE WROUGHT-IRON FLAMINGOS

"At the top of the list . . . a fearless protagonist, remarkable supporting characters, lively action, and a keen wit." —*Library Journal*

"What a light-hearted gem of a juggling act . . . with her trademark witty dialogue and fine sense of the ridiculous, Andrews keeps all her balls in the air with skill and verve." —*Publishers Weekly*

"Genuinely fascinating. A better-than-average entry in a consistently entertaining . . . series." —*Booklist*

MURDER WITH PUFFINS

"Muddy trails, old secrets, and plenty of homespun humor." —*St. Petersburg Times*

ACKNOWLEDGMENTS

Thanks, as always, to all the folks at St. Martins/Minotaur, including (but not limited to) Andrew Martin, Pete Wolverton, Hector DeJean, Matt Baldacci, Toni Plummer, and especially my longtime editor, Ruth Cavin.

Ellen Geiger and the staff at the Frances Goldin Literary Agency continue to make my life easy by taking care of the business side of writing. And special thanks to Dave Barbour at Curtis Brown for helping turn *Murder with Peacocks* into *Falscher Vogel fangt den Tod*.

My writing groups, the Rector Lane Irregulars (Carla Coupe, Ellen Crosby, Laura Durham, Peggy Hansen, Valerie Patterson, Noreen Wald, and Sandi Wilson) and the Hellebore Writers (Erin Bush, Meriah Crawford, M. Sindy Felin, Barb Goffman, and C. Ellett Logan), continue to be a source of much-needed help and advice, as do my blog sisters at the Femmes Fatales (Dana Cameron, Charlaine Harris, Toni L.P. Kelner, Kris Neri, Hank Phillipi Ryan, Mary Saums, and Elaine Viets). As always, my friends, including Chris Cowan, Kathy Deligianis, Suzanne Frisbee,

David Niemi, Dina Willner, and all the Teabuds, help keep me sane. Well, relatively sane.

When I realized that *Stork Raving Mad* was taking a direction that would require rather more medical expertise than usual, I called on the generosity of Dr. Doug Lyle, Luci Zahray (the Poison Lady), and Dr. Robin Waldron. To the extent I've achieved any degree of accuracy, it's due to their efforts to set me straight, and they should not be held responsible if I've blown it.

Finally, many thanks to Stuart and Elke for giving me the idea of inflicting twins on Meg and Michael in the first place, and to Liam and Aidan, the Andrews family's dynamic duo, for helping me realize how awesome twins can be.

ONE

"Meg? Are you asleep?"

I kept my eyes closed while I pondered my answer. If I said "Yes," would my husband, Michael, understand that I was only expressing how much my sleep-deprived body craved a few minutes of oblivion?

No, I'd probably just sound cranky. I felt cranky. Most women occasionally do when they're eight-and-a-half months pregnant, especially with twins. Any woman who says otherwise has obviously never been pregnant.

"Meg?"

"I'm thinking about it." I opened one eye and saw Michael's tall, lean frame silhouetted in the bedroom doorway. He was holding a small brown paper bag in one hand. "If that bag contains chocolate, then I'm definitely not asleep."

"Chocolate chip cookies from Geraldine's," Michael said, shaking the bag enticingly.

"Okay, I'm awake," I said. "It's not as if Heckle and Jeckle were going to let me get any sleep anyway."

I began the laborious process of hauling myself upright. Michael cleared some junk off the little folding table by my side of the bed, produced a plate from somewhere, poured half a dozen enormous soft chocolate chip cookies onto it, and placed a large glass of cold milk beside it. Then he pulled the curtains open, revealing that it was still fairly early in the morning, and a dreary gray winter morning at that.

"At times like this, I'm particularly glad I married you," I said, reaching for a cookie. "So what's the reason for this bribe?"

"There has to be a reason?" He snagged a cookie for himself and pulled a chair up to the other side of the table.

"As busy as you usually are in December grading exams and reading term papers and all that other end-of-semester stuff faculty have to do at the college, you still went all the way to Geraldine's for cookies?"

"Okay, there's a reason." He paused, then frowned as if puzzled. I took a big bite of cookie and washed it down with a swig of milk, to brace myself. Michael was rarely at a loss for words, so whatever he wanted to say must be momentous.

"Is it okay if we have another houseguest?" he finally asked. He sounded so anxious that I looked up in surprise.

"Is that all?" I said through a mouthful of cookie. His face relaxed into something more like its usual calm good humor. "Michael, I haven't the slightest idea how many houseguests we have already. There's Rob—"

"Your brother's not exactly a houseguest," Michael put in. "After two years, I think he qualifies as a resident."

"And Cousin Rose Noire—"

"Also more like a resident, unless you've changed your mind about accepting her offer to stay on and help us through that difficult adjustment to having the twins around."

"Right now, I have no objection if she stays on long enough to help us through the difficult adjustment to sending them off to college." I reached for a second cookie. "But there's still my grandfather, and of course all those displaced drama department students filling up the spare rooms and camping out in the living room. How many of them do we have, anyway?"

He frowned again.

"Maybe a dozen?" he said. "Or a dozen and a half?"

"Seems like more," I said. "There are at least a dozen sleeping in the living room."

"Two dozen, then," he said. Still probably a conservative estimate. "More or less. And before you ask, I have no idea how much longer they'll be here. Last time I heard, some critical piece of equipment down at the college heating plant was still in a million pieces on the floor, and the dean of facilities was running around with a harried look on his face and a bottle of Tums in his pocket."

I heard a series of thuds and thumps in the hallway. A month ago I'd have gone running to see what was happening, or at least sent Michael to check. Our weeks of living with students underfoot had made us blasé about such noises.

"You'd think a big place like Caerphilly College could figure out how to get a boiler repaired," I said. "It's been—what, three weeks now?"

"Three weeks tomorrow." Michael took another cookie. "Not that I'm counting or anything. Meanwhile, the whole campus is still without heat. And from the temperatures the weatherman is predicting next week, you'd think we lived in Antarctica instead of Virginia."

"Which means the students stay for the foreseeable future," I said. "And since the Caerphilly Inn is also full to overflowing with displaced students, and Grandfather can't get the suite he usually stays in when he comes to town, we're stuck with him, too. With all that going on, what's one more person?"

"You're a trouper," Michael said, with a smile that could have convinced me to invite the entire freshman class to move in.

I heard the crash of something breaking downstairs in the hall. I winced out of habit, even though I knew nearly everything of ours that the students could possibly have broken had long ago been locked up in the basement or the attic. By the time I got downstairs, the student would have picked up the broken object, whatever it was, and Rose Noire would probably have washed, waxed, and polished the patch of floor on which it had fallen.

"So who's our newest houseguest?" I asked.

"Remember Ramon Soto?" he asked. "One of my grad students?"

"The one who's been holding his play rehearsals in our library? Yes. I thought he was already living here."

"He is. As is most of his cast. Makes it convenient. Anyway, the play's part of his dissertation project. He's doing it on Ignacio Mendoza, the Spanish playwright."

Was Mendoza someone famous? The Spanish equivalent of Shakespeare, or Shaw, or at least Neil Simon? The name didn't sound familiar, but one side effect of pregnancy, at least for me, was that my hormone-enriched brain temporarily jettisoned every single bit of information it didn't think was useful in my present situation. At least I hoped it was temporary.

"Ignacio Mendoza?" I said aloud. "Is that a name I should recognize?"

"Not unless you're a fan of obscure mid-twentieth-

century Spanish playwrights," Michael said. He finished his cookie and moved to sit on the foot of the bed.
"For Ramon's dissertation project, in addition to the
critical study on Mendoza, he's done a new translation
of one of Mendoza's plays and is directing it. And one
thing he discovered while doing his research is that, to
everyone's amazement, Mendoza is still alive."

"Why amazement?"

"Because most people thought Generalissimo Franco
had Mendoza shot back in the fifties." He picked up my
right foot and began massaging it.

I closed my eyes, the better to enjoy the foot rub.
Carrying around an extra fifty or more pounds does a
number on your arches.

"Apparently he just went to ground in Catalonia and
kept a low profile for the last sixty years," Michael added.

"Sixty years?" I echoed. "How old is he, anyway?"

"Nearly ninety. Which is why Ramon thought it was
pretty safe to invite him to come to the opening night
of the play. He just assumed the old guy would be flat-
tered and send polite regrets. No one ever expected
Mendoza to accept—and at the last possible moment.
We've managed to scrape up some money from the
department to pay for his airfare, but even if we had
enough to cover a hotel stay—"

"Every single hotel room in town is full of refugee
students," I said. "Plus every spare room in just about
every private house. I'd have thought we were pretty full
ourselves."

"The students are going to rearrange themselves to
free up a room," Michael said.

Aha. That probably explained the earlier thumps and
thuds, along with the dragging noises I could hear out
in the hall. Michael switched to my left foot.

"We're also going to swap a few of our drama students who aren't in the play for a few more Spanish-speaking students," he went on. "That way there will always be someone around to translate for Señor Mendoza. And the students will chauffeur him around and cook for him or take him out to eat—in fact, your grandfather's promised to help as well. And if he's in his eighties, how much trouble can Señor Mendoza be?"

I thought of pointing out that even though my grandfather was over ninety, he regularly stirred up quite a lot of trouble. Of course, trouble was a way of life for Dr. Montgomery Blake, world famous zoologist, gadfly environmentalist, and animal-welfare activist. Why was Grandfather offering to help entertain our guest, anyway? Did he consider the elderly playwright a kind of endangered species?

But I had to admit, Michael had done everything possible to make sure our potential houseguest wouldn't cause me any work or stress.

"So it's really all right if we host Señor Mendoza?" he asked.

"It's fine. The more the merrier. Wait a minute—the play opens Friday and it's already Wednesday. How soon is he arriving?"

Michael glanced at his watch.

"In about half an hour."

TWO

Actually, the beat-up sedan carrying our latest guest pulled up just twenty minutes later, almost precisely at the stroke of ten. A slender, dark-haired young man of medium height stepped out. Ramon Soto—I recognized him from seeing some of the rehearsals. A pretty, dark-haired young woman sprang out of the front passenger seat and ran around to the driver's side so that she and Soto almost bumped heads in their haste to open the left rear door and assist a bent, gnarled figure out of the car and up the steps.

I saw this from upstairs, where I was in the middle of getting dressed, which seemed to take longer every day.

I sat back down on the bed and resumed trying to put on my shoes in spite of the fact that I couldn't see my feet—hadn't seen them in months. My cousin Rose Noire bustled in, looking, as usual, like a New Age Madonna, thanks to her long, flowing, cotton-print dress and her frizzy mane of hair.

"Look what I found for you!" she said. She was holding out a two-foot parcel wrapped in a length of mud-brown stenciled cloth and tied at several points with bits of raffia.

"What is it?" I asked.

"Open it and see. Oh, wait—it might be too heavy for you."

She set it down on the table and began unwrapping it herself. Ever since she'd learned of my pregnancy, Rose Noire had alternated between urging me to exercise, for the good of the babies, and deciding I was too fragile to lift anything heavier than a teacup. As she struggled with the bits of raffia, I gave thanks that she was in the latter mood at the moment.

"Ta da!" she exclaimed, lifting a large object out of the cloth. It looked like a statue of a heavily pregnant woman with the head of a hippopotamus.

"What is it?" I repeated.

"It's Tawaret! The Egyptian goddess who protects women during pregnancy and childbirth."

"She looks like a pregnant hippopotamus," I said. "A very irritated pregnant hippopotamus."

Rose Noire, to her credit, refrained from pointing out that at the moment I looked rather like a hippopotamus myself.

"She takes the form of a hippopotamus to protect young children from demons," she said instead, as she handed me the statue.

Yes, even demons would probably avoid tangling with a goddess who looked like that.

As Rose Noire swooped down to help with my shoes she chattered with enthusiasm about Tawaret's powers, her importance, and even her marital history. Apparently, after first marrying Apep, the god of evil, then Sobek, the crocodile god, she became the concubine of Set, who must have been more important, since Rose Noire didn't bother to explain who he was. And I didn't dare ask, for fear of setting her off again. It was like listening to someone talk about characters in a soap opera I didn't watch.

"Do you need anything else?" she asked.

I started guiltily. I'd been turning the statue around to study it and not liking what I saw. Tawaret was stout, with pendulous breasts, a bulging abdomen, frowning brows, and an open-mouthed snarl that revealed a large collection of sharp teeth. Her figure probably did resemble mine at the moment, but her expression reminded me of my Great Aunt Flo, who was so fond of telling me about ghastly things that had happened to women friends during childbirth and pregnancy. Not a happy association.

Perhaps my fleeting impulse to drop the statue showed on my face.

"I'll just put her here where you and she can get acquainted," Rose Noire said. She took Tawaret back and cleared a space for her on the dresser—which wasn't an easy task. In addition to Michael's and my relatively modest collection of grooming supplies, the dresser already held a large collection of pregnancy-related books, CDs, videos, statues, charms, amulets, herbs, organic stretch-mark creams, aromatherapy vials, and other gewgaws—most of them courtesy of Rose Noire, who seemed a great deal more enthusiastic about the whole pregnancy process than I was.

Of course, she wasn't living through it.

"Meg?"

I looked up to see Rose Noire frowning slightly at me. I was zoning out again.

"Do I look presentable?" I asked. "I don't want to embarrass anyone when I go downstairs to welcome our latest guest."

Rose Noire tweaked, tugged, and patted bits of hair and clothing that had looked perfectly fine to me, then nodded her approval and flitted off.

On my way out of the bedroom, I waddled over to the dresser and grabbed Tawaret. Even after five minutes' acquaintance, I'd decided she wasn't someone I wanted to share our bedroom with. I'd find a place downstairs to stash her. Correction: display her. If Rose Noire objected, I could say I wanted everyone to benefit from her demon-chasing powers.

When I reached the front hall I could hear torrents of Spanish outside. I peeked out one of the front windows and saw Michael, my grandfather, Rose Noire, and several of the students chatting with Señor Mendoza. Why were they keeping him out in the cold? Not waiting for me, I hoped.

I glanced around the front hall and winced. It was almost completely filled with the coatracks and coat trees we'd brought in for the students, and the chairs we'd moved out of the dining room when we turned it into another temporary bedroom. When you added in the half a dozen bushel baskets we'd set out for gloves, boots, and scarves, what had once been a gracious foyer now resembled the entrance to a thrift shop.

And now the students had decided to turn the dining room into Señor Mendoza's room, on the theory that our geriatric guest might not be able to make it to the second story. These days I wasn't too keen on going up and down stairs myself. When we bought our three-story Victorian house, Michael and I had been charmed by the twelve-foot ceilings on the ground floor, but now I was all too conscious of the twelve-foot stairway.

Half a dozen students swarmed in and out of the

dining room, clearing out the sleeping bags, suitcases, knapsacks, and other paraphernalia and hauling most of it upstairs. That accounted for the thumps and thuds. Another two students were assembling a bed frame in one corner.

"Make way!" I heard someone shout behind me. "Mattress coming through!" I lumbered out of the way as nimbly as I could, which wasn't very—these days I had the maneuverability and turning radius of an aircraft carrier.

"Oh, sorry, Mrs. Waterston," said one of the students carrying the mattress. "We didn't see it was you."

"No problem," I said. "Could someone do me a small favor?"

Three students leaped to my side. I handed Tawaret to a willowy redhead almost as tall as my five foot ten. I was fairly sure her name was Alice, but given how bad my short-term memory was at the moment, I decided to avoid testing that theory.

"Could you take this and put it on one of the shelves in the library?"

"What is it?"

"Good luck statue," I said. "Scares away demons."

"Awesome," Probable Alice said, and she disappeared with Tawaret under one arm.

"That would scare away anything," said a blond student whose name escaped me.

"Yes, and I have no intention of letting it scare Woodward and Bernstein," I said, patting my stomach.

"Is that really what you're going to call them?" the blonde asked. From the look on her face, I deduced she didn't approve.

"No," I said. "But we haven't settled on names yet

because we've chosen not to know the gender. My doctor refers to them as P and non-P, for presenting and non-presenting."

"Presenting what?" she asked.

"Presenting is doctor talk for positioned to come out first," I said.

"Whoa, you mean even in the womb, one of the kids is destined to be the younger?" she asked. "Who knew?"

"Maybe," I said. "I'm not betting on it. Non-P is pretty stubborn, and I wouldn't put it past him or her to thrash around and shove P out of the way. And as you can see, P and non-P are pretty impersonal, so we usually refer to them by whatever nicknames come to mind at the moment."

"Like Woodward and Bernstein," the blonde said.

"Or Tom and Jerry," I said. "Thelma and Louise. Tweedledum and Tweedledee."

"Cool," she said. Did she really think so, or was she only humoring her favorite professor's boring wife?

"How about Rosencrantz and Guildenstern?" she asked.

"Good one," I said. "I'll spring it on Michael later."

She beamed. Actually, we'd already used that one, but I didn't want to hurt her feelings.

I'd been maneuvering through the swarms of students toward the front door as we spoke. I almost tripped over Spike, our dog, who still hadn't figured out that in my present condition, I couldn't even see my own feet, much less an eight-and-a-half-pound fur ball dancing around them. Or maybe he was doing it deliberately. Spike had been known to bite the hand that fed him, so why should I be surprised if he tried to trip the owner of that hand?

"Someone get Spike out of the way," I said as I waddled over to the doorway to greet our guest. Or maybe I should drag Mendoza inside—why were they keeping an elderly visitor standing on the front porch so long? Did they want him to get pneumonia?

Just then the door opened with a burst of arctic air, and Señor Mendoza limped in, leaning heavily on a walking stick and bundled in a thick overcoat that was clearly intended for a much taller man—the hem dragged along the floor behind him. He was about five foot four, though he might have been taller if he weren't so stooped. He had a wild mane of white hair, a ragged white beard, and an irrepressible twinkle in his eyes.

He also reeked of tobacco, which probably explained what he'd been doing outside—having one last smoke before entering the house.

"Welcome to America!" he exclaimed, waving his stick in the air. "I am Ignacio Mendoza! Happy to meet you!"

Michael followed Señor Mendoza in, helped him out of the overcoat and hung it on one of the coatracks, all the while making conversation in rapid-fire Spanish.

I gazed at my husband in envy. At the moment, I could think of two Spanish words—*adiós* and *arriba*. Neither of them seemed even slightly apropos, so I worked on smiling in a welcoming fashion.

Then I recognized another phrase—*mi esposa*. Michael must be introducing me. I held out my hand.

Señor Mendoza lunged forward, grasped my hand, and thumped my belly several times.

The twins resented it. Someone should explain to strangers that it was rude to tickle babies before they were born.

"Sorry," I said, wrestling my hand free and taking a

step back. "But Butch and Sundance aren't up to shaking hands yet."

Actually, Butch might be trying to—he was squirming around with great enthusiasm. Sundance merely began the steady, rhythmic kicking he resorted to whenever Butch annoyed him. Why couldn't they wait until they were out in the world before beginning their sibling squabbles?

Michael stepped up and treated Señor Mendoza to a few more paragraphs of Spanish. I hoped he was explaining that while he was happy to welcome such a distinguished guest to his humble home, the guest should damn well keep his hands off the lady of the house. Whatever he said made Señor Mendoza beam at me with great approval.

"Meg!" my grandfather said, as he burst through the door with another blast of cold air. "This is going to be such fun. Nacio's going to make paella. And he's brought his guitar—did you know he's an expert flamenco player?"

Nacio? Must be Mendoza's nickname. Short for Ignacio, I supposed. Were they old friends or had they hit it off instantly? Either way, it was cause for alarm, given my grandfather's penchant for trouble.

And then the other part of his statement hit me: paella. A dish that normally contained copious amounts of seafood. No one in my family ever remembered my allergy to crustaceans and shellfish, so why should I expect them to believe that ever since I'd become pregnant, the mere smell nauseated me? I'd be avoiding the kitchen for a while.

And was there any hope that someone could convince him to play quiet, subdued, soothing flamenco music? Or was that an oxymoron?

Everybody seemed to be looking expectantly at me. Had I zoned out again and missed a question? I blinked, hoping someone would enlighten me. No one did.

The only creature in the hallway not staring expectantly at me was Spike, who was sniffing suspiciously at Señor Mendoza's shoes. To my horror, he uttered the briefest of growls before sinking his teeth into the playwright's left ankle.

Everyone was horrified except Mendoza.

"*Que diablito!*" He picked Spike up, not seeming to mind getting nipped in the process, and held him up at eye level. "What a ferocious watchdog!"

Spike was squirming madly. I wasn't sure whether he was uncomfortable or just frantic to get out of the playwright's grip so he could counterattack. Luckily Mendoza seemed to have a good hold on him.

And some of my linguistic ability surged back.

"*Chien mechant,*" I said finally, hoping my memory was working, and I had just called Spike a bad dog. "*Et maintenant, je dois dormir.*"

Never before had news of an impending nap been greeted with such laughter and enthusiasm, so I was more convinced than ever that I'd mistranslated. Time enough later to worry about it. At least Señor Mendoza, after chuckling, tucked Spike under one arm, and kissed my hand. Then he followed my grandfather to the kitchen, still carrying Spike.

I ignored the chuckles and cries of "*Brava!*" as I shuffled upstairs.

It wasn't till I was curling up in bed, trying to find a position that was comfortable for me and my two passengers, that I realized I'd spoken in French rather than Spanish.

Ah, well. Maybe they'd think I'd done it on purpose.

Catalonia was on the border with France, wasn't it? Or was it on the border with Portugal?

Normally I'd have fretted about this for hours while tossing and turning, but instead I fell asleep while trying to remember.

THREE

It was darker when I woke up. Had I slept till nightfall? Had I missed hearing that we were having a storm?

No, someone had tiptoed in while I was asleep and pulled all the blinds. Probably Rose Noire, since I also noticed a thermal mug on the bedside table. Another infusion of some obscure, healthy, herbal tea whose very smell would set my stomach churning. In the morning, the mug might contain a yogurt smoothie so laced with vitamins, supplements, and herbs that it had the same unsettling effect on my stomach. But luckily, in the afternoons the offerings were almost always herbal teas. I had to walk all the way to the bathroom to dump the smoothies, but unloading the teas was easier.

I shuffled to the windowsill with the mug and held my breath as I opened the top and poured the contents into the dirt around one of the potted plants. The Boston fern this time. The spider plant and the English ivy were looking distinctly unhealthy. Difficult to say whether this was due to some toxic effect from their daily doses of herbal teas, or whether they merely resented having their roots repeatedly scalded with hot liquid. The Boston fern, on the other hand, was thriving. Was this because it liked the herbal brews, or had I not been giving it as much as the others?

"Sorry," I said to the Boston fern. "But better you than me."

I allowed myself a moment of guilt about pouring out yet another well-intended offering from my cousin. I would be the first to admit that she had been immensely helpful throughout my pregnancy. And especially during the last two months, when she had waited on me hand and foot and enabled me to get the all-important rest my doctor recommended. I knew that the closer I could get to full term, the better it would be for Kirk and Spock, and whenever people congratulated me on how long I'd lasted, I gave full credit to Rose Noire. And it probably was just a coincidence that my morning sickness had finally ended the week I'd stopped trying to drink all her herbal offerings. She meant well.

I just sometimes wished she had an off switch.

I checked the clock. I'd been asleep less than an hour. Par for the course. These days I could nod off sitting up, but Boris and Natasha never let me sleep for long. They weren't even born yet, and already I was stumbling around in a constant state of sleep deprivation.

Time to see what was going on downstairs. Apologize to my houseguest—my latest houseguest—for my abrupt disappearance.

After a brief detour to the bathroom, I opened the bedroom door and almost keeled over at the strong, nauseating smell that permeated the hall outside.

Most people would have found the smell delectable, I suspected. As I leaned against the wall, patting P and non-P with one hand, I tried to untangle the components. Garlic, of course. Along with hypersensitivity to smell, my stomach's sudden hostility to garlic had been one of the first clues that I might be pregnant. I hoped neither was permanent. Along with the garlic I detected a rich potpourri of unfamiliar spices—unfamiliar and, at least for the moment, unappetizing. And, of course, an almost tangible reek of seafood.

Normally I merely found the smell of seafood distasteful. Now I wondered what would happen if my allergy worsened so the mere smell triggered a reaction. I'd ask Dad. Get him to give me an EpiPen, or if they weren't allowed during pregnancy, get him to enforce a total ban on seafood cooking for the rest of Señor Mendoza's visit. I sighed. That certainly wouldn't make me popular.

Along with the smells, sounds were drifting upstairs. I could hear the rise and fall of conversations, accompanied by flamenco music played on a guitar—no, make that several guitars—and a rhythmic staccato rattle that could only be someone dancing to the music.

I felt a wave of nostalgia mingled with resentment. Back in the B.P. days—before pregnancy—I'd have been down in the kitchen. I might not have eaten the seafood, but it wouldn't have bothered me so much. And I could have enjoyed the music, the conversation, the dancing, and the wine.

And I would again, I told myself, as I carefully descended the stairs. Just not for a while. And there was no reason for everyone else to do without just because I wasn't in the mood at the moment.

But at least they could turn on the kitchen exhaust fan to keep the odors from drifting upstairs with such intensity.

Just then the doorbell rang.

I paused on the second step from the bottom. I really

didn't feel like opening the door and having to deal with more visitors, not to mention the cold air.

"Can someone answer that?"

The flamenco music continued unabated. They probably hadn't even heard me.

"Hello, anyone?" I called.

The doorbell rang again, twice, in quick succession. Our would-be guests were getting impatient.

"Hold your damned horses," I muttered as I waddled to the door.

While unlocking the deadbolt, I tried to assume a polite, welcoming face. Or at least a neutral face. I'd save the scowl in case the impatient doorbell ringer was someone who really deserved it.

I swung the door open to find a man and a woman standing outside. Both wore frowns that matched my mood. And instead of saying anything, they both gawked at my protruding belly as if they'd never seen a pregnant woman before. They both had that hunched-against-the-cold look that so many people around campus wore these days, probably because they were only wearing light coats.

Okay, I understood their impatience, though it wasn't my fault they'd neglected to dress for the weather. But I wasn't letting them in till I knew they weren't trying to convert us or sell us something.

"May I help you?" I asked. I was polite, though certainly not warm.

"Is this the residence of Professor Waterston?" the woman said. She was forty-something and might have been attractive if she could lose the scowl, though the lines of her face hinted that it was habitual. She wasn't wearing a hat over her neatly permed brown hair or gloves on her well-manicured fingers.

"Yes," I said. "May I tell him who's calling?"

"I am Dr. Wright," she said. "From the English department. And this is Dr. Blanco, from administrative services." She indicated the man, who was tall and also fortyish, with a thin, anxious face. He was bareheaded, too, though at least he wore driving gloves.

"May we come in?" Dr. Blanco asked.

"Of course," I said, stepping back from the door. Blanco I'd never heard of before, but I had the sinking feeling I should know who Wright was. The drama department, where Michael taught, was technically an unloved subgroup of the English department.

They stepped inside with just enough haste to make me feel sorry for them. They both set down slim, expensive-looking briefcases, and the woman carefully set a purse atop hers—a small, sleek bit of leather, probably a designer brand that a more fashion-conscious woman would have recognized instantly. Then they shed their coats and tried to hand them to me.

I gestured to the coatracks, which still had a few free hangers, and stepped a little farther away. It wasn't just that I resented being treated like a maid. One of them was wearing an overly strong perfume or aftershave that was making my nose tickle. Hard to tell which of them was the culprit—the scent didn't seem particularly masculine or feminine. Just unpleasant.

"If you'll wait here in the hall, I'll tell—*achoo!*—tell my husband you're here." I fumbled in my pocket for a tissue and gestured at some of the dining room chairs.

"Actually," Dr. Blanco said, "we're looking for one of Professor Waterston's students. A Ramon Soto."

"We understand he lives here," Dr. Wright added. Her face frowned a little more, as if showing her disapproval of any unorthodox living arrangements. In fact, both of them were wearing the sort of disagreeable expressions my nephews used to call prune faces.

"Ramon Soto is staying here," I said. "Until the heating plant is back in order and the dorms are habitable. We've taken in quite a few students."

Neither professor appeared impressed. I'd bet anything there were no unruly students disturbing the pristine academic quiet of their homes.

"May we speak to Mr. Soto?" Dr. Blanco asked.

"I'll see if someone can find him." I turned and began waddling toward the kitchen, sneezing a few more times as I went.

"See if someone can find him?" Dr. Wright said. "Don't you understand the—"

"I'm sure it's just a figure of speech," Dr. Blanco said, in a soothing tone.

When I opened the door the noise, light, and smells almost overwhelmed me. I grabbed the door frame and closed my eyes for a few moments to fight the dizziness and nausea.

"Mrs. Waterston!" I felt hands gripping me, and had to fight the impulse to push them away. "Are you all right?"

"Just tired." I opened my eyes to find half a dozen solicitous students crowded around me. "Is Ramon here?"

Ramon emerged from the crowd. His face wore an anxious look that had become habitual over the last few weeks.

"What's wrong?" he asked.

"Nothing that I know of," I said. "Two professors are here to see you."

"Two professors?" From his tone of voice, you'd think I'd said two masked gunmen.

"Dr. Wright and Dr. Blanco," I said.

"Oh, God," he muttered, and rushed out of the kitchen and into the hall.

I looked around to see if anyone else had as strong a reaction, but they'd all returned to their conversations.

Señor Mendoza was standing at the stove, stirring a large pot. Was this some advance prep for the paella, or was he also inflicting a very fishy bouillabaisse on my twitching nose?

As I was turning to go, Mendoza fished something out of the pot with a slotted spoon.

"Hey! *Perro!*"

I heard a familiar gruff bark and looked down to see that Spike was sitting at Señor Mendoza's feet, looking up at him with fixed attention.

Mendoza picked something out of the spoon—some kind of shellfish. My stomach lurched.

Spike growled softly. A small stream of drool began dripping from his open mouth.

"Perro! Perro!"

Mendoza grabbed a dishcloth and waved it in front of Spike like a toreador's cape. He shook it slightly. Spike growled again and swallowed, never taking his eyes from the dishcloth.

"Perro!" Mendoza said again.

Spike lunged at the dishcloth. Mendoza swept it away in a dramatic arc. Spike braked, turned, and then popped up on his hind feet and whined.

Mendoza threw his head back with a laugh and tossed something at Spike, who leaped into the air to catch it.

I was relieved that Mendoza didn't seem to hold a grudge about Spike biting him.

Mendoza saw me watching.

"Oyster?" he asked, holding out the spoon.

"No thanks," I said as I ducked out of the kitchen. I wasn't retreating, of course. I wasn't sure whether my protective instincts were aroused or my curiosity, but I realized I should follow Ramon back to the front hall. By the time I got there, he was standing in front of the prunes, shifting uneasily from foot to foot.

"—highly unsatisfactory," Dr. Wright was saying. "We've been trying to reach you for weeks."

"Nine days, actually," Dr. Blanco said.

Ramon stopped shifting and hunched his shoulders as if expecting a blow. But he didn't say anything, and the prunes just sat there, waiting.

I glanced back to see if anyone else was around to help. I saw only one of the women students—the one who had arrived with Ramon. She was watching the scene with a worried frown on her face, but she didn't seem ready to intervene.

And someone should.

"He's been here for two weeks," I said. "And working almost full time on his dissertation and his play. Did you leave a message with the drama department secretary?"

"We e-mailed Mr. Soto," Dr. Wright said. She turned her frowns on me, and I heard Ramon take a deep breath of relief. "And precisely whom do you mean by the drama department secretary? The last time I checked, the drama curriculum was still under the English department. There is no drama department, and thus no drama department secretary."

Her prim, condescending manner set my teeth on edge. And, to my astonishment, I felt some combative, articulate part of my brain wake up for the first time in several months.

"I do beg your pardon," I said. "I should not have spoken carelessly. I meant Kathy Borgstrom, of course. As you surely know, she coordinates matters related to the drama curriculum and the students enrolled in it."

"Perhaps she does," Dr. Wright said. "But she has no formal position, other than as Dr. Sass's secretary, so I fail to see why we would have any reason to consult her."

Maybe because if Dr. Wright had half a brain, she'd know that after ten years as Abe's secretary, what Kathy Borgstrom didn't know about the drama department wasn't worth knowing. But before I opened my mouth to say so, I remembered where I'd heard of Dr. Wright before. She was on Michael's tenure committee. The committee that would start its final deliberations in a few weeks. The committee that would determine whether the twins would grow up with the security of a father who was a full professor at Caerphilly College or whether Michael would remain a mere associate professor, whose employment could be terminated at the first sign of a budget crunch.

Or whenever he ticked off someone like Dr. Wright.

Luckily, Ramon finally found his voice.

"I'm sorry," he said. "But my computer's in my room. It's a desktop, so it wasn't easy to move, and I just haven't had the time to bother with it. I know I could probably get into my e-mail someplace else, but it just didn't seem that important. I've been very busy with the show."

"Yes," Dr. Blanco said. "The show. I'm afraid—"

"First things first," Dr. Wright said. "You could have

saved us all a lot of trouble if you'd remained in proper communication with the department. But at least now we can formally notify you that your dissertation topic is unsuitable."

"Unsuitable?" Ramon echoed. "But—"

"We are the English department," Dr. Wright continued. "Of an English-language institution. We cannot possibly approve a dissertation in a foreign language."

"Then what's the problem?" I said. "As far as I know, he's writing it in English."

Dr. Wright fixed her frown on me.

"That is immaterial," she said. "The topic is foreign, and thus unsuitable for an English department degree. Mr. Soto will have to select another topic."

"But that would mean starting over!" Ramon exclaimed.

"Sadly, yes," Dr. Wright said. She didn't look sad. She looked as if this was the most fun she'd had since outgrowing childhood pastimes like pulling the wings off flies.

"But I got permission," Ramon said. "I submitted about a million forms two years ago."

Dr. Wright reached down and opened her purse. She pulled a couple of things out of it—a matching wallet and a worn pale-blue Caerphilly College envelope that had been folded in half. She located her target: a small electronic gadget. She stuffed the wallet and the envelope back in her purse, then began clicking buttons on the electronic device—presumably making notes of their conversation.

"Now," she said, glancing up from her PDA or whatever it was, "to what forms are you referring?"

"I don't know." Ramon shrugged. "The forms the

department secretary told me to submit. They were all on that stupid blue paper."

Not helpful. All official Caerphilly College papers were printed on a tasteful pale-blue paper stock, theoretically to make them stand out from other, less exalted papers. Which it would if the college didn't send out such a blizzard of official papers that every professor's desk was covered in blue snowdrifts.

But criticizing the blue paper wasn't very smart. For all we knew, Blanco and Wright could have been on the committee that came up with the idea. Ramon should be more diplomatic. In fact—

"Do you have a copy of this alleged permission?" Dr. Wright was saying.

"I don't know," Ramon said. "If I did it'd be back in my room. Look, can't this all wait till after my show? I've got a rehearsal in five minutes and—"

"Ah, yes, the show," Dr. Wright said. She turned to Dr. Blanco. He looked blank for a moment. She frowned and made an impatient gesture.

"Oh, yes," he said. "The show." He turned to Ramon. "I have the unfortunate duty to inform you that the show cannot continue. Regrettably, the administration has determined that the show contains offensive and unsuitable material."

"We're canceling it," Dr. Wright said.

"Canceling it!" Ramon echoed.

"That's crazy!" the woman student said, and then clapped her hands over her mouth and ran back into the kitchen, as if hoping not to be noticed.

Didn't Ramon realize he shouldn't be talking to these two by himself? I had to do something before he got even deeper in trouble, but the brain wasn't cooperating.

"Wait!" I shouted. They all turned to look at me, and both the jackals took a step back. Ramon merely looked anxiously at my protruding abdomen. In fact they were all staring. I glanced down to see one of P's feet outlined perfectly against the tautly stretched fabric of my maternity blouse.

I shoved him back into a more comfortable position, while frantically trying to think.

FOUR

"Is there some problem?" Dr. Wright asked.

I couldn't come up with anything to say that would rescue Ramon, so I decided to stall. I grabbed the back of a chair and tried to look faint. It wasn't a stretch. I started breathing as shallowly as I could, trying to keep the perfume reek from triggering a sneeze.

"I hate to interrupt your discussion, but I'm feeling unwell," I said. "I need someone to help me. I—I—*achoo!*"

Both professors flinched.

"If you have an infectious disease," Dr. Wright said, "it's highly inconsiderate to expose others to the possible contagion."

I wanted to tell her that it was equally inconsiderate to wear so much perfume that you polluted every room you entered, but I decided that wouldn't be politic.

"What I have isn't contagious," I said. "I'm sensitive to strong odors. Side effect of pregnancy. I must be reacting to all the seafood Señor Mendoza is cooking. Mr. Soto? Would you mind helping me?"

Looking even more anxious, Ramon gave me his arm. I leaned on it heavily and steered him back to the kitchen.

"Should we call a doctor?" he asked, as I sank into a chair in the kitchen. The noise level dropped as at least half the people in the kitchen turned to stare at me.

"I'm fine," I said. "Or as fine as anyone can be when she's swollen to the size of a Panzer tank. You, on the other hand, are in deep—um, big trouble. You shouldn't be talking to these people by yourself."

"You mean I need a lawyer or something?" he said, sounding incredulous.

"It might come to that, but right now—quick, someone find Professor Waterston!"

Several people ran in search of Michael.

"Did you know they were looking for you?" I asked Ramon.

"Not exactly," he said. "I knew someone from the English department had been trying to reach me, but they never said what it was about and I figured it was just some kind of bureaucratic thing that could wait until after the show was over."

"Well, the show is over for now, unless we—unless Professor Waterston can fix this," I said.

Something suddenly occurred to me. I'd been calling Wright and Blanco "doctor." They referred to Michael as "Professor Waterston." So did I, usually, when talking about him to anyone from the college. But why? As far as I knew, Caerphilly College had no rule, official or unspoken, that you only called tenured professors "doctor." I knew adjunct professors in several other departments whom everyone called doctor. As far as I could remember, there were only three Ph.D.s at Caerphilly College that everyone always called "professor" rather than "doctor"—Michael and his drama colleagues, Abe Sass and Art Rudmann. Maybe I was imagining things or being oversensitive, but this felt to me like a deliberate slight. From now on, I was going to fling Michael's doctorate in their faces at every opportunity.

Dr. Michael himself appeared at my side.

"You wanted me?" he said. "Time to head for the hospital?"

"Not yet," I said. "Though if Dr. Wright and Dr. Blanco continue to annoy me, you may need to take them."

"Annoy you? Wright and Blanco? How?"

"They say I can't do my dissertation on Señor Mendoza, and the play is canceled," Ramon said.

Michael's reaction was lost in a sudden outburst of exclamations and oaths in two languages from the crowd of students.

"Down with the English department!"

"Those jerks!"

"Censorship! Censorship!"

"Discrimination!"

I wasn't up to deciphering what was being said in Spanish, but I assumed the gist was about the same.

"Professor, can they do that?" one student asked.

"*Qué pasó?*" Señor Mendoza asked. "*Qué pasó?*"

Three of the students began explaining to him, simultaneously, in rapid-fire Spanish. At first he looked confused, then he seemed to catch on.

"Villains!" he shouted. "Infamy! Let me accost them!"

I was bracing myself to intervene—to leap out of my chair, or at least yell at him to stop. But I realized he didn't seem to be going anywhere. He began speaking loudly and rapidly in Spanish. The students gathered around him, but considering his vehement tone, they were strangely subdued, as if struggling to understand him.

"What's he saying?" I whispered to Michael.

"No idea," Michael whispered back. "When he gets excited, he lapses into Catalan. Which none of us speaks."

Probably just as well, since from watching him I deduced that he was trying to incite the students to do something. From the expressions on their faces, I suspected the students were just as far out at sea as I was, but apparently they all assumed everyone else understood every word and had begun applauding and cheering diligently.

"Then how do you know it's Catalan?" I whispered to Michael.

"He apologized the first time he lapsed into it."

Señor Mendoza began shouting things that ended with either *Sí?* or *No!* The students could take a hint. They began roaring back "*Sí!*" or "*No!*" whenever Señor Mendoza paused for a response.

Michael beckoned me into the pantry, where it was a little quieter.

"So just exactly what did they say—Blanco and Wright?"

"Wright said Ramon's dissertation topic was unsuitable because it was Spanish," I said. "Caerphilly is an English-language institution. And Blanco said the play was unsuitable and offensive, and it's off, too. Who is he, anyway?"

"One of the president's pet bureaucrats," Michael said. "Has his finger in everything. Spends all his time on projects no one either understands or wants. Big on introducing new paperwork—he's killed more trees than all the arsonists in California ever will. Sticks his nose in everything from academic standards to the portion sizes in the cafeteria. Currently about the least popular man on campus because his department hasn't been able to get the heating plant problem solved. And Wright, of course—"

"Is a member of your committee," I said.

"A problem member." He sighed. "Not to mention a serious contender for the position of English department chair the next time that becomes vacant. But we have to deal with her. Let's go see if we can straighten this out."

Was he really as confident as he sounded? I followed him back into the kitchen.

Apparently, news of the prunes' actions had spread throughout the house. Every student living with us and quite a few I didn't remember ever seeing before had crowded into the kitchen. The room was boiling with heated discussions in at least two languages. Señor Mendoza was still holding forth in a surprisingly loud bellow.

"You have no idea what he's going on about?" I asked.

"Something about marching and picketing in protest, I think," Michael said.

"I got that much."

I followed Michael into the hall—not so much because I wanted to eavesdrop, although I did, but I couldn't stand the idea of waiting in the kitchen with all the noise and the overwhelming smell of seafood.

"Professor Waterston," Dr. Wright said. She sounded surprised to see him.

"I understand you have some issues with the topic of Ramon Soto's dissertation," Michael said.

"His topic is—"

"Is a drama topic, rather than an English topic," Michael said. "As it should be, since he is working on a degree in drama, not English. What kind of drama curriculum could we have if we didn't include playwrights like Aeschylus, Sophocles, Moliere, Lope de Vega, Chekhov, Ibsen, Garcia Lorca, Pirandello, Brecht—"

"That's not the point of view we're taking on the subject," Dr. Wright began. "We feel—"

"I think I understand your point of view," Michael said. "And I'd be happy to discuss it. What I fail to see is why this issue wasn't brought to his dissertation committee before the department took such drastic action."

"Since your committee failed to take any action on his highly unsuitable topic—" Dr. Wright began.

"Our committee did not fail to act," Michael said. "We have followed every step of Mr. Soto's dissertation with great attention and we have been highly satisfied with his progress. Are you asserting that there is a formal departmental rule prohibiting use of foreign language materials in a dissertation to be submitted under the drama curriculum? If there is, I'd like to see it."

"The material is not just foreign," Dr. Blanco put in. "It's obscene!"

Michael and Dr. Wright both glanced at him briefly and then resumed their argument as if his interruption hadn't happened.

"And why is the department taking this action now, at the worst possible moment for Mr. Soto?" Michael went on. "Has no one in the department been reviewing the paperwork Mr. Soto has filed, as well as the reports of our committee?"

"There is some question of whether Mr. Soto has filed all his paperwork," Dr. Wright said.

"Then the department should have brought that to his attention and his committee's attention earlier," Michael said. "And I know damned well our committee has filed all its reports, because I'm the one who did it. What's more—"

"Michael," I said. I could tell he didn't like being interrupted, but I could also tell he'd lost his temper. This didn't happen very often, but when it did, the results were scary. Not only did he look every bit of his six foot four and more, but he used his powerful, theatrically trained voice as a weapon. So far he was only in the first stage, speaking with icy precision and cold sarcasm, but I could tell that King Lear and Vesuvius weren't far off.

"Sorry," he said. He flashed me a brief, grateful smile. "Am I too loud? Upsetting Bonnie and Clyde?"

"I only wanted to suggest that perhaps this is something Mr. Soto's whole doctoral committee should hear about. I could call Dr. Sass and Dr. Rudmann."

"An excellent idea," Michael said. "I'm sure we can sort this all out with their help."

Abe Sass and Art Rudmann, in addition to being the balance of Ramon's dissertation committee, were the two senior drama professors in the department and the only tenured ones. Both were somewhat elderly, since they'd been hired before the English department had begun what Michael referred to as its militant repression of the drama curriculum. And they were good friends and staunch allies of Michael's.

"I fail to see what there is to sort out," Dr. Wright said. "The department's decision on this is non-negotiable."

"But perhaps there is a value in explaining the issues

involved to the entire committee at once," Dr. Blanco said. "Let's schedule something."

Clearly he was a man more comfortable with compromise than open conflict. He reached into his pocket and pulled out his PDA. After frowning slightly—a small crack in the façade of bureaucractic solidarity!—Dr. Wright began tapping again on hers.

"As it happens, I was supposed to meet both of them this afternoon for a meeting on another subject," Michael said. "Why don't I call and suggest they come out here a little earlier, since you're already here."

"And since we have heat," I added. "We can find you a warm place to work in the meantime."

"I have a rather busy schedule today," Blanco began.

"But this is a rather important issue," Wright said. Was there a note of deliberate sarcasm in the way she echoed the word rather? Perhaps another crack? "And we'd have finished this by now if you'd been on time."

Definitely a crack.

"If you feel it's essential," Blanco murmured. His shoulders were hunched, making him look like a turtle trying to pull its head into its shell.

"I'll call right now," Michael said. He pulled out his cell phone and stepped into the living room, presumably to make his calls in greater privacy.

Wright and Blanco turned to me. Dr. Wright took a step closer to me, and I sneezed several times. Apparently she was the source of the perfume reek. Luckily my sneezing encouraged her to take a step back.

"We'll need someplace to work," Dr. Wright announced. "I will require a place where I can use my laptop."

"I'd like a room where I can make some phone calls," Blanco said. "Without disturbing Dr. Wright."

I got the impression that disturbing Dr. Wright was something he tried to avoid at all costs.

"Most of our rooms are dormitories right now," I said. "How about our library? It's a bit messy—the students have been using it as a sort of common area. But I'll keep them out for the time being. And Dr. Blanco, if you need a place to make calls where you won't disturb Dr. Wright, you could either use the sunporch off the library or my office."

"Your office might be preferable," Blanco began. "It's near the library?"

"No, it's out in the barn," I said. He blinked in surprise. "I'm a blacksmith," I explained, "so it makes sense for me to have my office near my forge. But don't worry; it's got a space heater."

"Well, if—" Blanco began.

Just then Señor Mendoza erupted from the kitchen. He was managing an impressive speed, especially considering that he was waving his walking stick over his head instead of using it for support. Behind him surged a crowd of students.

"What's going on here?" Michael asked, sticking his head out into the hall. His words were lost in the confusion.

Mendoza stumped over to Wright and Blanco and began shouting at them. In English.

"Philistines!" he shouted. "Book burners! Assassins of culture! Jackals without souls! Harpies!"

He kept on in much the same vein, and I found myself thinking that considering English was his second—if not third—language, he really did have quite a gift for fiery, nonobscene invective. I was just considering whether to fish my notebook out of my pocket and jot down a few choice insults when Mendoza stopped and clutched at his chest.

FIVE

The students seemed frozen in shock at seeing Señor Mendoza's distress.

"Someone help him," I shouted. "Where's Dad?"

"Fetch Dr. Langslow!" Michael said, as he hurried to Mendoza's side. "He's out in the yard."

Several students scurried to follow his orders. One, more quick-thinking than the rest, grabbed a chair and he and Michael eased the old playwright into it.

"Someone run to the bathroom and get the aspirin, in case he's having a heart attack," I called.

Several students ran off to follow my orders. Mendoza rattled off something in Spanish that seemed to reassure those who could understand it. Then he reached into his pocket and took out an enormous pill bottle and handed it to one of the students.

"Apparently he's not having an attack." Michael had returned with a chair for me. "His heart fluttered, and it reminded him that he's not supposed to excite himself and that he had not yet taken his heart pills today."

"Probably atrial fibrillation," I said, as I sank gratefully onto the chair. "Dad should still check him out."

"And maybe your father could give him a bottle that

doesn't have a childproof cap," Michael said. Even the student was having trouble opening the top.

"Oops!" the student said, as tiny white pills sprayed out like a fountain. About twenty people almost simultaneously dropped to their hands and knees and began scrabbling on the floor, like devotees of a strange religion abasing themselves.

"No hurry! No hurry!" Mendoza shouted. "See? I caught one!"

He held up a small white pill. A sublingual nitroglycerin tablet? Digoxin? As a doctor's daughter, I could hazard a guess what they might be, but I couldn't see well enough to tell. Whatever it was, he put it into his mouth. Someone put a wineglass into his hand—.

"Not wine!" I shouted. "Not with heart pills!" But no one appeared to hear me. Señor Mendoza washed the pill down with a healthy slug of red wine, and then leaned back in his chair to watch the pill retrieval. Students were swarming over every inch of the hall floor, looking for and occasionally finding the tiny pills.

Within seconds, Drs. Blanco and Wright were the only people, apart from Mendoza and me, not on their knees searching for the pills. At least Mendoza and I were interested bystanders—the prunes merely looked on disapprovingly. When one of the students came too close to Dr. Wright, she stepped back, slipped on something—probably a stray pill—and fell. Luckily she fell against one of the coatracks, so her landing was well cushioned.

"Look what you've done!" Blanco snapped, to no one in particular, as he swooped down to help his colleague. A good thing he was so eager because no one else seemed upset at her mishap.

"I'm fine," she said. "Stop fussing over me."

"Look out! *El perro!*" Mendoza shouted.

I looked down to see Spike licking the floor.

"He's trying to eat Señor Mendoza's heart pills!" I shouted. "Stop him!"

For once, I managed to move tolerably fast—or maybe I only beat everyone else because the students had been here long enough to have acquired a healthy fear of the Small Evil One, as we called him. Michael swooped down to grab Spike and held him while I pried open his jaws.

"Did he eat any of the pills?" Michael asked.

"There's nothing in his mouth, but that doesn't mean he couldn't have swallowed one," I said. Just then I spotted my father in the doorway with his black doctor's bag. "Dad! How fast would Señor Mendoza's heart medicine work?"

"Don't worry," he said. "Where's the patient?"

"Check Señor Mendoza out," I said, pointing. "And find out what those pills are and what to do if Spike ate one!"

Spike was struggling to get down, but I could see at least one more of the little pills on the floor, and the students all seemed to be watching Dad and Señor Mendoza, who were conversing in a mixture of Spanish and English.

"Get that one," I called, pointing to the stray pill. Michael handed Spike to me and stooped to retrieve the pill.

"Doctor!" Blanco called. "Please see to Dr. Wright. I am concerned that she may have broken something in her fall."

"Nonsense," Dr. Wright snapped. "I'm perfectly fine."

"Broken bones aren't nearly as dangerous as heart attacks," I said.

"Or digitalis overdoses," Dad said, looking stern. "If that's what those pills are—he doesn't have them in the original container, so I can't be sure. See if you can make him throw up. Spike, I mean," he added. "Señor Mendoza will be fine if he stops overexciting himself."

"Sardines," I said. "Spike loves them, but he chokes them down too fast and then pukes. Find some sardines."

"I'll get them," Rose Noire said, and ran for the kitchen. Thank goodness she was willing. All this talk of retching had me on the brink without even smelling the sardines.

"Better yet, syrup of ipecac," Dad said. "I have some in my bag. Ah, here." He handed Michael a bottle and a syringe. "Squirt some in his mouth—let's see, I think one and a half ccs should do the trick."

Dad turned back to Señor Mendoza, and from his calm expression I could tell that he wasn't unduly worried about his patient.

"If we could have some medical attention for Dr. Wright, please," Dr. Blanco said.

Dad smiled, shook hands with Señor Mendoza, and strode over to kneel down beside Dr. Wright. I felt myself relaxing. If Dad was taking his eyes off a patient, it meant he truly wasn't worried—not just because he was a painstakingly conscientious doctor, but because there was nothing Dad would enjoy more than a breakneck ambulance ride to the Caerphilly Hospital and a few hours working side by side with the emergency room staff. I headed out for the kitchen with Spike.

While I barged through the swarming students with Spike under one arm, out in the kitchen, Rose Noire had opened a tin of sardines and was dumping the fish onto a plate. These days I could bulldoze through crowds with remarkable ease. I wasn't sure if it was the physical effect of being five foot ten and temporarily almost as wide, or whether everyone just scrambled out of my way these days out of sheer terror that the slightest nudge would send me into labor, but whatever it was worked. I set Spike down on the kitchen table.

"Hold his mouth open," Michael said.

I suddenly realized that I was about to get sick. Maybe it was the smell of the sardines added to that of the paella.

"I have to sit down," I said. "Can someone take over here?"

The students who were crowded around the table took a few steps back and looked uneasily at each other.

"I'll do it," Rose Noire said. She was a seasoned Spike-wrangler. She distracted Spike by waving the sardines near his nose and then clamped her hands down on him while I let go. I sat down as far from the sardines as I could and still see what was going on. Michael grabbed a small piece of sardine, waved it near Spike's nose, and while the Small Evil One was snapping at it, Michael managed to squirt the syrup of ipecac into Spike's mouth. Then he tossed in the sardine scrap to keep Spike from spitting out the medicine.

"Do you think it's going to work?" one of the students asked.

No one answered. We all stood or sat staring at Spike until the Small Evil One stopped trying to bite Rose Noire and waited expectantly.

Or maybe he could feel the syrup of ipecac working. After a few moments he whined slightly, then vomited just as Dad came bustling into the kitchen.

"Good work!" Dad exclaimed.

Rose Noire, bless her heart, was already running to fetch cleaning supplies.

"Look!" Michael said, pointing. "It's one of the digitalis pills!"

"I'll take your word for it," I said. Its brief stay in Spike's stomach had not improved the smell of the sardine.

"Do you think he swallowed any more?" a student asked.

"I doubt he could have swallowed any long ago enough for them to make it out of the stomach and into the intestines," Dad said, peering over Michael's shoulder. "Too fast. Which is a lucky thing, because if he had, he'd be in bad shape. Meg, are you all right?"

"I will be if someone will take those sardines away," I said.

"I'll give them to Spike," Rose Noire said, as she continued mopping the table. "Poor sick little doggie!"

"No, they'll only make him sicker," I said. "And he wouldn't be sick if he hadn't stupidly gobbled up Señor Mendoza's heart medicine. Get his crate; we'll need to keep an eye on him, and we don't dare let him out until we've picked up all the pills."

"I'll do it," Rose Noire said.

"No, we should have him checked out a little more carefully," Dad said. "I'll take him—I'm sure Clarence can work him in. Just call my iPhone if you need me."

Dad tucked Spike under one arm and hurried out. I felt relieved, not only because Spike was going to see the vet—I could stop worrying about him—but also because I knew Dad wouldn't be going anywhere if he thought his human patients needed observation.

And maybe Clarence would insist on keeping Spike overnight. That thought made me downright cheerful.

"Okay, Dad's got Spike," I said. "We need to put Professors Wright and Blanco someplace. I was thinking the library, although that would delay Ramon's next rehearsal."

"I think it will have to be the library," Rose Noire said. I sighed. Normally I loved even the thought of our library. Having a whole room devoted to books and reading had always been my idea of ultimate luxury. And ours, which a previous owner had built as a ballroom, was large enough to hold any amount of books Michael and I could ever imagine accumulating. But so far, it only held half a dozen Ikea shelves and a lot of book boxes, and even those were now completely hidden by an ocean of clutter. The drama students had been using our library as their common room and rehearsal hall. In addition to Ramon's props and costumes, it was filled with piles of books, papers, CDs, pizza boxes, soda cans, coffee mugs, and stray items of clothing. Not a sight I relished showing to unfriendly eyes. But I couldn't think of an alternative.

"The library it is, then," I said. "Rose Noire, could you show Professor Wright there? I think Professor Blanco wanted some privacy to make phone calls, so perhaps someone could show him to my office."

"I'll take care of him," Probable Alice said.

"No problem," Rose Noire said. "Alice and I will take care of everything."

Neither of them seemed to notice the demotion I'd given the prunes.

"Make sure the door to Michael's office is still locked," I told Rose Noire in an undertone. "And the doors between his office and the library. And—"

"Of course," she said, and hurried toward the door to the hall.

I didn't have to give Alice any instructions about my office because anything sensitive or valuable had already been locked up months ago, when I got too large to get near my anvil and had to put my blacksmithing business on hold for the balance of my pregnancy.

"And you might open the French doors to the sun-porch and crack a few of the jalousies," I called after Rose Noire. "A little ventilation would be nice. She's wearing gallons of some ghastly perfume that makes me sneeze."

"The library will be freezing if I do that!" Rose Noire protested.

"True," I said.

"We'll give it a good airing as soon as she leaves," Michael said.

"Good idea," I said as Rose Noire tripped away. "Michael, can we talk for a moment?"

I indicated the pantry and Michael followed me in.

Of course, so did the smell of the sardines, mingling with the remnants of the paella. In the small space of the pantry, the odors seemed more overwhelming.

"We've got to stop meeting like this," he said. And then he noticed my face and scrambled to find something on the shelves.

"Here." He twisted open the top of a little jar of stick cinnamon and handed it to me.

"You're a mind reader," I said, holding the jar to my nose. "That helps."

"The zarzuela's a little overwhelming," he said.

"Zarzuela? I thought that was a kind of theater?"

"It's also a kind of Catalan fish stew—sort of like bouillabaisse."

I wrinkled my nose at the thought.

"I thought he was fixing paella."

"He's fixing both."

"Yuck."

"Just inhale the cinnamon," Michael said. He unfolded the stepping stool I kept in the pantry to reach the top shelves, and I perched on the seat. "It's supposed to stimulate the brain."

"Brain stimulation's good," I said. "Because we need to strategize."

"Art and Abe are on their way," he said. He had closed his eyes and was leaning against the door. "You realize that this could torpedo my bid for tenure."

There. One of us had said it aloud. According to all the new age books Rose Noire kept giving me, naming a worry was supposed to help you realize that it wasn't really as bad as you feared. But this was every bit that bad. It plopped down and brought our conversation to a dead stop as both of us thought about it.

"Yes," I said finally. "But Dr. Wright's probably already gunning for you. And anyway—can you live with yourself if you don't at least try to fix things?"

"No," he said, without hesitation. "We have to help Ramon. I just wanted to make sure you were okay with it."

"I'm fine with it," I said.

"And I think Groucho and Harpo would understand," Michael said.

"Oh, God," I said, clutching my belly. "Not Groucho and Harpo!"

"Why not? I thought you liked the Marx Brothers."

"Yes, but there were three of them—don't forget Chico. Haven't there been rare cases where people thought they were having twins and ended up with triplets? Don't jinx us!"

I began looking around for someplace to put my feet up.

"Actually, there were five of them—don't forget

Zeppo and Gummo. I'm pretty sure the doctors wouldn't overlook an extra three."

He pulled a twelve-pack of paper towels down from a top shelf and set it where I could use it as a footstool.

"Thanks," I said. "And humor me—let's stick to doubles only."

"So Winken and Blinken would be out, too."

"Since two of the hyenas at the zoo are already named that, I think not. But we're wandering. Back to the problem at hand. What do we do?"

"We can't just jump in without thinking. We need a plan."

And he was probably expecting me to help him formulate the plan. Normally, that was the sort of thing I was good at. Why did this crisis have to hit when I felt as if my brain was full of sludge?

Just then P squirmed, as if expressing his impatience, and non-P predictably delivered several thumping blows.

"Settle down and take a nap, kiddies," I said, patting them. "Mommy needs to think."

"More premature labor pains?" Michael asked. I'd been having something called Braxton-Hicks contractions for weeks now. After one late-night visit to the emergency room and several anxious calls to Dad and my ob-gyn, we'd stopped panicking.

"No," I said. "Just the kids doing their calisthenics. Just as well, since if I were getting contractions now, they might not be false."

Michael's face took on the anxious look he always got at the thought of me going into labor.

"And that's fine," I reminded him. "Remember, the kids are big and healthy and nearly full term, and at my last appointment, Dr. Waldron said if they came anytime from then on it would be just fine. Though obviously it would be better if Gin and Tonic delayed their arrival until the current crisis is over."

Michael took a deep breath.

"Sorry," he said. "When the time comes, I will do my best not to behave like a stereotypical new father. And I shouldn't be putting you under this much pressure right now."

"You're not, the prunes are," I said. "And remember, a problem shared is a problem halved. Many hands make light work and all that nonsense. So, one plan coming up."

I pulled out my notebook-that-tells-me-when-to-breathe, the worn notebook that serves me as a combination to-do list and address book. I started a new page and held my pen poised to begin making notes. Michael smiled, as if he found the appearance of the notebook as reassuring as I did, and took a comfortable position leaning against the pantry counter.

"So what kind of records do they keep in the English department about dissertations?" I asked. "Would Ramon's proposal be on file there after it was signed, sealed, and approved?"

Michael's smile disappeared.

"If he turned it in. He told me he did, but maybe I shouldn't have taken his word for it. From now on—"

"From now on, you don't trust your students on anything. They're drama students, not bureaucrats. And frankly, that kind of nitpicking isn't your forte, either, so why don't you get someone who is good at organization to come up with a system to do it for all the drama students and professors?"

"Kathy Borgstrom," he said. "She loves doing stuff like that, thank God."

And Dr. Wright didn't seem to like Kathy. Was that

really because Kathy had no official position, or had Kathy managed to turn in papers the prunes would rather have seen lost?

"That's good," I said, scribbling a couple of items in my notebook. "But right now, we've got to find Ramon's paperwork. Maybe it's in the files and maybe it's somewhere in his frozen room."

"And maybe it's in a landfill somewhere." Michael sounded discouraged.

"Think positively," I said. "I assume we can consider Kathy an ally?"

"Absolutely," he said. "She's militantly in the camp that thinks drama should be a separate department."

"Let's get her to see if the paperwork's on file in the English department."

"Excellent idea," Michael said. He pulled his cell phone out of his pocket and began pushing numbers. "Kathy? Michael Waterston. We've got a problem here."

While Michael explained what was going on, I scribbled a few more notes.

"Make sure she doesn't let the prunes know what she's up to," I called over to Michael. "Or anyone else on the English department side of the rift."

"She already said the same thing," Michael said. "And she says she's worried that they may already have gotten to the files."

"You mean she thinks they might deliberately destroy Ramon's paperwork if they got hold of it?"

"Kathy wouldn't put it past them."

"Trolls," I muttered. "Can I talk to Kathy a sec?"

Michael handed the cell phone over.

"Hey, how are the babies?" she asked.

"As eager as I am to protect their daddy's student," I said. "Not to mention their daddy's hopes of tenure.

They start kicking the second they see the prunes. I mean, Dr. Blanco and Dr. Wright."

"Prunes is better," she said. "What can I do for you?"

I peered down at my notebook, and Michael shifted his position so he could see over my shoulder. I pushed the speaker button so he could hear too.

"Is there someplace outside the English department where the paperwork on dissertations would be kept?" I asked.

"Someplace the prunes can't get at? Not until the department approves them."

"So if someone doesn't make the grade, only the English department has that person's files?"

"Well, I have my files," she said. "But no one considers them official. There's no official record outside the department until after they're approved."

I heard Michael mutter a couple of words I hoped he'd stop using once the twins arrived.

"But the college has some central record of people who get doctorates?" I asked.

"Yes, that would be on file in the registrar's office and the alumni office, and the dissertations are kept in the college library."

"For the whole college? Great!" I said. "Can you get someone reliable down to the library and the registrar's office to do some research?"

"What do you want?"

She sounded puzzled. For that matter, Michael looked puzzled. Maybe having a father who read detective novels by the bagful was rubbing off on me, just a little.

"It might be useful to have someone look at a whole lot of doctoral dissertations to establish that there's a precedent for using foreign language material in dissertations. Especially in the English department, but precedents in history, philosophy, art, and so forth might help."

"Gotcha."

Michael nodded his agreement.

"And is there some way we could compile statistics on the percentage of drama department grad students who complete their master's and doctoral degrees compared with other departments?"

"The attrition rate," Michael said, leaning over my shoulder so Kathy could hear him.

Silence on the other end.

"Is that not something we can get?" I asked.

"You need to talk to Abe," she said. "And Art."

"They have attrition statistics?" Michael asked.

"Some," she said. "They've been working on that as part of their campaign to secede from the English department. We've got statistics and they're not pretty, and the prunes are going to fight like hell to explain them away. But maybe it's time for the showdown."

Michael and I looked at each other. We both knew that the ongoing tension between the drama faculty and certain powerful members of the English department was a volcano waiting to erupt. Was Ramon's problem going to set off the eruption?

Michael squared his shoulders.

"I already called them about an emergency meeting of Ramon's dissertation committee," he said to Kathy. "Maybe you could get hold of them and warn them to come armed with the attrition statistics, in case they feel it's time to use them."

"Can do," Kathy said, and I could hear the tapping of keys. I suspected Kathy had an electronic equivalent of my notebook. "If they've already taken off, I can bring the papers out myself."

"You'd be more than welcome," Michael said. "We've got heat. And enough paella and sangria to feed the whole college."

"I'm already on my way," Kathy said. "I've been getting frostbite over here. Anything else?"

Michael shook his head.

"If we think of anything else, we'll call," I said.

"Up the rebels!" she said. "Death to the prunes!"

And with that she hung up.

SIX

"I think I feel better already," I said, as I made a few scribbles in my notebook. "What next? Should we try contacting the Spanish department?"

"Why?" Michael asked.

"Maybe we could enlist them to help in the battle?" I asked. "Surely someone there would be insulted at the slight to one of their most notable living dramatists."

A slow grin spread over Michael's face.

"Mendoza's not exactly the Spanish Shakespeare," he said. "More like the Spanish Three Stooges."

"Oh, great," I said. "Your tenure's on the line for the Spanish equivalent of 'Nyuck-nyuck-nyuck'."

"Or maybe the Spanish Benny Hill," Michael said. "There's a lot of mildly suggestive stuff in it—the sort of thing that would amuse a teenage boy. Bathroom humor."

"Benny Hill? This isn't making me feel any better about defending him. Wait—is Mendoza's play the one where all the actors keep hitting each other over the head with plastic zucchinis?"

Michael nodded. I closed my eyes and shuddered.

"They'll be using real zucchini in the show," he said.

"And for tonight's dress rehearsal. We just wanted to keep the zucchini budget as low as possible. See, we've got the real ones all ready."

He pointed toward a shelf at the back of the pantry. I craned my neck and saw zucchinis, dozens of them, stacked, row upon row. Their deep-green skins had a curiously menacing sheen, like some kind of sinister organic arsenal.

Michael must have seen the dismayed look on my face.

"There's political content, too," he said. He leaned over, picked up a zucchini, and began tossing it from hand to hand like a beginning juggler. "All anti-Franco, anti-Fascist stuff. Which means it's pretty obscure. Although I suppose Blanco and Wright could have picked up on the left-wing, antiauthoritarian tone and disliked that."

"That's assuming they even bothered to read it," I said. "They could have just said 'Oops, graduate drama student on the verge of actually completing a doctorate!' "

"Quick, Dr. Blanco!" Michael struck a pose, holding the zucchini up as if using it as a sword to lead a charge. " 'We must act quickly to preserve the purity of our department!' "

I giggled in spite of myself.

"I think Art and Abe are right," I said. "The drama department needs its independence. Wouldn't most of the English department be happy to see you leave?"

"Ah, but there are budget issues," Michael said. "They think we take up more than our share of the budget. Our expenditures are higher—putting on shows takes money."

"The produce alone could bankrupt the department," I said.

"What they can't seem to get into their thick heads is that the shows also generate income." He was suddenly serious, though since he was still gesticulating with the zucchini, I had to smother the urge to giggle. "Hell, they might even earn a profit for the college if our theater were a little larger. Right now we sell out every show, but there aren't enough seats to cover expenses. With a bigger theater—which we'll never get as long as we're in the English department—that could change."

"You could earn enough to pay for a new theater?" I asked.

"We could probably find a donor for the theater, and earn enough to cover ongoing expenses," he said. "At least that's what Abe thinks—he's the closest thing we have to an expert on practical stuff like budget."

"But getting back to the English department—if you're such a drain on their budget, why wouldn't they be happy to see you go?"

"Because then we'd be yet another department competing with them in the college budget process," Michael said. "And they're afraid we're cool enough to wow the budget committee into giving us more than our share."

"You are," I said.

He smiled faintly and shook his head. I didn't think he was disagreeing with me, just feeling bone weary of cutthroat academic politics.

"But all that can wait," he said. "Right now, I should have a talk with Ramon. See how bad things are."

He tossed the zucchini on the counter and turned toward the door.

"I'll make sure the prunes are out of the way," I said.

He helped me up from the stepladder and we slipped out of the pantry.

Out in the kitchen, groups of students were talking in small huddles.

I glanced out one of the back windows. Señor Mendoza was smoking a cigarette and deep in conversation with my grandfather. I tried not to worry about this.

My grandfather gestured, and the two of them strode off. Heading for the front porch, no doubt. Most of the student smokers had long ago figured out that the front porch was a lot more sheltered than the backyard, and they were even nice enough to stick to the far end.

I scowled at the barn. The thought of Blanco occupying my office annoyed me no end. And just for good measure, I scowled to the left, in the general direction of the library wing, although I couldn't really see it— just a corner of the sunporch on the far end.

And then one of the twins gave a small kick, and I realized how silly I looked, scowling at invisible menaces. I patted them and turned back to tackle whatever was coming next. I saw Rose Noire was standing at the stove, holding a plate and scowling as darkly as I had been.

"What's wrong?" I asked her.

"That woman," she said.

"Dr. Wright?"

"I have never met anyone with such negative energy."

"Neither have I," I said.

"Her aura is dark brown, almost black," Rose Noire said.

I could see a couple of the students gawking at the statement, but I'd become used to Rose Noire's apparent ability to assess people's auras as easily as their ward-robes.

"A person with an aura like that is capable of . . . well, anything," Rose Noire continued. "Even murder."

To say nothing of murdering the careers of Michael and his poor grad student.

"And do you know what she did?" Rose Noire went on.

I shook my head.

"She requested—no, demanded—that I bring her tea and toast. 'And don't let it steep too long',' Rose Noire said, in a fair imitation of Dr. Wright's precise, supercil-ious voice. " 'And be sure to bring it while it's still hot. And be careful not to burn the toast.' The nerve of some people. I was about to ask if she wanted anything—she didn't have to be so . . . so . . . Oh!"

The toast popped out of the toaster, startling her. Rose Noire arranged the slices on a plate, then placed the plate neatly on a small tray already loaded with a teacup and saucer, a spoon, a sugar bowl, a tray of lem-ons, a butter dish, a marmalade jar, a butter knife, and a lacy starched napkin. I wondered if the elegant tray was intended to improve Dr. Wright's aura or her mood, or whether Rose Noire was simply incapable of being as rude as I would have been to our guest.

"I'd have showed her the way to the kitchen and let her make her own weak tea and pale toast," I said.

"But then we'd all have to put up with her here," Rose Noire said. "Her and her negative energy. I already need to do a cleansing in the house as soon as she leaves."

"While you're at it, have the place fumigated," I said, blowing my nose. "That perfume of hers is driving me bonkers."

"Some sort of ghastly artificial scent, no doubt,"

Rose Noire said. "An essential oil would never do that to you. Where's the teapot?"

It took a couple of minutes for her to locate the teapot—a student was cutting up onions on the counter where Rose Noire had left it, and another student was kneading dough in the place where the first student thought she'd put the teapot. It finally turned up on the floor near the basement door. Rose Noire hurried to whisk the tea infuser out.

"Do you think it'll be too strong for her?" I asked.

"I only used about three tea leaves," Rose Noire said with a sniff. "She's more likely to mistake it for plain hot water."

I noticed she'd used our black Wedgwood teapot and a matching cup and saucer—was that because they were among the few impressively expensive bits of china we owned, or because she thought they matched Dr. Wright's poisonous aura?

She covered the pot with an incongruously cheerful quilted tea cozy and placed it on the tray. Dr. Wright would probably think Rose Noire was our housekeeper. In fact, I suspected she already thought that, which would account for her excessive rudeness.

Not a good idea to tell Rose Noire that. I just shook my head in sympathy and got a glass from the cabinet.

"Let me fix that," Rose Noire said.

"You've got Dr. Wright to worry about," I said.

"She can wait," Rose Noire said. "Juice?"

"Some ginger ale," I said. "My stomach's a little un-settled. Probably just the excitement."

"Damn, but that guy's rude," someone said behind me.

I turned to see a young woman bundled up like an arctic explorer coming in through the back door.

"You mean Dr. Blanco?" I asked.

She nodded. She pushed her hood back and I saw it was the young woman who'd arrived with Ramon and Señor Mendoza.

"What's wrong, Bronwyn?" Rose Noire asked.

"Dr. Blanco came in and complained that it was too cold out there in your office," Bronwyn said. "So I went out to show him where the space heater was," she said. "As soon as I got it going, he demanded some hot tea and snapped at me that he was busy and needed privacy and wasn't to be disturbed. So what am I supposed to do with the tea—slip it under the door?"

"Here." Rose Noire handed me a glass of ginger ale— probably organic ginger ale made from free-range ginger roots, if there was such a thing, but it tasted fine. In fact, it tasted delicious. I had to force myself to sip rather than gulp. I'd have to visit the bathroom soon enough as it was.

"He probably won't even notice if I don't bring him any tea," Bronwyn went on. "When I left, he was yelling into his cell phone. Something about the heating plant."

"If he's working on getting the heat back on, let's do anything we can to help him," I suggested. Blanco was probably the administrator Michael had mentioned earlier—the one running around with a roll of Tums in his pocket. And if he was the person in charge of solving the heating-plant problem, perhaps I should revise my already pessimistic estimate of how long the repairs would take.

Rose Noire finished fussing with the tea tray and carried it out. I glanced at the kitchen clock. Almost noon. We should probably offer some kind of lunch to Michael and the other professors. And by "we" I meant Rose Noire, who wouldn't let me fix a meal even if I had the energy to do so.

I followed her out of the kitchen and plunked myself down in one of the dining room chairs that cluttered our hall, my glass of ginger ale in hand. Time for another nap. Past time, in fact. But I didn't want to nod off while there was anything I could do to help Michael, and climbing the stairs wasn't something I did any more often than I had to.

I pulled out my cell phone and then paused to study it. At one point in my life, I'd refused to get a cell phone. The idea of being always interruptible appalled me. "I'm a blacksmith," I said. "How connected do I need to be?"

But the safety and convenience of having a cell phone when I traveled had made a dent in my resistance, and when Michael entered my life, I realized that there was at least one person I nearly always wanted to talk to, no matter where I was and what I was doing when he called. And now I wouldn't go two steps without it. I was deathly afraid of going into labor at a moment when everyone around me was doing such a good job of leaving me in peace and quiet that they wouldn't hear my cries for help. These days, the cell phone only left my pocket when I slipped it into the charger on my nightstand.

"What a negative person!" I looked up to see Rose Noire returning from the library. Evidently she hadn't lingered to chat with Dr. Wright. "I should start the cleansing now."

"Make it an exorcism," I said. "Maybe you can chase her out."

Rose Noire giggled at that, and returned to the kitchen in better spirits. I speed dialed my brother, Rob. Although he was devoid of any skill with computers or talent for business, his uncanny ability to come up with ideas that would turn into popular computer games had catapulted him into his present role as CEO and chief game theorist at Mutant Wizards, now an industry leader in designing what his head of public relations referred to as "infotainment."

Right now Rob's easy access to technologically savvy people was just what I needed.

"Hey," he said, as he answered his phone. "Do I have nieces and/or nephews yet?"

"Alas, no," I said. "Soon, but not yet."

"You don't want to wait too long," Rob said. "Don't do to them what Mother did to me and stick them with a birthday too close to Christmas."

Rob's upcoming mid-December birthday had always been a sore spot with him. He was convinced that everyone ignored his birthday, giving him a slightly larger Christmas present in lieu of two presents, so that his overall present haul suffered greatly. I was five years older and remembered events quite differently—it seemed to me that our parents had gone to great lengths to throw him quite elaborate birthday parties, and that our friends and relatives had brought heaps of presents out of pity for the poor December birthday boy.

But what seemed to matter decades later was his perception, not what really happened. For that matter, how could I be sure my own perception wasn't off base?

"If you like, I'll jog around the yard a few times after I hang up. See if I can bring on labor before the holidays get any closer," I said. "Right now, though, I need something."

"Your wish is my command," he said. "What do you need?"

"A tame hacker."

A small pause followed. I sipped my ginger ale as I waited for him.

"What for?" he asked. "Nothing illegal, I hope. Don't you just mean a techie?"

"I want someone who's absolutely expert at working with the college data systems," I said. "You know Ramon? Grad student who's been staying with us?"

"Of course," he said. "The one directing the play. With the gorgeous girlfriend."

"Gorgeous girlfriend?"

"Bronwyn Jones. She plays the prostitute with the heart of gold in the play. If she wasn't spoken for . . ."

So that was her name. I'd already marked her down as a potential ally.

"Getting back to Ramon," I said. "Some creeps from the college might be trying to pull a fast one and lose some forms that he needs to have filed for his dissertation."

"Typical. Jerks."

"So I want someone who can comb the college systems for useful information. Proof that Ramon's forms were submitted, if such a thing exists. Or proof that the creeps are trying to pull a fast one. I'd prefer finding stuff that's legitimately available, but don't find me anyone with too many scruples. If we exhaust the legit sources . . ."

"Yeah, I get it," he said. "If they're sending e-mails to each other saying, 'Okay, let's sabotage this Soto kid and that will help us prevent that horrible Michael Waterston from getting tenure,' you want to know about it. I think I know just the person, and he's probably already there. Have you met Danny Oh? That's O-H, last name, not a nickname."

"Not that I know of—should I have?"

"He's only been living in your basement for three weeks," Rob said. "One of our student interns. Remember when I asked if I could have some of the interns live in the basement until the heat came back on in the dorms?"

"I'd forgotten, actually," I said. "It's been weeks since I went down into the basement."

"Probably just as well," he said. "It's taken on a sort of frat-house ambiance. Nothing we can't fix with a few trash bags, of course," he added quickly. "But you might want to let me call Danny and have him come up to the ground floor."

"Call him and brief him," I said. "And tell him I'll drop down to his lair to see him a little later. I need him at his computer, not doing the flamenco in the kitchen, and I may want to look over his shoulder."

I also might want to take a look at the basement, to see if I thought getting it back to normal was going to take more than a few trash bags. I had visions of squalor that would take Dumpsters, fire hoses, and fumigation.

"Will do," Rob said, and hung up.

The doorbell rang. Again. What now?

SEVEN

I set down my ginger ale, waddled to the door, and opened it to find Abe Sass and Art Rudmann standing on the doorstep.

"Am I glad to see you two," I said. "Come in."

"Meg! You're looking wonderful!" Abe exclaimed. He was tall, lean, and Lincolnesque.

"But a little pale," Art added. "Don't you think she looks a little pale? Are you eating enough?" He was short, plump, and always looked as if he'd misplaced something and couldn't quite remember what.

"I'm fine and I'm eating more than enough to keep Gilbert and Sullivan happy," I said. "Come in; you're letting out all the warm air."

"Where's Michael?" Abe asked as they shed their coats and and hung them on one of the coatracks.

"In the kitchen with the students," I said, gesturing.

"And Dr. Wright?"

"In the library."

"We should probably have a short huddle with Michael before we tackle them," Art said. "If Wright's in the library, then I suppose Michael's office is out. Perhaps we could go out to the barn and use your office."

"Dr. Blanco's out in my office," I said. I noticed that they hadn't asked about him—clearly they shared my view that he was a lesser menace. "He wanted privacy for his important phone calls. If you want a room not already filled with either anxious students or hostile faculty, I'd suggest either the pantry or the nursery. Sorry, having all these students around does rather complicate things sometimes."

"It's the nursery, then," Abe said. "If you don't mind."

"Top of the stairs," I said. "I'll—"

"Oh, my God!" Art was pointing at something at my feet. A small puddle.

"Did your water break?" he asked. "Do you need to go to the hospital?" He had clutched Abe's arm and his eyes were as wide as I'd ever seen them.

"No, I'm fine," I said. "That's only some spilled ginger ale."

"Are you sure?" Art asked.

"Now, now," Abe said, patting his arm.

"If my water broke, it wouldn't contain ice cubes," I said, pointing to one sitting in the middle of the puddle. "Trust me, only ginger ale."

"That's a relief," he said. "I was so worried that your water had broken."

"Why worried?" I asked. "I'd be relieved. It would probably mean I was going into labor soon. I'm looking forward to getting this over with."

"Isn't it dangerous?" Art asked. "Wouldn't we have to rush you to the hospital if it broke?"

"Dangerous?" I echoed. "It's a normal part of pregnancy. Although it doesn't happen to everyone; according to Dad, seventy-five percent of the time it doesn't happen until well along in the delivery. And the only danger is that if you don't give birth within twenty-four hours of your water breaking, there's an increased risk of infection. So if it breaks, I call my doctor, very calmly, and do whatever she tells me to do."

"What if you can't reach her?" Art asked.

"Then we call my dad," I said. "Remember, he's a doctor, too."

"But they don't live here," he said. "I thought they lived in Yorktown. That's at least an hour away. What if—"

"He and Mother bought a farmhouse here so they can come to visit as often as they like without being a bother, as Mother puts it. And they've been staying here for the last few weeks, just in case. And Dad's been giving Michael and Rose Noire all kinds of lessons in what to do under every possible circumstance— Michael says it's the next best thing to med school. So there's no danger that I won't have help if I need it." Of course, there was some danger that I might trip over all the eager helpers and well-meaning worriers, but I decided it wouldn't be tactful to say so aloud.

"That's a relief," Art said.

"Don't worry," I said. "We've got everything covered. Why don't you go on upstairs? I'll send Michael up."

"We could fetch him," Art said. "So you don't have to exert yourself. How about—"

"I'm just going to call him," I said, holding up my cell phone. "These days, we both carry our cell phones twenty-four/seven."

"Let's go upstairs and let her make her call," Abe said. He was patting Art's shoulder in a reassuring manner. I found myself wondering how Art had survived his own children's births if the mere possibility that I might be going into labor unnerved him so much. I made a mental note to ask his wife one of these days.

They trooped upstairs. Abe seemed to take the stairs well enough, but Art lagged a little. Was he still worrying about me, or was he feeling unwell? He'd come through heart surgery last year just fine, but everyone was trying not to put too much stress on him. Everyone in the drama department, that is. I felt a sharp surge of anger and resentment against Drs. Wright and Blanco for causing Michael and his closest colleagues so many headaches. If they were fretting Art into some kind of stress-related medical problem . . .

Nothing I could do about it now. Except maybe ask Dad to take a look at him. But first, they had to have their conference.

A wave of tiredness washed over me. I could remember days when I'd have dashed out to the kitchen in a few seconds, but right now I felt too exhausted to stand up. I leaned back in my chair and called Michael.

"Meg?" he said. "Where are you?"

"Just out here in the hall," I said. "Art and Abe have arrived and they're upstairs in the nursery, since at the moment it's probably the only empty room in the house. Apart from our bedroom, of course, where I'm planning to take a nap before too long."

"Great," he said. "I'll be right there."

"By the way, did you know we have displaced programmers in the basement?" I asked.

"Is that something like carpenter ants?"

"No, it's more like I was so focused on the drama students occupying our extra bedrooms and living room, I never even noticed we had a whole extra colony of guests underground."

"Oh, Rob's people." Michael was standing in front of me now, so we both shut off our phones. "Yes, I found out about them a week ago. I chewed Rob out for not asking, then told him that under the circumstances, it was fine if they stayed. Should I have told you? I didn't want to worry you."

"No, it's fine," I said. "Maybe even useful."

"Do you want me to bring you another chair?" he asked. "Something more comfortable?"

"Nothing's all that comfortable right now, and I like this one. I can get out of it when I want to. Art and Abe are waiting."

"Just rest there, then." He planted a kiss on the top of my head and began galloping up the stairs, two steps at a time.

I leaned back. Maybe I'd rest for a few moments and then go up and join them. Or go out to the kitchen to check on events there.

The doorbell rang again.

"This is ridiculous," I said.

Michael came running back down the stairs.

"Stay put," he called. "I'll get it. I thought you said you let them in and sent them up to the nursery."

"I did," I said. "This must be someone else. Our lives are starting to resemble that scene in the Marx Brothers movie—you know the one where they have fifteen people in the ship's cabin?"

"*A Night at the Opera*. Good practice—when the kiddies arrive they'll be a crowd all by themselves. Oh, hello," he said as he opened the door. "Meg, it's your mother."

"Surprise!" Mother trilled.

Mother and her best friend and usual co-conspirator, Mrs. Fenniman, sailed into the foyer. Both of them were carrying bolts of fabric in shades of lavender and green. Behind them, I could see a small party of workmen carrying tool kits and lumber.

I had a bad feeling about this.

"Hello, dear," Mother said. "We've come to decorate your nursery."

She and Mrs. Fenniman both flourished their fabric bolts.

"Decorate the nursery?" I said, blinking with surprise. "It's already decorated."

Behind Mother, the workmen shuffled from foot to foot and looked sheepish. I recognized the tall, lean form of Randall Shiffley, owner of the Shiffley Construction Company. The other two workmen, equally tall and lean, were probably two of his many cousins. No wonder they looked sheepish. Randall and the rest of the Shiffleys should know by now how I felt about my mother's kamikaze decorating attacks.

"Meg, darling, it's not decorated. It's barely furnished." Mother kissed my cheek as she strolled past me toward the staircase. Her entourage followed.

"It's got cribs," I said, pulling my feet back to make sure the twins and I weren't jostled. "Cribs, a table for changing them, and a couple of chests for the clothes and diapers and stuff."

"The cribs don't even match," Mother said, in a tone that suggested that I was on the verge of committing child abuse.

"They don't need to match," I said. "Jeeves and

Wooster won't—they're fraternal. And I don't think it's a bad idea to have different cribs for the kids. Help them establish their independent identities from the start."

"Matching doesn't mean the cribs have to be identical," Mother said. "Matching means they coordinate. Look well together."

"Look like you didn't just buy them from the thrift shop," Mrs. Fenniman put in, with her usual tact.

"We didn't buy them in a thrift shop," I said. "They were gifts."

"Hand-me-downs," Mother said, with a sniff, as if to imply that hand-me-downs were not suitable for her grandchildren-to-be.

"And I'm not sure I approve of any decorating that requires a construction crew," I said. "No offense intended," I added to Randall.

"None taken," he said. "We're just here for the papering and painting and such."

Michael and I exchanged a look. Michael recognized the pleading in my eyes. I didn't want to deal with Mother.

"Why don't you show me what you have in mind?" Michael stepped forward and offered Mother his arm. "I don't think Meg has the energy to make decisions. And I have some pretty definite ideas about what we do and don't want for the nursery. Nothing frilly for example, in case they're boys."

"They can find that out these days, you know," Randall said. "They can do a test to find out whether you've got boys, or girls, or a mixed set."

"Meg and Michael have decided they want to be surprised, the old-fashioned way," Mother said. From the tone in her voice, you'd have thought she had agreed with us all along, instead of arguing with us for months. Probably, as I now realized, because it made her surprise decorating scheme more difficult.

"You'll have to evict Art and Abe from the nursery, then," I said. "Maybe they can have their meeting in our bedroom—it's about the only empty room I can think of."

"I'll take care of it," Michael said. "I'll let you know what I think of the plan after I've reviewed it."

He led the caravan upstairs. When they were out of sight, I closed my eyes and realized I had to go to the bathroom again. And as long as I was getting up, maybe I should see if Rob had recruited my tame hacker. Yes, that was the ticket. I'd visit the refugee computer science students in the basement. Art's and Abe's arrival had given me a new burst of energy, and I thought I could handle the stairs.

I passed through the kitchen on my way to the basement. Normally the kitchen would be alive with students reading lines to each other, debating the merits of the latest movies to hit town, and arguing over such timeless philosophical questions as whether killing another human being was ever justified and who was funnier, the Marx Brothers or the Three Stooges. And after Señor Mendoza's arrival, the kitchen had temporarily become a nonstop party. But the arrival of the prunes had cast a pall over the proceedings. Instead of the impromptu flamenco band, a single student sat in one corner, fingering soft, melancholy blues chords on his guitar. A few students sat in twos or threes, talking in undertones. Even Rose Noire seemed preoccupied as she listlessly stirred something on the stove.

Luckily she was too preoccupied to notice me or she'd have tried to keep me from climbing down to the basement. I slipped through the door, closed it behind me, and carefully began descending the stairs.

EIGHT

I heard melodramatic music coming from somewhere down in the basement.

"What is the name of this monster?" a tinny-sounding voice said.

"Godzilla."

More melodramatic music, followed abruptly by the loud music and louder voices of a commercial so familiar and annoying that I wanted to throw something at the TV every time I heard it. Clearly, at least some of the interns shared Rob's eccentric taste in cinema. The commercial continued as I slowly descended, and the volume was up so high that I doubted anyone would hear me coming. I was surprised I hadn't heard it up in the kitchen. No doubt the programmers had turned the volume up to hear over the flamenco music and never turned it down again when the prunes' arrival dampened the festivities.

When I was close to the bottom of the stairs and could see the main part of the basement, I peered around. Five—no, six—young men sat at makeshift desks made of boards and cinder blocks, peering intently at the monitors of their computers. Rob's interns.

None of them looked up.

I wasn't sure whether to be impressed with their dedication or feel sorry for them for having to work with all the excitement that had been going on upstairs. I wondered if I should have a word with Rob about driving his staff too hard.

Around and behind the desks I could see sleeping bags, air mattresses, and the same piles of clothes, books, and electronics the drama students had created in the rooms they occupied upstairs. The computer interns were no tidier, but certainly no worse.

I tried to pick Danny Oh out from the crowd, but I couldn't see any of their faces well enough. I was about to call out his name when one of the young men, who had been slouched back in his chair while studying something on his monitor, suddenly sat upright and slammed his fist down on the makeshift desk.

"Damn!" he exclaimed.

"What's wrong?" another asked, almost shouting to be heard over the sound of planes and bombs on the TV.

"Ajax just plundered my new city," the first one said.

"Lose much?" asked a third.

"Three million stone," the plundered one said.

"Stupid to keep that much around," one of the others said. "You knew he was going to hit you before long."

"Josh's right," another said.

"I was saving up to upgrade my wall," the first intern said. "Damn, but I hate Ajax."

"What in the world are you guys doing?" I asked.

Six startled faces turned up to look at me. Someone hit the TV mute and the basement became almost unnaturally quiet. I could hear the whirring of fans in the computers and languid chords from the guitar upstairs.

"Are we bothering you, Mrs. Waterston?" the one called Josh finally asked.

"How could you possibly be bothering me, lurking down here in the basement like . . . like . . ."

I groped to find a suitable metaphor. Rats, mice, bats—I couldn't think of anything likely to lurk in a basement that I'd want to call them. I decided to leave it dangling.

"I just wondered what this is all about," I said. "All this about Ajax plundering and building stone walls."

They all brightened.

"We're play-testing Rob's new online game," Josh said.

I peered at the monitor of the nearest computer, the one belonging to Josh. In the center of the screen was a picture of green countryside dotted with castles and around the perimeter were so many words, graphics, and numbers that the whole was about as intelligible as the control panel of a jet aircraft. Around the room, every screen showed a similar graphic. Okay, if Rob was having them play-test games, I didn't have to worry so much about him overworking them. They'd overwork themselves and consider themselves lucky. Rob's games tended to be addictive.

"Is one of you Danny Oh?" I asked.

One of the six raised his hand, as timidly as if I'd asked who hadn't done his homework last night.

"Did you get Rob's call?" I asked.

Danny nodded.

"Can you help?"

He nodded again. I was beginning to wonder if he had a voice. I stepped onto the basement floor and glanced down at the clutter littering it. Three of the students leaped up from their seats and cleared a path before me by picking up armfuls of paper and equipment and throwing them out of the way. One of them pulled over a chair.

"Thank you," I said. I didn't follow it with "Get lost!" but they all acted as if I had and scurried back to their desks.

Maybe Rob was right. Maybe impending motherhood had made me begin to take on Mother's commanding manner.

Scary thought.

"What did Rob tell you?" I asked Danny when the others were, if not out of earshot, at least not hanging over our shoulders.

"Find anything in the college system to prove Ramon filed all his paperwork and got approval for his dissertation," he said.

"Correct," I said. "And also, we're looking for any dirt—um, information—on Dr. Wright from the English department and Dr. Blanco from admin. services."

Danny nodded and scribbled something on a Post-it note.

"First names?" he asked.

"I'm not on first-name terms with them and probably never will be," I said. "I can try to find out if you like."

Danny scribbled. I heard keyboards rattling elsewhere in the room.

"Jean Wright," said one of the other interns.

"Enrique Blanco," Josh said.

I had a feeling I'd just enlisted six hackers instead of one.

"How . . . official do you want this?" Danny asked.

Keyboard rattling abruptly stopped, as if everyone else had paused to listen for the answer.

"Something we could take to court or to the police would be most useful," I said. "But knowing that something would turn up if we got a subpoena would also be useful."

"Gotcha," Danny said. "Want me to call you when I've got something?"

"Please," I said. I scribbled my cell phone number on another sticky note and affixed it to the wall behind his monitor.

As I turned to head back up the stairs, I looked around. I no longer saw any castle-strewn fields.

I felt strangely better. I had no idea if their searches would turn up any proof that Ramon had turned in his papers and gotten permission for his dissertation on Mendoza's plays. Or, for that matter, any dirt on the prunes. But at least we were doing something.

In the kitchen, small numbers of students were still talking together quietly. Actually, plotting might be the better choice of words. I overheard the words "petition" and "protest" several times. Yes, the home team was definitely at work. I nodded and waved to the ones who greeted me on my way to the bathroom.

As I was leaving the lavatory I felt another brief, slight contraction and paused for long minutes, waiting to see if it repeated. Nothing. Braxton-Hicks again.

Still, better to get off my feet. I'd been standing and walking more than usual today and my back hurt. I returned to my chair in the hall, opened my notebook, and began trying to think of something else we could do. Preferably something that I could do while sitting down.

I couldn't think of anything more, at least not until

my hacker team reported in. And until Michael and his colleagues finished their meeting. And . . .

I must have drifted off to sleep almost as soon as my body hit the chair.

NINE

"Mrs. Waterston? Are you all right?"

I started, and almost fell off my chair. A thin, pale young woman student was leaning over me with a concerned face.

"I'm fine," I said. "I just dozed off. What's wrong?"

"Nothing," the young woman said. "At least—well, nothing, except that I can't seem to get Dr. Wright to answer the door."

I glanced at the front door for a moment, puzzled. Then my brain shifted into gear again.

"The library door?"

The student nodded.

"I knocked and knocked, but she didn't answer."

"Maybe she didn't want to be bothered," I suggested.

"Yes, but Dr. Sass told me to go and ask her if she was ready for their meeting."

"And you told her that?"

"I yelled it through the door."

"Did you stick your head in to see what she was doing?"

"I didn't want to annoy her," the student said. "If she was busy, I mean."

"I'll go get her," I said. I waddled off toward the library.

"She won't like being disturbed," the student called after me.

"Then I'll get all the more fun out of disturbing her," I called back.

The student giggled.

Not a joking matter, I reminded myself. Dr. Wright had power over our future and she already didn't like us.

Polite. Businesslike. That's the ticket.

And I had plenty of time to calm down. The library was in a separate wing, at the end of a long corridor, about as far as it could be from the kitchen and still be in the same zip code. I was winded but positively mellow by the time I knocked on the door.

"Dr. Wright?"

No answer. After a few moments I took a deep breath and called to her again, projecting from the diaphragm, as Michael was always telling his students to do.

"Dr. Wright? Dr. Sass and Dr. Rudmann are here."

No answer.

"They're all in Dr. Waterston's office."

Even applying the D-word to three drama professors didn't seem to get a rise out of her.

"The meeting can begin as soon as you're ready."

Had she gone away? Snuck out through the sunroom and gone back to town, perhaps?

I opened the door, peered in, and winced at how untidy it was.

"Dr. Wright?"

No answer. But I felt my nose tickle from the faint odor of her annoying perfume.

I stepped inside and spotted her sitting at one of the work tables at the far end, near the doors to the sunroom, with her head down on the tabletop.

"Dr. Wright? Are you okay?"

She didn't move. As I picked my way across the room toward her, I fished a tissue out of my pocket and held it to my nose to keep her perfume from setting off sneezes. Thus armed, I leaned over and put my hand on her shoulder, intending to shake her gently awake if she didn't respond to my touch. But when I touched her, she slumped sideways out of the chair and fell to the floor. Her eyes were wide and staring, and there was a bloody gash on the left side of her head.

"Oh, no." I backed away. I wanted to sit down or maybe run away. It was probably just the sudden jump in my heart rate, but both P and non-P began wriggling frantically.

"Quiet down, kids," I said, patting my stomach. "Mommy's busy right now." In what was probably a bad omen for the future, they paid no attention and went on thrashing as I pulled my cell phone out and punched the key that would speed dial Dad's cell phone.

"Dad, where are you?" I said. "I need your help."

"Ah!" Dad exclaimed. "Are we having a blessed event?"

"No, we seem to be having a murder," I said. "Someone coshed one of the nasty visiting professors over the head."

"With what?" Dad asked.

"How should I know?" I asked. "Does it really matter? Just come quick. She looks pretty dead to me, but what do I know? Maybe she's still alive."

Even as I said it, I didn't believe it. And I realized

that maybe calling Dad wasn't the smartest thing to do. Maybe I should have called 911.

"I'm already on my way," Dad said. "Just pulling out of Clarence's parking lot."

Good. Clarence Rutledge's veterinary office was only five miles away.

"It's a pity you didn't call a few minutes ago," he said. "I've been sitting next to the chief in Clarence's waiting room. You could call their office and have them put him on."

"That's nice," I said. "That means the chief can get here soon, too. But he'd probably rather not advertise the murder to everyone in the waiting room. I'm going to hang up now and call 911."

"About that weapon . . ." Dad said.

"I have to call the police," I said.

"Just don't let anyone in until we figure out what it is."

Good point. I glanced around. I didn't see a lot of potential blunt instruments in the room. Then I took another step and my ankle connected with something.

"Oh, no," I said.

"What's wrong?" Dad asked.

"I think I tripped over the murder weapon," I said.

"What is it?"

"I'll show you when you get here," I said.

I hung up and looked down at where the statue of Tawaret lay near my feet. The strands of Dr. Wright's brown hair stuck in the statue's overlarge hippo teeth did not improve her appearance.

"Chief Burke isn't going to like you," I told her.

I sighed and called 911.

TEN

"Meg? Is something wrong? Do you need an ambulance?" Debbie Anne, the dispatcher, was normally unflappable, but she sounded distinctly rattled now.

"Nothing's wrong," I said. "At least not with me."

"I can have the ambulance out there in—"

"No ambulance," I said. "I'm not in labor. I just called to report a murder."

"Are you serious?" Debbie Anne asked.

"I'm standing here by a dead body!" I snapped. "Just tell Chief Burke!"

"Hang on for a second," she said. The line went silent, and I mentally kicked myself for shouting at Debbie Anne. I'd have to remember to apologize to her later. Then I heard the chief's voice.

"Yes, Ms. Langslow?"

"I'm standing here by a dead body," I said, this time more calmly. "I think she's been murdered."

"Where's here and who's she?"

"Our library, and she's Dr. Wright of the college English department. I'm sorry, I can't remember her first name right now."

"Never mind that," he said. "What happened?"

I gave him the CliffsNotes version of Dr. Wright's

arrival and her ill-fated stay in our house. As I spoke, I found myself staring at her hands to avoid those un-nerving open eyes.

"Are you sure she's dead?" the chief asked.

"Pretty sure," I said. "But Dad's on his way. I called him first, in case she was actually alive. I'll let him check her vitals. I'm going to sit down someplace that isn't part of your crime scene."

"Anything else?"

"Jean!" I said.

"I beg your pardon?"

"Her first name's Jean," I said. "Dr. Wright. The victim. I knew I should be able to remember that."

"Very good," the chief said. He sounded as if he thought I needed humoring. Maybe I did. "Don't move anything until I get there," he added.

With that he hung up.

"Did you get the chief?" Dad popped into the library, medical bag in hand. He must have set a new speed re-cord on the small country road between our house and the vet.

"What the hell's going on?" Grandfather said, ap-pearing in his wake.

"I called the chief and he says don't move anything," I said. "He'd probably like to keep as many people as possible out of his crime scene," I added to my grand-father, who had followed Dad in and was peering over his shoulder.

"Right, right." He didn't look as if he planned on go-ing anywhere.

"Could you maybe find me a chair?" I asked.

"Plenty of chairs here," my grandfather said.

"Yes but they're part of the crime scene, and I want to sit outside the crime scene, in a chair that was never in the crime scene. Could you get one from the kitchen?"

He frowned, turned, and stumped off.

"Do you need anything?" I asked Dad.

"Call your cousin Horace," Dad said. "The chief might need him. He's in town this week."

I nodded. Horace was a crime-scene investigator in the sheriff's department back in Yorktown, where I grew up. Since he was spending more and more of his free time here in Caerphilly, the chief had taken to borrowing him whenever he had a case that needed forensic assistance. As I picked my way through all the students' clutter to the door, I felt sorry for Horace. He'd probably have to process most of the stuff in the room. And for the chief, who would have to deal with the owners of the stuff.

Outside the library, I took a deep breath, leaned against the wall, and dialed Horace's cell phone.

"Meg, what's up?" he asked. "Are you—"

"The chief needs you," I said.

Normally I responded patiently to everyone's constant inquiries about how soon I planned to go into labor, but seeing a dead body had used up a lot of my usual reserve of calm. Even if it was the dead body of someone I'd come to dislike so intensely in our brief acquaintance.

"What's wrong?" he said, all business.

"We have a body in the library," I said.

"A real one?" he said.

"Yes," I said. "One of the professors."

"A professor? In the library? That sounds like—"

"Yes, someone killed a professor in our library," I said. "And no, it wasn't Professor Plum, and they didn't use the candlestick, the lead pipe, or the wrench. Get all the Clue jokes out of your system before you get here—I don't think the chief will like them."

"Roger," he said, and hung up.

Michael answered on the first ring.

"Everything okay?" he asked. "Or are you, I hope, calling to say that our departmental prima donna is ready for our meeting?"

"Meeting's off," I said.

"Don't tell me she went home!"

"Not quite," I said. "She's dead."

A pause. My grandfather appeared at the end of the hall, dragging a kitchen chair.

"You're serious?"

"Someone hit her over the head with Tawaret."

"With what? A toilet?"

"No, Tawaret. Egyptian goddess of pregnancy and childbirth. Not the real thing, of course—a statue. One of Rose Noire's presents."

I heard him telling Abe and Art, and their exclamations.

"Hang on, Meg," Michael said. "Abe wants to talk to you."

"Meg, are you all right?" Abe asked.

"Tell her she should sit down," I heard Art say in the background. "She's had a shock; she shouldn't be on her feet."

"I'm fine," I said. "And Grandfather just brought me a chair—thank you," I added to Grandfather. "Hang on a sec."

I pressed the mute button on my phone.

"Grandfather," I said. He was, predictably, heading back to the library. "Can you make sure no one leaves the premises until the chief gets here?"

"Leaves the premises?" he said. "You think this is a murder investigation?"

Had he somehow missed the bloodstained hippo statue?

"Looks that way to me," I said. "Until the chief says it isn't, we need to act on the assumption it is. We need to make sure people don't leave. Normally I'd do it, but I'm a little out of it right now. You take charge. Round everyone up and keep them in the kitchen—most of them are probably hanging out there anyway."

"Right," he said, and stalked back down the hall toward the kitchen.

I pressed the button to unmute my phone.

"Sorry, Abe," I said. "What's up?"

"Should I notify the department chair?" he asked. "The death of a member of his department—he's going to want to know about that."

"Especially when it's murder and most of the suspects are going to be faculty or students in his department," I said. "But I think maybe the chief would rather break the news."

"Are you sure it's murder?" he asked.

I closed my eyes for a few moments. Fragments skittered across the inside of my eyeballs. The statue of Tawaret falling from a high shelf—only the shelves were all across the room. Dr. Wright succumbing to a sudden suicidal urge and clubbing herself to death with the statue—also unlikely. I even had a vision, worthy of Rose Noire, of Tawaret coming suddenly to life and leaping onto Dr. Wright's head.

"I can't figure out any way for it not to be murder," I said aloud. "And that's going to cause trouble in the department, isn't it?"

Abe sighed.

"I do hope Art and I can alibi each other for the time of death, whenever that turns out to be," he said.

"Abe!" Art said.

"Because the way things have been going in the department, Chief Burke would be a fool if he didn't put us at the top of his suspect list."

Just then I saw the chief's portly form appear at the other end of the long hallway. Rose Noire was almost running to keep up with him.

"Speaking of the chief, he's here now," I said. "Talk to you later."

"Take care of yourself," Abe said. "You don't need this right now. And there's plenty of other people around to handle whatever problems this causes. Just yell if you need help."

"Thanks." I hung up.

". . . at the end of the hallway," Rose Noire was saying. "Meg! Are you all right?"

"I'm fine," I said. "Dr. Wright isn't. Dad's in there checking to see if she's really dead," I added to the chief. "And I put in a call to my cousin Horace. And I sent my grandfather to the kitchen to make sure all your suspects stay put until you're ready to deal with them."

"All my suspects," he repeated. "So you already know who my potential suspects are?"

I winced. The chief was touchy about even the suggestion of a civilian interfering with one of his cases. His round, brown face was already creased in the frown he usually wore when investigating a crime.

"Sorry," I said. "I should have said 'everyone who was in the house when this happened.' Whether they're suspects or potential witnesses or just people who might

get in your way, I figured you wouldn't want them showing up here. Whatever you want to call them, Grandfather is rounding all of them up in the kitchen."

"You keep saying all," he said. "Just how many
people are here at the moment?"

"Let's see . . ." I began counting on my fingers, and
the chief began scribbling names in his notebook.
"Me. Michael. Rose Noire. Mother. Dad. Grandfather.
Mrs. Fenniman. Three Shiffleys. Señor Mendoza. Art
Sass. Abe Rudmann. Dr. Blanco. Five or six of Rob's
student interns. And an estimated two dozen drama students. Oh, and an unknown number of additional Spanish and drama students who are just visiting to translate
and eat paella and join in the party. At least fifty people."

The chief had stopped scribbling midway through
my listing. By the time I finished, he was staring at me
with an expression of dismay.

"I'm sorry there are so many of them," I said.

"Not your fault," he said. "Any of them with some
particular reason to dislike the deceased?"

"All of them," I said. "Well, all of them who know her.
Dr. Wright is—was—an extremely difficult person."

The chief scribbled some notes.

"Let me take a look at the crime scene," he said.
"Then we can continue this."

"Fine," I said. "By the way, is Scout okay?"

"Scout?" The chief blinked. He was devoted to his
recently adopted hound, and normally would have
beamed that I'd asked. But clearly his mind was on the
murder. "He's fine. Why?"

"Dad mentioned that he'd seen you at the vet's," I
said. "It only just occurred to me to worry about why
Scout was there."

"He was just getting his annual checkup," the chief

said. "But thank you for asking. I hope it's okay that I left him in your kitchen with one of my deputies."

"Absolutely fine," I said. "Just make sure he doesn't eat any of the spilled pills."

"Spilled what? Never mind. You can tell me in a minute. Right now I'm going to inspect the crime scene."

I sat back in my chair and closed my eyes. Probably just as well I had a few moments to gather my thoughts before talking anymore to the chief. I needed to figure out where to begin—with Señor Mendoza's arrival? With the prunes' arrival? Or just with my arrival at the library? And should I tell the chief about Ramon's—and for that matter, Michael's—possible motive? Probably better to be honest about the many reasons everyone had to dislike Dr. Wright. He'd find it out anyway, so better if it came from me. And—

"Meg?"

Art, Abe, and Michael appeared at the other end of the hallway, with Sammy Wendell, one of Chief Burke's officers, trailing behind them.

"Meg? Are you all right?" Art called.

The chief stuck his head out of the door.

"Chief Burke, thank goodness you're here," Abe said.

Michael just strode on ahead of them until he arrived at my side, then knelt down beside my chair and put his arms around me. I suddenly realized how shaky I felt, as if even sitting down I was in danger of keeling over.

"Should she be sitting here?" Art fretted. "Shouldn't she be lying down?"

"May we inform the chairman of the English department?" Abe asked. "He should be told as soon as possible."

"Maybe we should send someone out to the barn to check on Dr. Blanco," Michael said, lifting his head. "After all, a lot of the people who have it in for Dr. Wright don't like him very much either."

"Oh my God," I said. "You're right! And he probably knows Dr. Wright better than any of us."

"Sammy," the chief said. "Go to the barn and fetch this Dr. Blanco person they're so worried about. Put him in the kitchen with the rest."

"Yes, sir," Sammy said, and disappeared down the hallway.

"If you don't mind," the chief said to Michael and me, "I'd like to set up a work area here at your house for now. More convenient, until we finish processing the crime scene and interviewing all these witnesses."

"No problem," I said. "Would you like to use the nursery? With any luck, you'll have solved the crime before Bonnie and Clyde arrive to occupy it. And meanwhile, I'm sure Mother would understand if she has to postpone her decorating for the time being."

"No thank you," the chief said. "I'm not getting between your mother and a decorating project. Besides, I'm too old to go traipsing up and down those stairs every five minutes."

"Then what about my office?" Michael suggested. "It's right here next to the library."

"Maybe a little too close," the chief said. "How can we be sure it's not a part of the crime scene?"

"Because we've been keeping it locked up ever since the students moved in," Michael said. "When we offered to let the students stay here, we realized it could create a security problem—we'd have dozens, maybe hundreds of people coming and going. Most of them perfectly honest of course, but it only takes one crook."

"So we locked everything valuable or confidential in the closet in Michael's office, and we keep the office itself locked," I added. "There are French doors between the office and the library, but they're locked from the office side."

"Any chance someone could have made a key to the office door?" the chief asked.

"It's a combination lock on a padlock," I said. "So it's unlikely."

"Smart," he said. "I'm having to keep my office locked up these days. Got twenty-seven criminal justice majors living in the jail wing until that damned heating plant is fixed. It's as if we put the police station in the middle of a blasted dorm."

"I know what you mean," Abe said. "We have a house full, too. Rivka must have taken in the whole library science department. All through dinner last night they were planning a demonstration against library funding cuts."

"We just took freshmen," Art said. "They do get younger every year, don't they? And none of them eat properly. It's a wonder they're not all deathly ill."

We all sighed and shook our heads for a few moments.

"When you see Dr. Blanco, you can ask him about the heating plant," I said.

"Why?" the chief said. "He's in the English department, right? What do they have to do with the heating plant?"

"Dr. Wright, the victim, was in the English department," I said. "Blanco's in administrative services."

"Then what was—never mind," the chief said. "I'll find out when I question him. Gentlemen, why don't you wait for me in the kitchen? I understand Dr. Blake is gathering my potential witnesses there. You can help

keep all those students in order. Ms. Langslow can let
me into the office, and I'll take a brief statement from
her. If she shows any signs of tiring, Dr. Waterston, I'll
give you a call."

Dr. Waterston. That was more like it. I beamed ap-
provingly at the chief, which seemed to unnerve him so
I schooled my face into the more serious look he would
consider suitable for a participant in a murder investigation.

Michael and his fellow professors reluctantly shuffled
back down the hallway. I took the smaller passageway
that led to Michael's office, which the previous owner
had called the music room. It occupied the same place
at one end of the library that the sunroom did at the
other. I was punching the combination into the lock
when we heard a disturbance outside in the main hall.

"What in tarnation?" the chief muttered, as he strode
back toward the sounds. I followed more slowly.

ELEVEN

Outside, about halfway down the long hallway, Dr. Blanco and my grandfather were standing nose to nose, glaring at each other. Well, more like nose to chin, since my grandfather was half a head taller.

"I insist on talking to the chief," Dr. Blanco was saying.

"And I'm telling you, he wants everyone to wait in the kitchen," Grandfather was saying.

"What's going on here?" the chief said.

Blanco made a quick feint to the left and then broke right, getting past my grandfather and heading for the library door. The chief planted himself in front of the door, feet apart, hands on hips, with a stern look on his face.

Dr. Blanco pulled up short a few feet from the chief. He was panting heavily and before speaking he paused for a moment to catch his breath, pull a handkerchief out of his pocket, and wipe the sweat from his forehead.

"I suppose we should be relieved that at least he's okay," I murmured.

"Am I to understand that something has happened to Dr. Wright?" Dr. Blanco asked.

"Coshed on the head with a bookend," my grandfather said, before the chief could answer. The chief glared at him. Dr. Blanco's mouth fell open in shock.

"It wasn't a bookend," I said, momentarily disconcerted by the thought of having a matched set of Tawarets. "There's only the one of her. Just a statue."

"Coshed on the head?" Dr. Blanco repeated. "Are you sure? By whom?"

"We're not sure of anything yet," the chief said. "And by whom is exactly what we're trying to figure out. Dr. Blake, if you could go back to the kitchen to keep an eye on things?"

"Roger," my grandfather said, and strode back down the hall.

"Oh my," Dr. Blanco said, as if he'd finally taken the news in. His shoulders slumped and he visibly wilted.

"I'm sorry you had to learn the news in this way," the chief said. "But I'm afraid Dr. Wright is dead. We are investigating the possibility of foul play."

"I knew he was upset," Blanco said, shaking his head as if in disbelief. "We knew he wouldn't take the news well but I would never have expected him to do anything like this."

"Who's that?" the chief asked.

"Ramon Soto."

"Ramon Soto?" The chief glanced at me. "Is this one of the people your grandfather's got corralled in the kitchen for me?"

"Probably," I said.

The chief pulled out his cell phone, peered over his glasses at it, and punched a few numbers.

"Sammy? Make sure there's a Ramon Soto there. Uh-huh. No, just make sure he's there and stays put like the rest of them."

The chief hung up and turned back to Dr. Blanco.

"I'd like to hear more about why you suspect this Mr. Soto," he said. "But we're still processing the crime scene so for right now, I'd like you to wait in the kitchen."

"With the rest of the suspects," Dr. Blanco said. "You suspect me of harming Dr. Wright? She was a colleague!"

Colleague? That was fairly tepid. He could at least have said friend.

Blanco must have realized how weak it sounded.

"A trusted colleague," he added. "We worked very closely together on a number of difficult projects."

Better.

"In fact," he added, "I may have been the closest friend she had at the college."

I got the curious impression that he was mentally totting up his own social circle, to reassure himself that he wasn't as isolated as his colleague.

"You have my condolences," the chief said. "I was about to ask if you could wait in the kitchen with the rest of the good people who have had the bad luck to be here when Dr. Wright met her unfortunate end."

"I see," Dr. Blanco said. He sounded somewhat mollified. "I will, as instructed, proceed to the kitchen to await my turn to be interviewed."

He turned and started down the hall.

Just then two figures appeared at the far end. Randall Shiffley, accompanied by Deputy Sammy.

"Chief," Randall called. "We've got a delivery truck outside—some of the stuff Mrs. Langslow ordered for the nursery."

"Oh, bother," I muttered. I closed my eyes and leaned against the wall.

"If we don't let 'em deliver it, I'm not sure when we

can get the stuff back. Is it okay if we—you! What are
you doing here, you miserable rat?"

I opened my eyes to see Randall Shiffley and Dr.
Blanco looking at each other from opposite ends of
the hall. Randall was glaring fiercely, and Blanco was
hunching again.

"So this is where you've been hiding when I try to
reach you," Randall went on. He began striding down
the hall toward us.

"I've been completely available by cell phone at all
times," Blanco said. "I'm not hiding. But I choose not
to respond to abusive, harassing phone calls."

"I've been calling to demand the money that's due to
me," Randall said. "Is that what you call abusive?"

"That check was sent weeks ago—" Blanco began.

"And never got to me, so just cancel the damned
thing—" Randall shouted back. Apparently it was his
turn to stand chin to nose with Blanco. I glanced at the
chief. He was simply listening quietly. I decided to follow suit.

"And the college is not paying you another dime until
you deal with the heating plant!" Blanco snapped back.
He was probably aiming to appear stern and fierce, but
only looked as if he had indigestion.

"Deal with it? Deal with it? I've been trying, you
miserable cheat!"

I winced as the two kept shouting at each other.
No, Randall was shouting. Blanco was merely speaking a little louder than usual. And he was leaning slightly
away from Randall, shoulders hunched defensively, looking more like a turtle than ever.

But if Randall thought he could beat a bureaucrat
solely with decibels, he was naïve. Even if he won the
current battle by shouting, Blanco could retire to his of-

fice, issue a few memoranda, and win the war. I knew that Caerphilly College was a major source of revenue for the Shiffley Construction Company, as it was for all the contractors in the county. Did Randall really mean to antagonize someone who probably had the ear of the college president, and thus a lot of influence on which vendors were chosen?

Was he calm enough even to think that way?

And why was the chief letting this go on? Didn't he have better things to do? Like investigate the murder?

"Quiet!" I shouted. They both stopped talking immediately and looked at me. Randall looked calm and expectant. Blanco, the ingrate, looked as if he resented the interruption.

"This is of no concern of yours," he said, and pursed his lips again.

"It damn well is if it's about to make you come to blows in our house," I said. "Not to mention the fact that you're upsetting my unborn kids."

"I think it's very much Meg's business," Randall said. "Since, like most of the good people in this town, she's dealing with the consequences. Blanco's been going around blaming us for the problems with the college heating plant."

He pronounced it Blank-o, with a flat, American "A." Why did I suspect it was deliberate?

"I hardly think it's unreasonable to blame you, since your company has failed to complete the repairs for weeks now," Blanco said.

"We'd be happy to complete it anytime you like," Randall said. "But either the college has to order the part, or you have to pay some of our back invoices so we can afford to order it."

"Parts and materials are to be supplied by the vendor,"

Blanco said. His tone was mechanical, as if parroting an often-quoted sentence from a contract.

"And the customer's supposed to pay the vendors on time," Randall said. "Some of our invoices are six months past due."

"I explained the problem we were having in accounts payable," Blanco began.

"Stupid problem to have," Randall said. "If a woman's going out on maternity leave, you can usually spot that problem far enough in advance to arrange for someone else to take over."

"The unfortunate logjam has been resolved," Blanco said. "And your check has been mailed."

"The check's in the mail," Randall said. "Been hearing that for six weeks. Meanwhile, I'm getting hounded by my suppliers for what I owe them on parts and materials we used on your jobs eight or nine months ago. I've got payroll, I've got overhead—I can't afford to keep carrying this."

"You have to—" Blanco began.

"Hold it," the chief said. "Is this why there's no heat at the college?"

Blanco pursed his lips. Randall nodded.

"Blanko's right about one thing," Randall said. "The main boiler's been in pieces on the floor for weeks now. What he doesn't ever mention is that the reason it's been in pieces is that we can't afford to fix it. College owes us nigh onto half a million dollars in back invoices."

"Which you'll have as soon as you find the check we sent you," Blanco repeated.

Randall shot him an angry glance and continued.

"I can't fix the boiler without a piece that costs nearly a hundred grand, and thanks to Blanko there, I'm so far in the hole I can't afford to buy a hammer at the hardware store. If I don't get what's due me soon, I'm going to go under."

"The check has been issued," Blanco repeated.

"And it hasn't been received, so cancel it and issue another one," Randall said. "People do it all the time. You don't know how, the bank can walk you through it. And if you give me a call, I'll pick it up myself and save you the postage."

"That shouldn't be necessary," Blanco said. "There's a lot of paperwork involved in canceling a check, and a fee, and if you'd only—"

"Damn the fee!" Randall shouted.

"I agree," I said. "You mean the heat has been off for a month now because you're too cheap to pay a stop-check fee? How much is it? I'd be happy to donate that much to the cause."

"It's not that simple," Blanco said. "But I'll look into it."

He scuttled down the hall. Sammy followed, presumably to see that he went to the kitchen as instructed.

"Not that simple?" I repeated. "Is the man an idiot?"

"Just incompetent," Randall said.

"Interesting," the chief said.

"I've been hearing that sniveling liar make excuses for six months," Randall said. "You know what I'm starting to think? Maybe the college is having a cash-flow problem. Maybe they're not paying me because they can't."

My stomach churned at the thought. Cash-flow problems at the college? Right now, with me unable to work at my blacksmithing because of my pregnancy, Michael's paycheck from the college was our only reliable source of income. I had a brief, melodramatic mental image of myself like a character out of Dickens, wearing rags, struggling through snowdrifts, carrying a swaddled infant in each arm, begging for alms.

Hormones again. I took a deep breath, banished the image, and focused on Randall's problem.

"You need a lawyer," I said. I reached into my pocket for my notebook, pulled it out, and tore out a blank page. Then I flipped to the section in the back where I kept names and addresses and wrote down the names of two attorneys.

"Here," I said. "Cousins of mine. Call one of them, say I sent you, and they should do a good job for you."

"Thanks," Randall said. He was about to put the sheet of paper in his pocket, then seemed to change his mind and pulled out his cell phone. "You recommend one over another?"

"Victor's nicer," I said. "Hermione's a shark."

"I want Hermione then," he said. "Thanks."

He strolled away, already dialing.

I winced slightly. I wouldn't have minded siccing my cousin Hermione on someone I didn't like. The late Dr. Wright, for example. But Blanco? He might be spineless and ineffectual, but I suddenly began to feel sorry for him.

"That was interesting," the chief said.

"Do you think it has anything to do with the murder?" I asked. "Oh, never mind. I should know better than to ask that."

"Could Dr. Wright have had something to do with Randall's problem?" he asked.

"Seems unlikely," I said. "Blanco's in administrative services—they deal with facilities. But Wright's a dean in the English department. I can't imagine what she could have to do with the boiler."

"We'll look into it," the chief said. "Meanwhile, Sammy?"

"Yes, sir," the deputy replied. He was still lurking cautiously at the other end of the hall.

"Guard the door to my crime scene," the chief said. "When Horace Hollingsworth gets here, let him in. No one else."

"Yes, sir," Sammy said. He began striding toward the library door. His gangly frame and awkward, jerky way of walking made you overlook the fact that he could move quite rapidly when he wanted to.

"Chief?" Randall again, sticking his head around the corner at the far end of the hall. "About that delivery . . ."

"Can we have them put it in the barn for now?" I suggested. "Whatever it is."

The chief nodded. Randall disappeared.

"Now, Ms. Langslow, if you don't mind."

I led the chief into Michael's office.

"I'm taking the desk chair for now," I said, as I plopped down in Michael's huge leather chair. "You can have it when I leave, but right now, I'm sitting for three."

"That's fine," he said.

"And you might not want to sit there," I said, as he pulled up one of Michael's four guest chairs.

"Why not?" he asked, glancing down at the chair as if expecting to find something dangerous in the seat.

"They may look comfy—in fact, for the first five minutes, they aren't too bad. But they're next to impossible to get out of," I said. "I've seen able-bodied people take two or three tries, and for anyone with weak knees or low upper-body strength, forget it."

"I'll save them for any witnesses I want to be sure of

holding onto," the chief said. He pulled up a nearby book box and sat on that instead. "Now tell me what the devil's been happening around here."

I took a deep breath and dived in.

I'd gotten as far as telling the chief about the confrontation between Ramon Soto and the prunes when someone knocked on the door.

"Who is it?" the chief snapped, in a tone of voice clearly intended to make casual curiosity seekers flee.

Sammy stuck his head in.

"We appear to have found the murder weapon," he said.

He held up the pregnant hippopotamus statue in one gloved hand.

TWELVE

"What the hell is that?" the chief asked.

"She's the Egyptian goddess of pregnancy and child-birth," I said.

The chief studied the statue with a look of vague distaste on his face.

"This thing belongs to you?" he asked.

"Don't look at me," I said. "It was a present."

"Who the dickens would give a pregnant woman a thing like that?"

"Rose Noire. It's supposed to protect me and the kids from demons. And if you want to know how I felt about it—well, there's a reason I exiled it to the library."

The chief shook his head.

"There seems to be hair on the hippo," Sammy said. "Human hair, I mean. And if you ask me, the dent in the victim's skull matches the hippo's snout."

"We'll have Horace look at the hair when he gets here," the chief said.

"He's already here," Sammy said. "He wouldn't let me bring this to show you till he took about a million photos of it lying there on the floor."

"Good," the chief said. "Give that nasty thing back

to him. I'm sure he and the medical examiner will want to do some tests to confirm the match to the wound. But from the look of things, I expect you're right."

"Does this mean you'll have to confiscate the statue?" I asked. I tried not to sound too cheerful.

"I'm sorry," the chief said. "I'm afraid so."

"Don't be sorry," I said. "I'd be absolutely thrilled if you ended up having to keep it indefinitely."

"That shouldn't be necessary," the chief said. He turned back to Sammy. "Where did you find this?"

"Lying there right by the body," Sammy said. "Like whoever did it just hit her and dropped the hippo right away."

"Show me," the chief said. "If you don't mind," he added to me.

"I'm not going anywhere until Starsky and Hutch decide to show up," I said. The chief looked blank for a moment, so I patted my stomach.

"You're not having labor pains, are you?" he asked, looking anxious. "If you think you're going to need to go to the hospital soon, we could finish our interview now."

"I'm fine," I said. "If the shock of finding a dead body didn't send me into labor, I think I can manage to hold off a few minutes while Sammy shows you where he found the murder weapon. But there's just one thing," I said to his back.

He turned around and frowned.

"You might want to tell Horace that where he found it may not be precisely where the killer left it," I said. "I remember stumbling over the thing as I was backing away from the body. Sorry," I added, seeing the slight frown on his face.

"Not exactly your fault," he said. "Did you pick it up?"

"No." I shook my head vigorously. "I knew better. I left it where it landed. I don't think it moved much, if that helps."

He nodded and disappeared.

I leaned back, closed my eyes, and hoped he took a good long time examining the scene.

"Meg, dear."

I winced involuntarily, then opened my eyes to see my mother standing in the open doorway of the office.

"Meg, would you like to see the plans for the nursery?"

I was opening my mouth to shriek, "Not now, Mother." But I stifled the urge and counted to ten before saying anything.

"Maybe later," I said finally. "Has Michael seen them?"

"He thinks they're fine," she said. "But I would feel better if you saw them before we get started, and we need to do that soon if—"

"Right now, I'm not sure Chief Burke will even let you do any decorating," I said. "He might consider the whole house part of the crime scene."

"Crime scene?" Mother asked. Her hand flew to her throat in a characteristic gesture of genteel astonishment. I sighed. I'd forgotten that the rest of the household might not have heard about Dr. Wright. Mother, for example, had probably been too busy with her decorating plans to notice.

"We've had a suspicious death," I said. "Probably no one you know," I added, to quell the growing alarm on her face. "A Dr. Wright from the English department."

"Oh, dear," Mother said. "The English department? Is this apt to have any unfortunate effect on, well, circumstances?"

"You mean on Michael's tenure prospects?" I've never been noted for subtlety. "If anything, this should improve them, since it would be hard to find anyone in the English department who hated him more than Dr. Wright."

"I see," Mother said. I could tell she disapproved of my bluntness at the same time as she appreciated the information. And I hoped she wasn't about to say anything about a silver lining.

"Of course, this means Michael is a suspect," I said. "We all are."

"I'm sure that the chief will sort everything out," Mother said. "Such a nice man. Where is he? I'll just make sure he's comfortable with our continuing the work on the nursery."

"He's in the library," I said. "With the body."

She sailed off. I wondered if Mother's current positive opinion of the chief would survive if he vetoed her plan to redecorate the nursery, or worse, blasted her for interrupting his investigation.

Not my problem.

I heard them talking out in the hall for a few minutes. I felt curiously indifferent to the outcome of their conversation. If I'd known this morning that Mother was planning a kamikaze decorating raid, I'd have reacted with angst and anger. But now? I found it hard to care.

"Sorry to keep you waiting," the chief said. I opened my eyes to see him seating himself in one of Michael's guest chairs. Had he forgotten my warning, or did he think I was exaggerating? He'd find out. "Now, let's— hang on a second."

Something beeped, and he reached in his pocket and pulled out a cell phone. He flipped it open and frowned at the screen.

"Text message," he said. "I hate text messages." He peered over his glasses at the phone, tentatively punched a few keys, and then frowned more deeply and continued staring at his cell phone as if expecting it to turn into an adder and bite him.

"What's wrong?" I asked.

"I called Dr. Smoot," the chief said. "And I left a message for him to call me back ASAP on police business. Does that seem unreasonable?"

"No," I said. "You've got a murder. You need the medical examiner."

"Acting medical examiner," the chief corrected. There was no love lost between the two at the best of times. "And he texted me back—is that a verb, texted?"

"If it isn't, it will be eventually," I said. "What did he text—er, say?"

"That he couldn't because he was in no this week. What does he mean, 'in no'? Is that some kind of flippant refusal? Like get lost?"

"Probably just a typo," I said. "Maybe he was typing something that began with n-o and hit send before he finished."

"Well if that's the case, he should have sent a follow-up message to explain," the chief grumbled. "And he was pretty emphatic. Not just no but NO, in caps."

"Oh, he means New Orleans," I said.

"Well, how the dickens am I supposed to know that?" the chief said. "And what the devil is he doing there?"

"Taking that tour of the famous vampire hangouts in New Orleans," I said. "He's been talking about doing that for ages. Fictional vampire hangouts, of course," I added, seeing the chief's reaction. Chief Burke had little sympathy with his acting medical examiner's passion for the supernatural.

"Fine way for a grown man to spend his time," the chief said. "Not to mention the fact that he's not around when I need him."

"Next time I plan a murder, I'll make sure he's on the invitation list," I murmured.

"I'll have to call the mayor and get him to deputize someone again," he said. "Might as well be your father, if you think he'd be willing."

"I'm sure he'd be ecstatic," I said. "As long as you don't consider him a suspect."

The chief sighed. "No, he's well alibied," he said. "We've been together down at the vet's office for most of the last two hours."

I was immensely relieved. Dad was an avid reader of mystery books and always loved the idea of being involved in a real-life case, even—or perhaps especially—if he was a suspect. But he could hardly nominate himself as the killer if the chief himself could alibi him.

The chief punched a few buttons on his cell phone. I closed my eyes and tried to demonstrate my complete lack of interest in eavesdropping during the chief's brief conversation with the mayor.

"Lucky thing, your dad being with me at the vet's," the chief said, after he and the mayor had said their goodbyes. "That makes him practically the only person associated with this household who isn't a suspect."

"Including me," I said.

"Including you," he echoed. "Though I have to admit, I can't help but consider you a long shot."

"Because of your profound respect for my character, or because you don't think a pregnant woman capable of murder?" I asked.

"Never mind," he said. "Shall we continue our discussion?"

"What about Horace?" I asked. "If you're having Horace do the forensic work—"

"Horace and Sammy were at the veterinarian's office with your father and me," the chief said. "Some fool tourist ran over Sammy's dog, Hawkeye, this morning. Didn't even stop to see if the poor beast was all right. Which he will be," he added, noticing my anxious face. "But it took Doc Clarence an hour and a half of surgery, with your Dad helping out, while Horace and I calmed Sammy down and got a description of the car. Been a lively morning already."

"And now this," I said, shaking my head. "By the way, don't you want to tell Dad about his temporary appointment?"

"Good point." He started to sit up, realized the chair wasn't about to let him, and then tried again. He managed to lever himself out, which was more than a lot of people could, but he gave it a thunderous glance once he'd escaped. "Though I don't know why I bother. He's been acting as if he already had the job from the moment he arrived on the scene. But still, your father's—"

"Chief?"

Cousin Horace. With Dad right behind him.

"We have good news, sort of," Horace said.

"Sort of?" the chief echoed. He glanced back at the chair, then changed his mind and leaned against the desk.

"Tawaret didn't do it."

"Tawaret?" the chief asked. He pulled out his notebook and flipped a few pages forward. "Who the hell's Tawaret?"

He glared at me, as if rebuking me for leaving out a critical suspect.

"Meg's hippopotamus statue," Horace said. "It wasn't the murder weapon."

"You're sure?" the chief said.

"Reasonably sure," Horace said.

"We'll know more at the autopsy, of course," Dad said. "But I think the evidence is fairly conclusive."

"I thought you found strands of her hair on the hippo, and the dent in her head matches the thing's snout," the chief said. "If she wasn't hit over the head with it—"

"She was," Horace said. "But that's not what killed her. She was already dead when the blow was struck. No bleeding."

"Exactly," Dad said. "It could be a natural death, but more likely she was poisoned. You might want to secure the kitchen."

Bad news for the paella makers. The chief pulled out his cell phone again.

"What was she eating?" he asked, as he pushed one of his speed-dial numbers.

"Weak tea," I said. "And lightly buttered toast. You might want to see if Rose Noire took the same thing to the other prune."

"The other what?" the chief said, frowning.

Oops. Better not explain. I'd just let him try to figure out if he'd misheard or I'd misspoke.

"The other professor," I said. "Dr. Blanco, the one who came with Dr. Wright. I could be wrong, but I think they both ordered weak tea and toast."

"And prunes?" the chief asked.

"I don't know," I said, wincing. "Ask Rose Noire."

"Great," the chief said. "Which reminds me—Dr. Langslow, the mayor sends his regards and asks if you'll fill in as acting medical examiner while Smoot's away."

"Shouldn't that be acting acting medical examiner?" I said. "Since Smoot—never mind."

The chief was glowering at me.

"Splendid," Dad said.

"So carry on, and keep me posted," the chief said. "One other thing—"

Dad and Horace both paused in the doorway and looked back expectantly.

"We don't tell anyone about this," the chief said. "Apparently Dr. Blake has already spread the word that she died from being hit over the head. So let's leave it that way. Let everybody think that's what we think."

"To weed out false confessions," Dad said, nodding vigorously.

"And to create a false impression of security in our killer," the chief said. "If he doesn't know we know about the poison, maybe he'll think he's got plenty of time to dispose of the evidence. So don't say anything to anyone about poison. What should we say she died of?"

"Blunt force trauma to the upper right portion of the occipital bone," Dad said.

"Too specific," the chief said.

"I'm the one most people are going to be interrogating," I said. "How about if I just say it looked to me as if she was hit on the back of the head with something."

"That's probably best," the chief said. "Holding back information is one thing; deliberately spreading inaccurate information might be counterproductive."

"All right." Dad sounded disappointed. "I'd better get back to my examination."

He and Horace popped back into the library.

"There's also the fact that anyone with half a brain could figure out that he's lying," the chief said.

"Yes," I said. "Dad's enthusiasm for intrigue far exceeds his acting skills."

"I hope he's not going to sulk about it," the chief said.

"He is," I said. "But only for about five minutes. And I see your point. After all, if someone saw some-one else deliberately putting poison in her tea—oh, my God!"

"What?" the chief asked.

"Señor Mendoza's heart medicine. Did I mention that?"

"No," the chief said.

"Of course I didn't," I said. "Because I thought she was killed with a blunt instrument. But now that we know she might have been poisoned—"

"Just tell me about the blamed heart medicine," the chief said.

"He spilled it," I said. "He handed the pill bottle to a student to open, and suddenly there were little white pills all over the foyer floor. And people crawling around everywhere picking them up."

"When you say people, you mean all those . . . potential suspects sitting around in your kitchen?"

"Most of them," I said. "I don't think Art and Abe were here yet, or Mother and the Shiffleys."

The chief scribbled in his notebook.

"Of course, that doesn't mean there weren't still pills lying around when they got here," I said. "Señor Mendoza didn't seem at all worried about getting them all back. That's why Dad was at the vet, incidentally; be-cause Spike swallowed one, and we were worried about what it would do to him."

"He mentioned Spike might have swallowed some-thing," the chief said. "But just then Sammy came run-ning in with Hawkeye, so I never heard the details."

"Anyway, there were pills all over the front hall and probably still are some. I hope Clarence keeps Spike until we can give the hall a thorough vacuuming. You might not know what they were—unless you talked to any of the dozens of people who saw what happened. But—"

"Did the pills look something like this?" he asked. He held up a small yellowish-white pill.

"Yes," I said. "I didn't know you had a heart problem."

"I don't." He tucked the pill back in his pocket. "I almost stepped on this in your foyer when I first arrived. So we make sure the tox screen looks for digitalis."

He glanced up and caught me suppressing a yawn.

"You should rest," he said.

"If you're finished with me, I could certainly use a nap," I said.

"Take care of yourself," he said, shooing me in the direction of the door. "If you think of anything else, you let me know after your nap."

"Will do," I said.

I made my way down the long hallway, wondering all the while what it would take to install one of those rolling walkways they used in airports to move passengers from one end of the terminal to the other. Probably not very useful in the long run, so I returned to trying to figure out how we could install an elevator without ruining the look of the front hallway.

I was still thinking about the elevator when I found myself at the bottom of the stairs. To my surprise, the siren call of my nice, comfortable bed wasn't as strong as it had been a few minutes ago. Okay, my eyelids were still drooping, but I was also dying to find out what all those witnesses, suspects, and innocent bystanders were up to in our kitchen.

And also to my surprise, I was hungry. I couldn't remember the last time I'd eaten—breakfast? Had I had a midmorning snack? Even if I had, odds were it was time for lunch.

I braced myself in case the kitchen still reeked of seafood and flung open the door.

Dozens of anxious faces looked at me. And I seemed to have interrupted a migration in process. People were slowly filing out the back door, many of them carrying kitchen chairs. Sammy was standing by the door, holding a clipboard, supervising the departure.

"What's up?" I asked.

"Chief's orders," Sammy said. "He said he wants everybody out of his crime scene until Horace has a chance to check it out, and until Horace says otherwise, the whole house is the crime scene. So we're taking everyone out to the barn."

Wasn't the chief worried that some of these people— including the poisoner—might begin to suspect that he had a particular interest in the kitchen?

"He's probably just tired of people sneaking out of the kitchen and coming to the library to bother him," I said.

Sammy chuckled slightly.

"You could be right," he said. "We'll have an easier time keeping them out of his hair if they aren't in the house."

I wasn't sure how much evidence they'd find in the kitchen, though, even if the murderer had done something there to poison Dr. Wright. Clearly someone had made a start at cleaning it. Probably Rose Noire, who cleaned furiously whenever she had to get something out of her system—like Dr. Wright's rude treatment of her.

Though it would be interesting to see if anyone had insisted on helping her.

"By the way, I was sorry to hear about Hawkeye," I said to Sammy. "How is he?"

His face fell.

"He'll be fine, thanks to Clarence and your dad," he said. "But I'm worried that we won't be able to catch the guy who did it, with all this going on. All our officers are here, and I'm not sure the state police are really taking the search seriously."

"Hey, if you got enough information for any kind of a search, that's good, right?" I asked.

"It was a dark blue SUV," he said. "But I only got a partial license plate. Debbie Anne's going to get the DMV to give us a list of possible vehicles, but the more time passes, the smaller our chances of getting useful evidence."

I didn't know what to say, so I patted him on the shoulder. I understood why the chief was putting all his officers on the murder investigation. But I also understood how Sammy felt about his dog.

Just then I spotted the tea kettle on the stove and realized I hadn't told the chief everything I knew.

I ducked out into the hall, fished my cell phone out of my pocket, and called the chief.

"I thought of something I should have told you," I said. "I don't know how I overlooked it—except when I was telling you about what happened, I thought Dr. Wright had been killed with the statue. So the tea didn't seem important."

"What tea?"

I glanced up to make sure there was no one in the living room and cupped my hand around the cell phone.

"The weak tea Dr. Wright drank, along with her dry toast. Rose Noire made it for her," I said as softly as possible. "I think that might be how she got the poison."

A pause.

"You think your cousin poisoned Dr. Wright?"

"Good heavens, no! She wouldn't poison a fly. At least not deliberately." I thought, briefly, of all those noxious healthy drinks she kept bringing me. But that didn't really count.

"Then why do you think I should know about the tea?"

"She was making it in the kitchen," I said. "Weak tea and light toast. I wasn't there the whole time she was doing it, but when I was there, she was fussing nonstop about how rude and obnoxious Dr. Wright was and making it clear how much she resented having to take a tea tray to her."

"And there were other people in the kitchen?"

"There are always other people in the kitchen," I said. "The kitchen and the library are where people hang out, and just then Dr. Wright was tying up the library. So anyone could have been in the kitchen. And Rose Noire wasn't just brewing tea and slopping it into a mug; she was running from the kitchen to the pantry, arranging the sort of gracious tea tray Mother always insists on."

"Yes, I saw it in the library," the chief said. "The black china made a nice, gruesome touch in the crime scene photos. Did anyone help Rose Noire?"

"Not that I saw," I said. "But everyone would have known who it was for, and anyone who wanted to spike the tea or the sugar bowl would have had plenty of chances while Rose Noire was fussing over the napkins and arranging the flowers."

Another pause. A long pause.

"So if the poison is in the tea—" he began.

"Or the toast, or the sugar bowl, or anything else on the tray."

"—you want me to know that Rose Noire didn't do it."

"I want you to know that Rose Noire isn't the only one who could have done it," I said. "That's all. And that she might have some idea about who was hanging around and had the opportunity."

"Thank you," he said. "Anything else?"

"All I can think of for now," I said.

"Thank you," he said. "Now get some rest."

It sounded like an order. And, while he probably wouldn't believe it, an order I planned to obey.

As soon as I figured out what the loud voices in the kitchen were all about.

THIRTEEN

I stuck my head back into the kitchen. The last few of its former occupants were filing out—Ramon Soto, Bronwyn Jones, and Dr. Blanco, supervised by Sammy and a deputy I recognized as one of Randall Shiffley's cousins.

"I insist that you present my request to Chief Burke immediately," Blanco was saying to the deputies. He could have used some speech lessons. His voice, normally rather high and thin, had a tendency to squeak when he tried to raise it in emphasis.

"I'll do that, sir," Sammy said. "I'm sure he'll get to you as soon as possible."

"I have a very busy day," Blanco said. "And this disruption is intolerable!"

Ramon muttered something in Spanish. Bronwyn tittered. Blanco shot him a dirty look but didn't reply. He strode out the back door, presumably to join the rest of the suspects in the barn.

"What a jerk," Ramon said. "Thinks he's more important than everybody else."

I'd have diagnosed Blanco as having an inferiority complex myself.

"Mr. Soto?" Sammy said. "Chief's waiting."

"Right," he said. Head down, shoulders hunched, he stumbled toward the door to the hall. Sammy followed him.

"See her out to the barn, will you?" he said over his shoulder to Deputy Shiffley.

The door closed. Bronwyn turned to stare at me and the deputy with arms crossed and a frown on her face.

"Don't look at me," I said. I looked longingly at the refrigerator. I'd intended to rummage in it for something suitable to eat. At the moment, suitable meant anything my temporarily picky appetite could tolerate that was still in its original sealed container. But I'd forgotten that it was an integral part of the crime scene. And I wasn't sure I wanted to eat anything from there anyway—not until the police figured out how Dr. Wright was poisoned.

"If you could follow me to the barn, ma'am," Deputy Shiffley said to Bronwyn.

"What about her?" she said, pointing to me.

"I've already been interrogated and released," I said.

I could hear Bronwyn still arguing with the officer as I drifted out into the hallway.

Something to eat and a place to sleep. I had some snacks stashed in my bedroom. But I stared up at the stairs in dismay. It had been a long morning. I wasn't sure I wanted to go upstairs. If I did, I'd probably be too tired to come down later, which would mean I'd miss everything that was going on.

As I was dithering over whether to climb the stairs, the doorbell rang.

"Serves me right for hesitating," I muttered as I made my slow way to the door.

But when I opened the door and saw who was standing outside, my mood lifted.

"Kathy!" I exclaimed.

Kathy Borgstrom was dressed, as usual, almost entirely in black—black velvet coat, black tights, black wool cap, black platform boots, and black velvet gloves. A cobwebby scarf in neon pink added the one note of color—though very little warmth. But while her wardrobe might look as if she'd raided the crypt of a Goth-obsessed vampire, Kathy herself could never be described as anything but wholesome and perky. Not to her face, of course.

"Meg!" she said. "You look enormous. How much longer?"

"Anytime now," I said. "Come in."

"I was kidding about the enormous part," she said. "I hope you realized that. Most of you looks fine; you haven't gained a lot of weight in your face or your hands or—"

"It's okay," I said. "Come in so I can shut the door. You're letting all the heat out."

"Is this a bad time?" she asked as she followed my orders. "I could come back later if this is a bad time."

"It's a horrible time, and don't you dare leave," I said. "Abe needs you. We've had a murder."

"A murder!" Her hands flew to her face in a dramatic gesture of alarm. "Who?"

"Dr. Wright," I said.

"Oh," she said, in a much less agitated tone. "That's terrible," she added, about a second too late.

"You think so? Nobody else does."

"Just because none of us likes her doesn't mean it's okay for some nut to knock her off," she said, as she shed her coat, revealing a tight-fitting black knit garment that she probably thought of as a dress. I would have called it a tunic. "Besides, you know this is only going to cause trouble for all of us on the drama side of the divide. The police are bound to suspect us. Hell, I suspect us."

"Yeah," I said. "Here's hoping we all have alibis for the time of death."

"Oh, God," she said, her face suddenly falling. "I probably don't. Assuming it happened between the time you called me and now, that is. And it's all The Face's fault."

The Face was what most people called the president of Caerphilly College. He was a kindhearted man of great charm and personal dignity and arguably not a single brain cell. He owed his position to his inexplicable ability to extract large amounts of money from wealthy people and institutions. As long as he stuck to doing that and left running the college to people with some kind of administrative skills, things went smoothly. But Kathy Borgstrom wasn't a wealthy potential benefactor, so the fact that she'd even encountered The Face was unsettling news.

"What did he want?" I asked.

"I have no idea," Kathy said. "I mean, who ever does? He kept asking to see Abe, and I must have explained about fifteen times that Abe was out of the office but that I'd track him down as soon as possible. I didn't want to tell him where Abe was—the last thing you need is him showing up on your doorstep. And he kept wandering around, picking up papers and putting them down in the wrong places, reading stuff on the bulletin board, and asking questions about whether I was happy and did I think that the building needed painting and had I taken enough of a vacation this year. It was . . . unnerving."

Studying her face I could see that she really was

rattled. Which was odd. Normally an encounter with The Face produced monumental irritation, not anxiety.

"What does he care how happy I am?" she was asking. "I mean, do you suppose that's what he asks people before he fires them?"

"He doesn't fire people," I said in my most reassuring voice.

"No, he leaves that to his minions," she said. "Like Dr. Blanco. The most obsequious toady ever to slime his way into administrative services, and considering some of his predecessors, that's really saying something. Anyway, the whole conversation with him was so creepy that I drove halfway out here before I realized that I'd left behind the files I was supposed to bring. I locked them in my desk drawer as soon as The Face showed up, of course, so it's not as if they fell into the wrong hands or anything. But he was there a half an hour—maybe more—and then all that time driving around on top of the time I spent dealing with him, and only my word for it that any of it happened. And it's not as if The Face would remember that he was talking to me if you asked him five minutes after he left my office, much less hours later. And—"

"Calm down," I said, in my most soothing tones. "So you don't have an alibi. Hardly anyone here has an alibi. You'll fit in perfectly. Take a few deep breaths."

"Sorry," she said. "Look, what should I do?"

"Go around to the barn," I said. "Abe's probably still out there, and you can identify yourself to the deputies and explain that you only just arrived. Don't go volunteering the fact that you don't have an alibi unless they ask you."

"Okay." She retrieved her coat and tried to struggle into it while opening the front door, a maneuver that ended up costing time instead of saving it. "Will do. Why don't you get some rest? You really look done in."

"That's just what I plan to do," I said as I shut the door behind her.

The second she was out of sight, something struck me: She hadn't asked how Dr. Wright was killed. If I were arriving at a house where a murder had just taken place, I think I'd be full of questions about how it happened—especially if I knew the murderer was still on the loose. Kathy hadn't asked a single thing. Her first reaction to hearing about the murder had been to worry that she didn't have an alibi. Did she have a reason to worry?

I pulled out my cell phone and checked the time: 1:30. Art and Abe had arrived around noon. Michael had called her a few minutes after he called them, and even considering that she probably had to walk from the drama building to wherever she parked her car, it shouldn't have taken her more than twenty minutes to get here. Had she really lost over an hour entertaining The Face and returning to get the files?

I peered out the window and saw that she was near the hedge at the front of our lawn, talking to a uniformed deputy. The deputy was probably there to keep people from just wandering up to the front door during the chief's investigation—so how had Kathy slipped past him?

I sighed. I hated to admit it, but Kathy was a suspect.

I couldn't see her as the murderer. She'd have been a lot more plausible for that role back when I thought Dr. Wright had been killed by a blow to the head. Kathy had been to our house dozens of times in the last several years, so she'd had plenty of chances to notice that the sunporch at the back of the library could be used by someone who wanted to get into the library without coming through the rest of the house. And given Kathy's fierce devotion to Abe Sass and the department, I could even imagine her trying to take some action on her own. Sneaking in to confront Dr. Wright, for example. And Kathy had a temper. I could see her long-standing grudge with Dr. Wright erupting into sudden intolerable rage, impelling her to grab the nearest weapon.

But poisoning? There my vision of Kathy as the killer fell apart. Unlike the students, who were here most of the time when not actually in classes and had vast piles of their worldly belongings close at hand, she'd either have had to find a poison on the spur of the moment—unlikely—or come already armed with it, on the off chance she'd get a chance to use it—equally unlikely. Even if she were planning to kill Dr. Wright and had brought poison for the purpose, someone surely would have noticed and greeted her when she showed up in the kitchen. And she was too smart to believe she could sneak away and not have someone mention she'd been hanging around the kitchen. Not a very promising plan.

Devising a flimsy plan would be completely out of character for Kathy. My family praised how organized and efficient I was, but I was nothing compared to Kathy. Her incredible organizational skills made her invaluable to the drama faculty and students—so many of them highly creative right-brain types who couldn't organize their way out of a wet tissue. If Kathy came up with a plan, you could be certain she'd researched it thoroughly, had worked out contingency plans for any possible snags it might hit, and would execute it flawlessly. Wandering into the library in the hope that she'd get a chance to

poison her potential victim was not something Kathy
would do.

But marching into the library to confront Dr.
Wright—that I could see Kathy doing. And if, once
there, she saw Dr. Wright apparently asleep and calcu-
lated that there was no serious obstacle to getting away
with murder?

Maybe. And if Kathy thought she'd killed Dr. Wright
or realized she'd just attempted to kill somebody who
was already dead, that could account for her unusually
agitated state. She'd been almost babbling, and that
was completely unlike Kathy. Unless Kathy, like me,
was cool and calm in action and sometimes got the
shakes afterward. I could see that, too.

I should probably mention all this to the chief.

Later. I was way overdue for my nap. But by now I
couldn't even bear to look at the stairs. I went into the
living room instead. It was a cluttered mess, since about
fifteen students were sleeping there—though at least it
was empty, since the students were all out in the barn,
nervously awaiting their turn to be questioned. Or
possibly singing "Ding, dong, the witch is dead!" and
coordinating their alibis.

Their sleeping bags and air mattresses were still
there, along with their other belongings. The few organized ones had stuffed their possessions in cardboard
boxes or plastic bins. The rest just surrounded their beds
with huge deltas of clothes, books, cosmetics, and other
paraphernalia.

The students' belongings! Surely some of them had
food stashed away that I could eat. I'd replace it later.
Tenfold.

I searched the students' belongings until I found a

couple of unopened packages of cheese crackers and an orange soda. Both items from what Michael and I referred to as the neon-orange food group, processed as hell and not normally to my taste. Rose Noire would slap my hands if she saw me reach for them. But she was out in the barn, waiting her turn for interrogation. I pounced.

I picked my way through the debris to the far corner, where a quirk in the architecture made a nook that Michael and I had filled with a particularly comfy couch with its back to the room, making a lovely, private little niche. Assuming the students hadn't moved it. . . .

No, it was still there, under only a moderate layer of pizza boxes and laundry. I cleared it with a few quick shoves and settled down for my rest.

I had to rearrange my position three times before I found one that Castor, Pollux, and I all liked. Then I opened the orange soda and took a long swig. Ambrosia. And where had I gotten the idea that packaged cheese crackers were junk food? I'd had artisan cheeses that hadn't tasted this good.

I ate and drank until I could hold no more—which took less than ever these days, with the kids squishing my stomach to miniscule proportions. Then I pulled an afghan over me and curled up for a well-deserved nap.

FOURTEEN

"Are you sure you don't want a nice cup of tea?" Rose Noire kept asking me. "Just one cup of tea?"

She was holding out a teacup. Toxic fumes billowed out of it and bubbles rose to the oily surface and popped, as if some small but sinister aquatic monster lurked and breathed in the depths of the cup. She began lifting it to my mouth as if to help me drink.

I woke up and saw with relief that I was still alone in the alcove. Nobody was bending over me proffering glasses of herbal swill or dainty cups of poisoned tea.

"Tell me what you put in her tea," a woman's voice said out in the main part of the room.

I glanced down. No tea on the floor beside my sofa, only the empty orange soda can.

"Forget it."

I recognized Ramon's voice.

"Danny saw you." Bronwyn. "From the basement door. I made him promise not to tell the police until I talked to you."

"Yeah, right. He's probably already gone running to the cops."

"No, he'll do anything for me. So tell me."

I held my breath. Danny would do anything for

Bronwyn? Was Ramon reluctant to speak or was he, like me, pondering how Bronwyn had managed to win that kind of loyalty?

"Some of my sleeping medicine," Ramon said finally. "Just a couple of pills. I didn't want to hurt her. I just wanted to buy some time until I could figure out what to do."

"How many pills?" Bronwyn asked. I almost nodded in approval.

"Three," he said. "The stuff's not very strong—I usually have to take two of them myself to get any effect. I've taken three on a bad night. It couldn't have killed her."

"No," Bronwyn said. "From what I heard, she was hit over the head with that horrible hippopotamus statue. Of course, they don't yet know why she just sat there and let someone whack her on the head with the hippo. She didn't strike me as the type to just take a nap when she was in the middle of screwing with someone's life. So there must be some reason she was snoozing."

"My sleeping pills?" Ramon asked. Bronwyn must have nodded. He groaned.

"Don't tell anyone," Bronwyn said. "I'll get Danny to keep quiet. It's not your fault what the killer did, and with luck they'll never figure out about the sleeping pills."

"Thanks," Ramon said.

I heard a few soft murmurs and giggles—Bronwyn and Ramon kissing and making up, probably. I tuned them out and thought about what I'd heard. Was Ramon telling the truth about the pills? Or had he slipped something deadly into Dr. Wright's tea? If he was the poisoner, was the rumor that she'd been hit over the head reassuring him or making him more wary?

"Come on," Bronwyn said. "Nearly time for rehearsal."

"How can we have a rehearsal with the police camped in the library?" Ramon asked.

"Professor Waterston said we could use the barn."

"You really think Blanco will let us do the show?" Their voices were beginning to fade as they walked toward the other end of the living room.

"Blanco? He's not going to give us any problems," Bronwyn said. "Without Dr. Wright to give him a backbone, I bet he doesn't have the guts to stop the show."

"And if you're wrong?"

"Then maybe the killer will come back and bash him, too."

"Bron, that's horrible."

"I'm only saying what we're all thinking," she said. "Come on—we should start the rehearsal on time."

I heard their footsteps disappear in the distance.

Apparently, while I was asleep, the chief had made progress in his interviews, if Bronwyn and Ramon were at large and even thinking about starting a rehearsal. And maybe it was a good thing they were moving the rehearsals to the barn before they began using the real zucchini.

How long had I been asleep? I glanced at the clock on the mantel, which said a quarter past twelve, as it had for the last month—it was an antique clock Mother had given us that required winding weekly, which no one had bothered to do since the students moved in. Probably not a practical clock for the busy family we were about to become, and absolutely no help at the moment.

I pulled out my cell phone and checked the time on that—2:40 p.m. Which meant I'd been sleeping for over an hour. I didn't feel particularly rested, but then I rarely did these days.

I began to pick my way through the debris to the doorway.

Halfway there a thought stopped me. If memory served, Ramon was one of the students sleeping here in the living room. With everyone else either being interrogated or attending a rehearsal, now might be a good time to see if his sleeping pills were still findable—before it occurred to him to dispose of them.

I poked around the room until I figured out where Ramon's stuff was. They'd put together a ring with everyone's mailbox keys on it, and apparently someone had just made a mail run to the dorms and thrown small bundles of letters and flyers on some of the sleeping bags and air mattresses. I scanned the addresses until I found a pale pink envelope addressed to Ramon lying on one of the sleeping bags. The return address was a Mrs. Angelica Soto in San Antonio.

I glanced over my shoulder. Still no one around. If the living room had a door I'd have closed and locked it, but there was only the huge open archway. I felt incredibly exposed as I rummaged through the heaps of stuff around Ramon's sleeping bag.

Eventually I found a pill bottle tucked under his pillow. Diazepam, two mg to be taken at bedtime.

I pulled a tissue out of my pocket, picked the bottle up with it, then heaved myself back to my feet and studied it.

Diazepam? Wasn't that the generic name for Valium? If Ramon's sleeping pills had been some kind of barbiturates, dosing Dr. Wright with three of them might well have had serious ill effects. But I seemed to recall Dad saying that one benefit of Valium was that overdoses, though serious, were rarely fatal. So if Ramon really had used only three of these, then unless his doctor had prescribed a particularly high dose, they weren't likely to have been the cause of Dr. Wright's death. Was two mg a high or low dose?

A question for Dad—Dad, and of course, the chief, who would doubtless like to see the bottle. I wrapped the tissue around it and tucked it away in my pocket.

As I passed through the foyer I heard noises coming from the coat closet. It sounded as if things were falling off the shelves. I strode over and pulled the door open.

Dr. Blanco was lying on the closet floor on a pile of boots and shoes. Scattered around his head were several Frisbees, half a dozen flashlights, a softball glove, a tennis racket, and the bag containing Rob's bowling ball.

"Are you all right?" I asked.

"That thing could have killed me!" he exclaimed.

"The bowling ball?" I said. "Yes, I imagine it could if it landed right on your head. But then, as bowling balls go, it's pretty mild mannered. Most of the time it just stays up there on the shelf where we put it. I've never known it to lie in wait and pounce on an innocent bystander before."

Of course, storing the bowling ball on an upper shelf wasn't a particularly clever idea, but I'd discuss that with Rob later.

"I hope I don't have a concussion," Blanco said.

"Then again, bowling balls can be pretty territorial," I went on. "I can't answer for what it would do if it caught someone ransacking its closet. Just why were you ransacking the closet?"

"I wasn't ransacking," Blanco said. "I was gesticulating. I must have bumped the shelf."

"Gesticulating," I repeated. "And you normally hide in closets to practice your gesticulating?"

"I was having a conversation. An animated conversation. On my cell phone." His tone was petulant rather than guilty, so perhaps he was telling the truth. "Since there doesn't seem to be a single room in this entire house not filled with dozens of boisterous, inquisitive people, I was attempting to use your coat closet to obtain some small measure of privacy."

I considered asking why he didn't go back to his own office to make his calls. After all, the planned emergency meeting of Ramon's dissertation committee was presumably postponed for the time being. But perhaps he had his reasons. The lack of heat in his office. Or orders from the chief to stick around for a while.

He had begun to thrash around, dislodging the sports equipment that had landed on him. He looked up at me as if expecting help. I patted the twins and watched as he struggled to his feet.

"If the bowling ball did hit you on the head, you could ask Dad to take a look at it," I said.

"Thank you," he said. "But I think I would prefer to see my own physician. But—"

He paused as if deep in thought.

"This incident has made me wonder. About Dr. Wright's death, I mean. Could she possibly have hit her head in the fall?"

"In the fall?" I echoed. Had I described Dr. Wright's body falling over when I found her? I didn't think so. I frowned suspiciously at him. And then the light dawned.

"You mean when she tripped over one of Señor Mendoza's pills?"

Blanco nodded.

"I think Dad would have noticed if she'd wounded herself then," I said.

Blanco pursed his lips. My temper flared. Was his snide expression intended to cast aspersions on Dad's medical skill? His commitment to the welfare of his patients?

Or was I just reading too much into Blanco's habitual sour, anxious expression? I took a deep breath and told myself to chill.

"I understand it can be very difficult to diagnose head injuries," he said. "And Jean—Dr. Wright—she was very resistant to the idea of going to the hospital."

"In general? Or did Dad suggest it this morning?"

"In general," he said. "Like so many people who enjoy robust health, she rather looked down on anyone who went running to the doctor with every scratch."

It sounded like a quote. And he was absently fingering his coat pocket. Was it just my imagination or did I see a small lump there, the size and shape of a roll of Tums?

"And your father did suggest it—both to Dr. Wright and to Mr. Mendoza," Blanco said. "I got the impression he was disappointed that they both refused."

"I'm sure he was," I said. "He loves riding in the ambulance."

"So his disappointment wasn't necessarily due to any reservations over their condition?"

"If he'd had any reservations about their condition, he'd have kept nagging till they agreed to go to the hospital," I said.

"I don't know about Mr. Mendoza, but Dr. Wright is very strong willed," he said. "She's hardly ever sick and when she is, she does her best to carry on as if there were nothing wrong with her."

I suspected I knew the type—the people who wouldn't stay home when they caught cold, but insisted on dragging themselves to work, shedding germs and damp tissues everywhere. I'd gone through a phase of being like that myself, until I'd realized that the world could usually manage to get along without me for a day or two. Dr. Wright seemed like the type who had liked feeling indispensable.

"I should have insisted that she go to the hospital," Blanco said.

"And if you had, would she have listened to you?"

Blanco sighed and shook his head.

"If Dad thought she was injured, either she'd be in the hospital right now or he'd still be following her around, nagging her," I said. "You have no idea how persistent he can be."

"Isn't that possible—for someone to hit their head and feel fine initially and then later have some complication?"

"Like a subdural hematoma," I said. "Yes, I suppose that's possible."

Possible, but I hoped it didn't turn out to be true. Dad would never forgive himself if he'd failed to hospitalize a patient who turned out to have had a traumatic head injury.

"You should suggest that to Dad and the chief," I said. "If you haven't already."

"It would be so much easier to understand," he said, "if it were all a horrible accident. I can't imagine why anyone would actually kill her."

Clearly he hadn't been eavesdropping on Ramon and Bronwyn.

"Not everyone agrees with the actions she's taken on Ramon Soto's case," I said.

"But that's hardly a life-or-death issue," Blanco said.

"It could be for Ramon," I said.

"He could do another dissertation, couldn't he?" Blanco's expression was puzzled. Maybe tossing off major research projects was a breeze for him.

"He's spent three years on this one," I said. "That's probably an eighth of his entire life. And what's more, it's three years of tuition. Unless he's on full scholarship, Ramon has probably racked up some pretty serious student loans. Another three years of work, more tens of thousands of debt."

I suddenly realized that I was probably making too good a case for Ramon as a suspect. I could feel Ramon's pill bottle pressing against my leg.

"And Ramon's just the one we know about," I said. "How many other students and former students might be walking around feeling that Dr. Wright ruined their lives?"

"Oh, dear," he said. "I never considered that. The fact that someone could have some violent, irrational grudge."

Irrational? Well, it was all in your point of view.

"Watch your back, then," I said as I turned to leave. "We wouldn't want anything to happen to you."

"To me?" His voice rose to a squeak. "Why should anything happen to me?"

"Right now, a lot of people associate the two of you," I said. "For all some of these people know, you were helping Dr. Wright with whatever she was doing that they don't like. So be careful. We don't want more trouble."

He gave me a startled look and scurried back to the kitchen, clutching his cell phone like a talisman.

Okay, it was a mean thing to say, but he'd angered

me, with his slurs on Dad's professionalism and his automatic assumption that anyone who didn't like Dr. Wright was irrational.

Still, he was looking less and less like a credible threat to Ramon's dissertation. I had been wrong in thinking that we were facing two formidable adversaries. Dr. Wright might have been formidable. Dr. Blanco was merely the faithful sidekick.

Or perhaps he was only a weapon Dr. Wright had planned to use—a weapon now harmless with no hand to wield it.

A weapon someone else could use for good, perhaps? I'd leave that to Art, Abe, and Michael, who presumably knew Dr. Blanco better than I did.

I was about to shuffle out of the hall when an impulse struck me. I reached into my pocket for my key ring. I didn't know if it was an old-fashioned custom or an eccentricity of the previous owner, but most of the doors in our house had keyed locks, even the closets— and all with different keys. The coat closet was supposed to be for Michael's and my stuff, which was why the entire hall was crammed with borrowed coatracks. We hadn't been locking it, but whether Dr. Blanco had really been using it as a phone booth or whether he'd been snooping, I could keep him from doing it again. I sorted through my keys till I found the right one and locked the door.

If Dr. Blanco wanted privacy for his phone calls, he could go out in the yard as the students did.

As I turned away from the door, I ran into Ramon and Bronwyn coming back from the kitchen.

"Rehearsal over?" I asked.

"About to begin," Ramon said. "Would you like to come and watch?"

"No thanks," I said. "Farther than I want to walk right now and I've seen a couple of rehearsals already."

"I don't suppose you could keep Dr. Blanco here in the house with you, then," Bronwyn said. "We don't want him interrupting the rehearsals telling us how obscene and offensive the play is."

It had puzzled me before when Blanco said that. I'd have called the play merely bawdy. I planned to discourage Mother from seeing it. But I wouldn't have called it obscene. Clearly Blanco's literary taste matched his rather prim and priggish exterior.

"He's entitled to his opinion," Ramon said.

"But he's not entitled to force his opinion down everyone else's throat," Bronwyn said. "That's censorship."

"He probably likes censorship," Ramon said. "And anyway, he's been pretty quiet since Dr. Wright died."

Perhaps Blanco was making a few token protests to prove he wasn't a pawn.

"He's obnoxious," Bronwyn said, turning to me. "When Ramon or any of the other students speak Spanish to him, he ignores them. Pretends he doesn't understand."

"Maybe he's not pretending," Ramon said. "Not everyone with Latino heritage actually speaks Spanish."

"Then it's dishonest of him to take advantage of an accident of birth if he doesn't honor his heritage enough to speak the language or learn about the culture," Bronwyn said. "Have you looked at his CV?"

"His what?" Ramon echoed.

"CV—curriculum vitae," I put in. "It's what they use in academia instead of resumé."

"Never use an English word when a Latin one will do," Bronwyn said with a sniff.

"Actually, resumé is French, but I know what you

mean," I said. "Where'd you see his CV, and what's so interesting about it?"

"It's posted on the college Web site," she said. "It lists a lot of awards and honors. First Latino professor on the staff of this college, certificate of thanks from some Hispanic cultural association. I mean, it looked encouraging. We knew Dr. Wright was going to be hard to deal with, but when we heard that the other professor assigned to deal with Ramon's case was a Latino, we were relieved. We thought he'd be sympathetic."

I frowned suspiciously. Ramon had managed to give the impression that the prunes' arrival was a horrible surprise. But how could that be if he and Bronwyn had known Blanco was assigned to the case—or even that there was a case to begin with? Maybe the prunes were right and Ramon had been deliberately avoiding them.

Clearly Ramon had done well in his acting classes. Or maybe it was Bronwyn who had been busy gathering intelligence about the enemy.

"But instead of being helpful, he's as bad as she was," Bronwyn said. "He's nothing but a Tío Taco."

"Stop calling him that," Ramon snapped.

"What is it?" I asked.

"It's a term for someone who's sold out his Latino heritage," Bronwyn said. "Like Uncle Tom or Oreo for blacks."

"It's a nasty insult and I wish you'd stop saying it," Ramon said. I got the feeling I was seeing the latest round of an old argument.

"Even if the guy deserves it? Look at him—turns up his nose on every aspect of Spanish culture—"

"How do you know he deserves it?" Ramon snapped back. "How do you know what the guy went through to get where he is? You don't know what kind of economic barriers he had to overcome, what kind of prejudice and discrimination he experienced. None of us do."

"If he's suffered and struggled so much, how come he isn't more sympathetic to other Hispanics?"

Ramon just closed his eyes as if tired of arguing, so I spoke up.

"Suffering and struggling don't automatically ennoble someone," I said. "Sometimes it just beats people down. Makes them anxious. Fearful. Protective of what they have."

"Yeah," Ramon said. "Believe it or not, 'I made it, so let me help you' is a lot less common than 'I got where I am under my own power—what's wrong with you?'"

"But does he have to be so hostile to his fellow Hispanics?"

"He probably doesn't see it as hostile," Ramon said. "He probably sees it as making sure he isn't seen to be favoring one group over another."

"I can't believe you're defending him," Bronwyn said.

"I'm not defending him," Ramon said. "I'm just trying to explain why I'm not condemning him. I'd like to think I'll do things differently if I'm ever in a position of power—"

"When, not if," Bronwyn put in.

"But in the meantime, I'm not going to come down on the guy for doing what he thinks he has to. And hey— even if we don't think he's a very good role model, when outsiders look at the college staff directory, they see a Spanish name with 'doctor' in front of it and a fancy title after it. He doesn't have to be a nice guy to break glass ceilings. Just hardheaded."

"And if he cancels your play and does what he can to sabotage your dissertation?" Bronwyn said softly.

Ramon shook his head.

"You can't just sit back and do nothing," Bronwyn said. "You have to fight to preserve your culture. Look what's happening to whales!"

I tried to make sense of what she was saying. Had I taken another brief power nap? At what point had the conversation jumped from ethnic discrimination to conservation and animal welfare?

Ramon simply rolled his eyes as if to say, "Not that again." I could understand his point of view—Bronwyn was strident and singularly persistent.

Then light dawned.

"You mean the country of Wales?" I asked.

"Well, of course the country," she said. "A country where due to generations of discrimination against it, the native language has become all but obsolete. My family's originally Welsh but none of them has spoken our native language for generations. Of course, that's not surprising. Did you know that only twenty percent of the population of Wales can speak Welsh?"

A sudden though hit me.

"That's why you came to school here, isn't it?" I asked. "Because the college has a Welsh name."

"Yes," she said. "Caerphilly. Such a beautiful name."

I was struck by the way she said the word. Not just that she was pronouncing it right, "car-FIL-ly," instead of "care-FIL-ly" or, worse, "CARE-ful-ly." But when she said it, there was a lilt, a hint of music, an echo of—

"It's Welsh?" Ramon asked.

"Of course it is, you dolt," Bronwyn snapped.

"What did you think it was?"

"I always figured it was Native American," Ramon said.

"It's a town in Wales," I said. "When we're not man-gling Indian place names, Virginians like stealing place names from the British Isles."

"And pretty soon, that will be all that's left of Wales," Bronwyn said. "Beautiful place names that no one can pronounce, because all the Welsh turned their back on their culture. Just the way you—"

"Give it a rest, dammit!" Ramon said. He grabbed a coat from one of the racks, strode over to the front door, and stormed out, slamming it behind him.

Bronwyn looked after him, frowning. Then she glanced at me.

"The guy is trouble," she said.

"Oh," I said noncommittally, glancing at the front door, which I could almost imagine still quivering. Yes, with a temper like that, he could be.

"He's out to get Ramon," she said.

I should have realized she wouldn't criticize Ramon, at least not to me. From my point of view, Blanco looked less likely to cause trouble than to become the next mur-der victim. Perhaps Bronwyn had already formed her opinion and wasn't seeing his current mild-mannered behavior.

"We expected it from Dr. Wright, but we were hop-ing for better from Dr. Blanco," she went on. With that, she followed Ramon out, though at least she closed the front door more quietly.

I stared at the closed door, frowning. Bronwyn had been studying Dr. Blanco's CV. And so far, Danny, who was supposed to be my researcher, hadn't brought me a single bit of information. Granted, he probably hadn't had much time at his computer, given the murder inves-tigation.

Still, he'd found time to talk to Bronwyn. He'd told her about seeing Ramon put something in Dr. Wright's tea. And he'd promised not to tell anyone.

I needed to talk to Danny. And possibly do a little online research of my own.

Time to visit the basement again.

FIFTEEN

I had to pass through the kitchen on my way to the basement. I stopped for a few moments to look around. Only a lingering hint of the paella smell remained, and that seemed to be coming from the remarkable mountain of dirty dishes in and around the sink. The room was empty, and peering out the back windows, I could see why. A few people were milling about outside the barn, and bright light spilled out of the door as someone slid it open to go inside. I could see Señor Mendoza and my grandfather inside, laughing in the center of a group of people. I saw a couple of students turn to the door, no doubt to complain about the arctic air coming into the warmer interior of the barn. The people outside hurried to enter and slid the door closed again.

I realized I felt ever so slightly lonely. When the students had first arrived, I'd felt the occasional twinge of resentment, feeling that they were spoiling the last few weeks Michael and I would ever have together as just a couple. But I'd gotten used to having them around day and night. When they were gone, it would probably feel downright peaceful and cozy with only Michael, the twins, and Rob and Rose Noire underfoot.

Of course that sounded rather like a half-remembered

joke of Rob's, about a man hitting himself over the head with a two by four because it felt so good when he stopped. Still, to my surprise, I realized I'd miss the students.

I peered down into the basement. The TV was on again, and I could hear melodramatic music.

Danny might not be at his computer, but even if he wasn't, I could use his computer—or one of the other computers down there—to do a little Googling.

I began to descend, slowly and carefully.

"The neck's broken," came a voice from the television. "The brain is useless. We must find another brain."

Was this some kind of omen? Warning me to watch my step so I didn't break my neck?

More likely, if it was an omen, it was warning me that I'd made the wrong choice of researchers. I needed another brain—one that wasn't obsessed with the beautiful but potentially untrustworthy Bronwyn.

I breathed a sigh of relief when I stepped down safely onto the basement floor. I began looking around, trying to remember which computer Danny had been sitting at. It wasn't easy. All the makeshift tables were liberally strewn with desk kibble, those random bits of flotsam and jetsam that seem to accumulate within five minutes after you sit a human being down at a desk. Instead of the kids' pictures, award plaques, and vacation souvenirs you'd find in a typical office, the students seemed to have accumulated rather a lot of action figures, signs with incomprehensible slogans, and pictures of buxom female anime figures. The desks probably seemed incredibly personal to their owners, redolent with the flavor of their unique talents and interests, but they all blended into one to me. And I realized with a pang that

I couldn't even tell if their displays were cool or lame; I was the wrong gender and generation.

"Just let me find Danny's desk," I muttered.

As I was still pondering, I heard voices above.

"Bron? We need to talk."

Danny Oh.

"Not so loud," Bronwyn said. "Someone could come in."

"There's nobody here," he said. "But we could go in the basement."

"Good idea," she said. "More private."

She was using her flirtatious voice, the one that subtly suggested she had more in mind than a private conversation. Just force of habit, or was the lovely Bron two-timing Ramon?

I quickly ducked into the laundry room and hid myself behind the door, turning the light off but leaving the door open so I could overhear.

Steps sounded on the stairway. I glanced down and realized that while I might be well hidden, Holmes and Watson jutted out into the open doorway rather obviously. I looked behind me and saw a mountain of dirty laundry. Was that all ours? Surely we weren't letting the students use the machines again. I thought we'd laid down the law about them going to the Laundromat in town after the first week, when we'd had major problems with our septic system.

No time to worry about that now. I eased myself back onto the laundry and, for good measure, grabbed an empty plastic laundry basket, turned it upside down, and pulled it on top of my head. Better than hiding behind the door. Not only was I sitting down, but I could peek out through the ventilation holes in the laundry

basket and see at least some of what was happening in
the basement.

The hollow sound of steps on the wooden stairs gave
way to a few dull steps on the concrete of the basement
floor. Then Bronwyn appeared. Luckily she decided to
stop while she was still within my limited field of vision. Danny joined her.

"What did you want to ask me, Danny?" Bronwyn
said. She probably was a wonderful actress. It was the
voice—warm, intimate, caressing. The little tremor when
she said his name was priceless. And from the poleaxed
look on his face, he was falling for it, completely.

"I saw something," Danny said. "At least I thought I
did."

"What?" Bronwyn said in an almost inaudible whis-
per.

"It looked like—but it couldn't be . . ."

His voice faded away. He shook his head slightly but
didn't take his eyes from hers.

"You know you can tell me, Danny," Bronwyn cooed.
"What did you see?"

"It looked like you were putting something in Dr.
Wright's tea." It wasn't an accusation—more a plea for
her to tell him it wasn't so.

"Only some of Ramon's sleeping medicine," Bronwyn
said. "Just a couple of pills. We—I didn't want to hurt
her. Just to knock her out for a while until we could figure out how to handle the problem."

I digested this for a while and assumed Danny
was doing the same. It was a masterful little bit of
manipulation—the change from "we" to "I" suggesting,
of course, that she was taking the blame for something
that was ultimately Ramon's idea.

Actually, from the look of it, Danny wasn't digesting

it. Bron was running her fingers across his chest, tracing the letters on his T-shirt, and from the look on his face, Danny wasn't thinking much.

So apparently Bronwyn had also put something in Dr. Wright's tea. Before or after she saw Ramon drugging it? And why did Bronwyn lie to Ramon, telling him that Danny had seen him put something in the tea? Was she just trying to pry an admission out of Ramon? Then why not say that she'd seen him? Why bring Danny into it? Or had Danny seen both of them?

I decided I could learn to dislike Bronwyn.

"You should tell the police," Danny said. His voice sounded a little hoarse.

"They'd get the wrong idea," Bronwyn said.

"You don't know what those sleeping pills did to her."

I had to hand it to Danny. He was clearly trying. And also clearly so besotted with Bronwyn that there was no danger he'd spill the beans.

"I'm going to tell Chief Burke, but I need to do it myself," she said. "At the right time. You know how people would react if they knew I'd done that. I know now it was a stupid thing to do. So maybe after I've had a chance to talk to the chief, I can persuade him to keep it private. Just give me a chance to do that."

"Okay," Danny said. "And he'll understand when you tell him about how evil she was, won't he? How many lives she was ruining?"

"Of course he will," Bronwyn said. "Now I've got to go—I'm late for the rehearsal."

She turned and disappeared from my view. Footsteps began ascending the stairs. Danny's eyes followed her, and the naked yearning on his face was painful to see.

"Rehearsal?" he said, after a few moments. "I thought the library was a crime scene."

"We're using the barn," Bronwyn called down. "Come on. You can watch."

"Okay." From the expression of rapture on his face, you'd have thought she'd just conferred an enormous honor on him. He bounded away and his footsteps, like hers, faded into the distance.

I remained ensconced in the laundry, brain running furiously, like a hamster in a wheel.

Danny had seen Bronwyn putting something in Dr. Wright's tea. Something that Bronwyn said was Ramon's sleeping medicine.

And Ramon had admitted to putting his sleeping medicine in Dr. Wright's tea.

Had they both done it, giving Dr. Wright an overdose?

Or was one—or both—of them lying about what they'd put in the tea? If you substituted a couple of Señor Mendoza's heart pills for sleeping meds, would that be enough to kill her? Either alone or in combination with a dose of sleeping medicine?

And how many people had been drugging Dr. Wright's tea, anyway? Were Ramon and Bronwyn the only ones? Even if they'd all only been using sleeping medicine rather than Señor Mendoza's heart pills, what if the total dosage had reached a lethal level? Ramon's Valium probably wasn't going to kill anyone, but I didn't know for sure that was what they'd been using. A question for Dad.

And clearly I needed to rethink using Danny Oh as my main source of online dirt. He had too much incentive to protect Bronwyn. He'd clearly do anything for her, including lying about what he'd seen her do.

And maybe doing what he could to make Ramon look guilty?

And—

"Meg? You okay?"

I started and looked up to see Josh, the leader of the interns, peering into the laundry room.

"Josh! How long have you been there?" I pulled the laundry basket off my head.

"Here in the doorway about thirty seconds," he said. "In the basement since you came in. I was behind some boxes, hooking up some cables. I was going to come out and see what you wanted, but then you ducked into the laundry room and I figured if you wanted to eavesdrop on Danny and Bron, why should I spoil it for you?"

"Thanks," I said.

"Do you need a hand?"

I pondered the question.

"Probably," I said.

With Josh's help, I managed to extract myself from the laundry heap. He courteously pulled up a chair that looked sturdy enough to hold me, and I sat down with murmured thanks.

"Did you just come in to spy on Danny?" he asked.

"Yes and no," I said. I glanced around. "Anyone else hiding under their desk?"

"The others all went off to a database management class," he said. "Except for Danny, who's been cutting class, as usual, so he could hang around and maybe get a glance from Bronwyn."

"You're not taking database management?"

He laughed and sat down in a chair at one of the computers.

"I took it three years ago, when I was a junior," he said. "I'm the token grown-up here. Regular Mutant Wizards staff. Assigned to oversee the student interns."

He didn't look appreciably older than the others to me.

Of course, ever since I'd hit thirty-five, I'd had a hard time telling college students from junior high schoolers.

"I may need your help," I said. "I'm beginning to rethink the wisdom of using Danny Oh as my sole information source."

"Rob was right to recommend him," Josh said. "He has the right skill set. He did a lot of work on some enhancements we did to the college e-mail system."

"Mutant Wizards is doing work for the college?" I said in surprise. "Since when?"

"Since we set up that new corporate subsidiary a few months ago," he said. "Data Wizards. Someone pointed out to Rob that we had the personnel to do it, and an inside track due to having such close connections to the computer science department."

Clearly I needed to catch up on what Rob was up to.

"But getting back to Danny," I said. "He might have had the right skill set, but at the time I talked to Rob, we didn't have a murder, and Danny didn't have a crush on one of the prime suspects."

"A crush?" Josh said. "That's rich. Like calling World War II a skirmish. I'm relieved to hear it was Bronwyn who poisoned Dr. Wright. I'm sure Danny would have volunteered to do it if he knew Bron wanted it."

"We don't know that Bron poisoned her," I said. "She might have been telling the truth about what she put in the tea."

Josh snorted.

"I gather Bron doesn't seem like an improbable killer to you?" I asked.

"Just the opposite," he said. "She's a manipulative bi—er, she's manipulative. It would be one thing if Danny just had this random unrequited crush on her, but she's lured him on to the point he's barely sane. So yeah, if Bron's a suspect, you can't trust Danny to dig up any dirt on her. And if he digs up any on Ramon, I'd be very suspicious. In fact, I've been wondering if I should tell someone about this."

He got up and led me over to a computer.

"This is Danny's," he said. "And look what someone's been using it for."

He studied the screen for a few minutes, clicked a few keys, and pointed to the site he'd called up.

The headline read "Digitalis Overdose."

SIXTEEN

I studied the page on digitalis. Sounded authentic—not that I was an expert, but since Dad was not only a doctor but also an avid reader of mysteries, I'd managed to pick up a fair amount of normally useless trivia about poisons. Even better, the page was from the Web site of a major medical school. And it gave fairly specific information on clinical and toxic doses. Anyone with half a brain could probably figure out how many of Señor Mendoza's little heart pills it would take to make sure Dr. Wright wouldn't survive to meet with Ramon's dissertation committee.

"Danny was looking at this?" I asked.

"Either Danny or someone he was letting use his computer," Josh said.

"And was he letting anyone else use his computer?"

"Only Bron, that I saw," Josh said. "Of course, the other students living in the house are always coming down trying to cadge a little computer time, and not all the guys are careful about password-protecting their machines. But Danny's more careful than most—more paranoid, maybe. And his desk is the farthest from the stairs, so not as many people go all that way to mess with it."

"Probably Bron or Danny, then," I said.

"Not that you could prove it in court," he said. "But yeah."

I studied the evidence. Pretty damning. But was it maybe a little too damning, not to mention awfully convenient? After all, if Bron or Danny were planning on killing Dr. Wright with Señor Mendoza's heart medicine, it would be fairly stupid to leave a page like this open. Even if they hadn't left it open and Josh had found it by looking at the computer's history, there were ways of wiping that kind of information trail clean. Even I know that, so wouldn't a cyber-savvy killer know it?

Then again, Danny seemed a pretty unlikely killer, and I had no idea how tech-savvy Bronwyn was. It was possible that one or the other had not realized that someone like Josh would be checking up behind them.

And also possible that Josh had planted the evidence. He'd been here the whole time, too. I didn't know what grudge he could have against Dr. Wright, but that didn't mean he couldn't have one. If he had killed Dr. Wright and wanted to divert suspicion from himself, what better way to do it than to show me this page and claim Bron or Danny had been looking at it? Even if he wasn't the killer, what if he had it in for Bron and Danny and wanted to cast suspicion on them?

"Of course, you probably don't want to take my word for it," Josh said. "For all you know, I could be the one who was looking at the digitalis information."

Was the man a mind reader? Or had my sudden flash of doubt been all too visible on my face?

"I'll keep that in mind," I said. "You might want to tell the chief about this."

"I only just found it a few minutes ago," he said. "You think he'd be interested?"

I nodded.

"Okay," he said. He leaned over to reach behind the makeshift computer table. The monitor went dark.

"You don't want to save that stuff first?" I asked.

"No, anything I did on the machine would muddy the waters," he said. "Best way to preserve whatever evidence is on it is to just pull the plug. Leaves all the temporary files in place, and sometimes that's your best source of forensic data."

As I watched, he unplugged various cables and wires from Danny's computer.

"Won't Danny be suspicious when he finds his machine gone?"

"It belongs to the company, not him," he said as he hefted the CPU under one arm. "I'll tell him we had to take it back to the office for some kind of maintenance. You still interested in learning what you can about Drs. Wright and Blanco?"

I nodded.

"I'll see what I can dig up," he said. He put the CPU down under his own desk. "Danny might be a little distracted right now."

"Thanks," I said. "After you take that to the chief. Or if you like, I could tell him about it."

"That'd be good," he said. "Maybe he could send someone down to fetch it. I'd rather keep an eye on things here, if you don't mind. Make sure no one else sneaks down and uses corporate property to research a murder. And I should probably show him this."

He handed me a paper. I glanced down. It was an e-mail from Dr. Wright to Ramon. I read it quickly. She was acknowledging receipt of his paperwork and giving him permission to do his dissertation on Mendoza's work. Her permission sounded grudging and was hedged with at least a dozen cautions and requirements, and I had no idea if he'd paid attention to them, but the core issue—whether he'd gotten permission for his topic—was there in black and white.

Either Dr. Wright had been mistaken or she'd been lying.

"Did you get this legally?" I asked.

"As far as I know," he said. "Since Danny was clearly too distracted to do much, I thought I'd help out. I asked Ramon if I could search his e-mail for proof that he'd gotten permission for his dissertation and he wrote down his e-mail ID and password. Some friends in the college systems department helped a bit by restoring all his deleted e-mail from the archives, and voila."

"You'd think he'd have kept a copy of this somewhere he could find it," I said.

"I would," he said. "Then again, I write code, not plays."

"Can I take this to my husband?" I asked.

"Sure," he said. "I can run another copy."

"Thanks."

I got up and shuffled back across the basement to the stairs.

"Careful," he said, frowning a little as I reached the basement stairs. "Shouldn't you be lying down more?"

"Yes," I said as I heaved myself upward once again.

I glanced back down from the top of the stairs. Josh's face looked rather eerie, lit only by the light from the monitor, and as I watched, he pushed the same key over and over again a few seconds apart. Something to the right of the keyboard—possibly the page-down key. From his frown, he didn't seem to like what he was seeing.

Was the e-mail from Dr. Wright real? I was at least

ninety percent sure it was. I'd learned enough about computer security from some of my brother's technical staff to know that it would be hard to fake something like that well enough to hold up under a forensic examination of the college mail system.

But right now I wasn't going to trust anything a hundred percent. Josh had been here all day and for all I knew, he could have been holding a grudge if Dr. Wright had flunked him back in his all-too-recent college days. I needed some information that wasn't coming from a possible murder suspect. I needed my own laptop.

Which, last I'd seen it, was locked up in the secure closet in Michael's office. I should probably share what I'd learned with the chief anyway. As I passed by the stairs I glanced longingly up, thinking of our bedroom. Later. For now, I made a quick pit stop then shuffled down the long corridor toward the library.

SEVENTEEN

"Shouldn't you be resting?" Sammy called to me as I came down the hallway.

"Is there an echo in here?" I muttered.

Sammy was sitting in a chair at the far end of the hall, guarding the library door. Combined with the crime scene tape behind him and the chain and padlock wrapped around the knobs of the double doors, his guard post gave off a definite message: keep out. I ignored the message.

"I wanted to get my laptop from Michael's office," I said. And then, remembering the pill bottle in my purse, I added, "And I'd like to see the chief for a few moments."

Sammy nodded and gestured toward the small hallway that led to Michael's office. He looked glum. I suddenly remembered why.

"Any more news on Hawkeye?" I asked. Sammy's face clouded.

"Still doing well, thanks to Clarence and your dad," he said. "It was touch-and-go for a while, though. And you know what really burns me?"

I shook my head.

"The guy who did it didn't even stop," Sammy said.

"And I'm not even sure we could charge him with much if we manage to locate him. The chief's going to check with the DA, but I know what will happen. They'll say it's only a dog and he wasn't killed. Except he almost was."

"At least he'll be all right," I said, patting Sammy's shoulder.

He nodded. I could see that he was deeply upset but pretended not to notice and plodded down the hall toward Michael's office.

I found the chief sitting back in Michael's desk chair, his feet up on a trash can. One hand held a cell phone to his ear while the other was scratching Scout, who sat leaning against the chair.

"You look comfortable," I said.

"That doesn't mean I'm not busy," he said. He turned to sit up straight, feet on the floor.

"I was talking to Scout," I said, reaching down to pet the dog. His short, light-brown tail thumped softly on the rug as I did so. "You, on the other hand, look overworked. Put your feet up again."

"Hope it's okay to have him in here," the chief said, nodding at Scout. "We've all been too busy for me to assign anyone to take him home."

"He can stay as long as you like," I said. "Spike's staying overnight at the vet's for observation, so the coast is clear." I sat down on an ottoman, which I knew from experience was a lot easier to get out of than the pseudo-comfy guest chairs. "I brought you something."

I pulled the paper-wrapped pill bottle out of my pocket and put it on the desk in front of him.

"What's this?" he asked, peering over his glasses at it.

"Ramon Soto's sleeping medication. Which I overheard him admit slipping into Dr. Wright's tea."

"Overheard?" His voice was sharp. "You weren't interrogating him?"

"I was trying to nap in the living room while you were interrogating people," I said. "He and his girlfriend woke me up discussing it."

I gave the chief a rundown of what I'd overheard between Ramon and Bronwyn, and for good measure Bronwyn's conversation with Danny and the page on digitalis Josh had shown me.

When I finished, the chief continued frowning and scratching Scout's head for a few moments.

"When you left here I thought you were going to rest," he said finally.

"I was resting," I said. "Can I help it if some of your suspects chose to wake me up with their plotting?"

A fleeting hint of a smile interrupted his scowl, so quickly that I wasn't entirely sure I'd seen it.

"You weren't resting when you found this," he said, nodding at the pill bottle.

"The kitchen was off-limits the last time I checked," I said. "I was rummaging through the students' stuff for something safe to eat." Which was only a small lie, I figured. The chief didn't know I'd rummaged twice— once for food and once for incriminating evidence.

He nodded absently then picked up his cell phone and poked a couple of buttons.

"Dr. Langslow?" he said. "Could you step in here for a few moments? Thanks."

He put the cell phone back on the desk. Then he reached into his pocket, pulled out a pair of plastic gloves, and began putting them on.

A few seconds later, Dad appeared through the French doors between the library and Michael's office. Well, that explained the chain and padlock.

"Meg!" he exclaimed. "Do you need me?"

"No," I said. "The chief does."

The chief picked up the pill bottle in one gloved hand and held it out to Dad, whose hands were also gloved. Dad peered at the pill bottle's label, then smiled and held it up with a flourish, as if the chief had just handed him some kind of trophy.

"Diazepam!" he exclaimed, as if this alone solved the case.

"Meg says that's generic for Valium," the chief said.

"Very good," Dad said, beaming at me. He opened the pill bottle, inspected the contents, and nodded.

"So this could be the murder weapon?" the chief asked.

"Oh no," Dad said. And then, seeing how the chief's face fell, he added, "But they could be another very useful piece in the puzzle."

The chief didn't look very happy to see the number of puzzle pieces multiplying.

"So what would happen if someone slipped two or three of these in our victim's tea?" the chief asked.

"She'd feel sleepy," Dad said. "Might even fall asleep, though that's a pretty minimal dose. And she'd probably be just fine when she woke up, as long as no one came along while she was asleep and did something else to her. Which appears to be what happened."

"But I thought Valium was for anxiety, not insomnia," the chief said.

"A lot of insomnia is caused by anxiety," Dad said. "Dull the anxiety and the body's natural sleep mechanisms take over. And the diazepam itself acts as a mild sedative. It can be very effective in the short term. In the longer term, patients tend to develop tolerance to the sedative effects."

The chief pondered this briefly.

"So," he said. "If Ramon's doctor thought his insomnia was due to, say, the stress of trying to finish his dissertation and direct the play, he might prescribe this in the short term?"

Dad nodded.

"Or perhaps Ramon prefers to think of himself as taking sleeping medication rather than anxiety medication," Dad suggested. "So many of us find physical ailments more socially acceptable than even the mildest form of mental illness."

"So two or three of these wouldn't kill her," the chief said. "What about five or six?"

"Even a dozen wouldn't necessarily kill someone," Dad said. "Certainly not as rapidly as Dr. Wright's death appears to have been."

"What if they were combined with something else?" I asked. "Subdural hematoma, for example?"

"It wouldn't be good on top of subdural hematoma," he said. "But I think it's unlikely she had that."

"Dr. Blanco has been wondering aloud if she died from a subdural hematoma caused by the fall she took in our hallway," I said.

"Unlikely," Dad repeated. "Most people keep their brains in their skulls. She landed on her derriere, not her head."

"You're sure?" the chief asked.

"I cross-checked it with half a dozen witnesses," Dad said. "If she'd landed on her head, I'd have insisted she go to the hospital, and if she refused, I'd have kept her under close observation. Can't be too careful with a head injury."

"So Ramon and Bronwyn could chuck handfuls of his sleeping meds into her tea with relative impunity," I said. "But what if one or both of them is lying? What effect would it have if they used a couple of Señor Mendoza's heart pills?"

"That would depend on what his heart pills are," Dad said. "We should confiscate his pill bottle so we can test it!"

"We already confiscated it," the chief said.

"Great!" Dad said. "Let's have a look at it!"

"It's already on its way by courier to the State Bureau of Investigation in Richmond," the chief said. "Since we don't actually have testing facilities here in Caerphilly."

Dad's face fell.

"Oh," he said. "Yes, that makes sense. I don't suppose you took note of what it said on the label."

The chief's face softened.

"I did, but it wasn't any use," he said. "To start with, it was in Spanish. And Señor Mendoza admitted that he was not carrying the pills in the original prescription container. He combined the contents of two smaller bottles of heart medicine into the big one we all saw. So even though I now have a translation of what the label says, it's completely irrelevant. It's for some over-the-counter antacid tablets."

"Unwise," Dad said, shaking his head. "Anyone treating him would have no idea what medication he was on, or the dosage."

"And blasted inconvenient for my investigation," the chief said. "But under the circumstances, you can see why I didn't think showing it to you would be of any use."

"Still, I'd have liked to have seen them," Dad said.

"The pills? Is there really much you can tell from visual inspection?" the chief asked. "Assuming the name isn't stenciled on the pills, and I can tell you that wasn't the case."

"It's possible I could learn something," Dad said. "If I'd had a chance to see them."

"Then examine this," the chief said, pulling something out of his pocket. "Dr. Waterston gave it to me. He says it's one of Señor Mendoza's, picked up after the spill in the front hallway. As far as Horace and I could see, it looks exactly the same as the ones in the bottle we sent in."

He dropped the tiny pill into Dad's outstretched palm.

"Excellent!" Dad retreated to the other end of Michael's desk and trained the desk lamp on the pill.

Chief Burke shook his head slightly, as if exhausted by such enthusiasm.

"Meg," he said. "I have a question for you. Was Dr. Wright carrying a handbag when she arrived?"

I closed my eyes and tried to remember.

"I know she had a briefcase," I said. "They both did."

"We found that," he said.

I thought some more.

"Yes, a very small leather handbag," I said. "Probably something designer."

"Would you recognize it if you saw it?"

I pondered.

"Maybe," I said. "Why?"

"We didn't find a purse near her body," he said. "Her wallet was in the briefcase, but everything else in it was neatly arranged and the wallet was just wedged in. Seemed odd."

I nodded.

"And there wasn't any other feminine stuff in the

briefcase," the chief said. "She had on makeup and her hair was nicely done, but there wasn't a lipstick or a compact or a comb or anything like that in the briefcase. It seemed to suggest that there might have been a purse, though we didn't find one near her body."

"I'll keep my eyes open for it," I said.

"You can't remember anything else about it?"

I shook my head.

"Well," he said. "Perhaps you could—"

"Aha! There you are!"

We all started and turned to see Señor Mendoza standing in the office doorway.

"Can I help you, Señor?" the chief asked.

"Just the people I wanted to see," Mendoza said. "*El jefe de policía*, and my poor hostess."

The chief sighed, got up from the desk chair, and courteously offered one of the evil guest chairs to Mendoza. Mendoza seated himself with a flourish, planted his cane in front of him with a brisk tap, and leaned both hands on it. The chief reseated himself and pulled out his notebook.

"First, Señora, I must apologize for having so terribly abused your hospitality," Mendoza said to me. "How can I possibly make amends?"

"That depends on what you've done," I said. "If it's about the fish, you had no way of knowing."

"Fish?" Mendoza seemed puzzled. "No, this is not about fish, but murder!"

"You have more evidence for me, Señor?" the chief asked.

"I have a confession!" Mendoza exclaimed. "I did it!"

"Did what?" the chief asked, peering over his glasses.

"It!" Mendoza repeated. "The assassination of Señora Wright."

The chief sighed, took his glasses off, and rubbed his eyes. I found myself thinking, not for the first time, how good Mendoza's English was. He probably understood a lot more of what was going on around him than some of the students gave him credit for.

"Aren't you going to arrest me?" Mendoza asked.

"We like to take our time about things like that," the chief said.

"Since we don't get that many murders in a small town like Caerphilly," Dad added. "When we do get one, we like to savor it."

The chief winced and cast a sharp glance at Dad, who didn't notice. Life was finally providing the kind of drama Dad loved in his beloved mystery books, and he sat there beaming happily at Señor Mendoza from his ringside seat.

"Let's take things one step at a time," the chief said, settling the glasses back on his temples. "Just tell me, in your own words, what happened."

"Well, if you like," Señor Mendoza said. His shrug and the expression on his face seemed to suggest that he was puzzled at the chief's lack of enthusiasm for his confession. "I became enraged at her villainous treatment of young Ramon—her and her friend, the one who has a Spanish name but not, in my opinion, a Spanish soul! To reward his years of patient labor and his courteous treatment of me in this way! The villains! The ingrates! I cannot say how angry I was to hear it. To think that these . . . these . . ."

"You became enraged," the chief said. "Got it. Go on."

"And I entered the room in which she had hidden herself and confronted her. I rebuked her for her treatment of Ramon and implored her to keep her word to him. But she would not relent. I was enraged. Somehow

I found that hideous statue in my hands and before I realized, I had struck her with it."

"Hmm," the chief said. He looked up from his notebook. "You were confronting her, you say? So you struck her . . . where?"

"On the head," Señor Mendoza said.

"Yes, but where on the head? The front? The side? The back?"

Mendoza frowned. I was already suspicious of his confession. Now I was sure he was lying. I'd bet the chief thought so, too, and had just posed what Mendoza clearly recognized as a trick question.

"To be truthful, I do not know," Mendoza said finally. "I was facing her, so it could have been the front. But equally she might have turned away at seeing my rage, or tried to. I really don't remember. It was all a red blur."

"A red blur," the chief repeated. "Do you mean there was a lot of blood?"

Clearly Señor Mendoza was on his guard.

"I have the impression of a great deal of red," he said. "But I have no idea if I am recalling blood or whether it was merely the force of my rage that made me think so."

The chief rubbed one temple absently. I wondered if he was getting a headache. Should I offer him some aspirin? Probably better to wait until he was finished with Señor Mendoza. And considering how many people had been slipping unidentified pills to each other, maybe I should find a brand-new, sealed bottle.

"And what did you do next?" the chief asked.

"Next? There is no next! She is dead! I can see that very clearly."

"After you saw that she was dead," the chief said.

"I go back to the kitchen to continue preparing the paella," he said. "And the fish stew."

"No one noticed your absence?" the chief said.

"Who notices when an old man leaves the room?" Mendoza said, with a shrug. "No doubt they assume I go to the lavatory."

The chief nodded.

"You didn't do anything else?" he asked.

"What else is there to do?" Mendoza said.

"You didn't, for example, move the body?"

"No!"

"Or take any of her belongings? Her briefcase? Her purse?"

"I am a murderer, not a common thief!" Mendoza drew himself up as tall as he could and pounded his cane on the floor, sending the chair skittering back an inch or so on the polished floor.

"I wasn't implying—" the chief said.

"This is an outrage! I have never been so insulted!"

"Señor Mendoza—"

"I will not stay here to be abused by the *policía!*" Mendoza said, followed by several exclamations in Spanish that had the singsong sound of oft-used slogans. He seemed to be making an effort to rise, but the inescapable guest chair had him firmly in its clutches.

"No one thinks you are a thief," I said, in my most soothing voice. "But of course, even an enraged killer might have the wit and clearheadedness to hide something if he realized it could be used as evidence against him."

"*Sí,*" he said, more calmly. "But her purse, her belongings—how could they be evidence?"

"The chief is only asking," I said. Actually, I was doing the asking, and the chief, seeing that Mendoza responded to my questioning more calmly, was nodding and scribbling in his notebook. "In case you noticed whether any of her belongings were missing."

"I care not for belongings!" Mendoza said. "So I would not notice them."

"Just one more thing," I asked. "Why are you telling us now? Since you seem to have gotten away without anyone catching you—why not keep silent and hope to get away with it?"

"Ah, that was my plan," he said. "Until I realized that suspicion would fall upon young Ramon."

"So you confessed to save Ramon," the chief said.

"To save him from being blamed for my crime," Mendoza said. "I cannot allow his young life to be ruined because of me. So take me away!"

He held out his hands as if for handcuffs. The chief sighed and rubbed the bridge of his nose.

"Thank you, Señor Mendoza," he said. "We'll be in touch."

"You do not want to arrest me?" Mendoza looked quite disappointed.

"We have to wait for the results of the autopsy before we arrest anyone," the chief said. "And I need to check on the protocol. I don't know if I have the authority to arrest a foreign citizen. For now, just give me your word that you won't leave the premises without my permission."

"On my honor," Mendoza said, holding his hand over his heart. "And now, if you do not wish to arrest me, I will return to my lodgings!"

He made another effort to extricate himself from the chair, and both Dad and the chief leaped to his assistance.

"Not leaving the premises means I'd like you to stay

here in the house for the time being," the chief said, as they steadied Mendoza on his feet.

"It's okay," I said. "His lodgings are our dining room."

"That's fine, then," the chief said. "Just one little thing."

Mendoza turned and held his head up, as if he expected the one more thing would lead to a battle of wits.

"Just what are those pills of yours?" the chief said. "The ones you spilled earlier today."

Mendoza blinked and frowned slightly.

"My heart pills," he said.

"Do you know the name of the medication?" the chief asked.

"No." Mendoza shrugged slightly. "My doctor prescribes them, I take them. For the heart. Why?"

"We're still trying to figure out whether to worry if there are any more of them lying around," the chief said. "I've got my dog with me," he added, indicating Scout, who, realizing he was the topic of conversation, lifted his head and thumped his tail on the carpet a few times.

"A noble animal!" Señor Mendoza said.

"And you know dogs. Eat anything in sight, whether it looks like food or not."

"Shall I have the students scour the hall for the pills?" Mendoza asked.

"No," the chief said. "We're already doing that as part of our forensic work. But it would help if we knew what the blamed pills were."

"Ah." Mendoza shrugged again, more eloquently. "I cannot help you. I leave that to my doctor."

"Not wise," I said. "Anyone who's taking any kind of medicine—even over-the-counter medicine—should be an informed consumer. Look up what the effects and

side effects are, and whether it has interactions with
other drugs you might be taking or—"

"I cannot be bothered with that!" Mendoza exclaimed. "If my doctor decides to poison me, so be it!"

With that, he strode out of the room. We could hear
the brisk tap of his cane disappearing down the hallway.

EIGHTEEN

"So, do you believe a word of Señor Mendoza's confession?" I asked.

"No," the chief said, with a sigh. "But I suppose it's rude to tell a distinguished foreign visitor point-blank that he's a bald-faced liar."

"Of course, it's always possible that he poisoned her and decided to confess to the bludgeoning to throw you off the track," I suggested.

"Always possible," the chief agreed. "But I think if he did poison her, he'd react a little more when asked about the pills. Let's hope he's content with having made his confession and doesn't keeping popping back in here every five minutes demanding to be arrested."

"Placate him," I said. "Send Horace to confiscate his clothes for testing or something dramatic like that."

"It's an idea," the chief said. "I just wish I knew what those blasted pills are."

"You could call his doctor," I said.

"I did," he said. "Actually, I had Debbie Anne do the actual calling, since her Spanish is better than mine. But Barcelona's six hours ahead of us, so the doctor's office hours were over by the time we got his contact information. It's unlikely we'll hear before tomorrow."

He picked up his notebook and began flipping through it. Was that intended as a dismissal? Probably. But since he hadn't actually ordered me out, I could take my time and decide what I wanted to do. Nap? Or eat? Both ideas had merit. But both required getting up and moving. And I was strangely comfortable. My back hurt less than usual. And—

"Ms. Langslow?"

I started and opened my eyes.

"Sorry," I said. "I was just trying to decide where to go when I left here."

"You were asleep," he said.

"Just resting my eyes and thinking," I said. "When you're as big as I am, you like to plan your movements."

"You always snore when you're thinking?"

I winced.

"I was trying to decide between taking a nap and getting something to eat." I braced and heaved myself up. "I guess my body decided for me."

"Take care of yourself," he said as I waddled out.

Of course, halfway down the long hallway to the rest of the house, I realized I was more hungry than sleepy. And I had no idea whether the kitchen was still off-limits. Or whether I really wanted to eat anything in it, since we still had a poisoner on the loose.

I'd figure that out when I got there.

I made another pit stop in the front hall bathroom and when I came out, I ran into my grandfather searching the coatracks and muttering under his breath. He was, of course, looking on the wrong rack. I walked over to the right one and plucked out his overcoat.

"Here," I said. "And where are you going, anyway?"

"Just out for a long walk to cool off," he said.

"Cool off?" I repeated. "The house doesn't feel over-heated to me, so I assume you mean your temper."

He scowled instead of answering, but he didn't storm out, so I waited. Having someone to vent to would probably improve his temper even faster than a brisk walk, and I wasn't at all sure anyone his age should be gallivanting about in twenty-degree temperatures.

I found myself wondering, once again, why he had turned up to visit us at this inconvenient moment. Was it just to see his great-grandchildren as soon as they were born? That seemed unlikely—he was fond enough of my older sister's six kids, but he certainly wasn't gaga over them. More likely he was in the planning stages for another installment of his "Animals in Peril" TV series. Were there any endangered species in Caerphilly, Virginia? Or was this going to be an exposé of animal abuse, like last year's dogfighting documentary?

"When the hell is the chief going to solve this thing?" he asked finally. Even more suspicious—he normally didn't share Dad's interest in murder mysteries.

"As soon as he can, I'm sure," I said. "It's only been a few hours."

"He's probably working on a bogus theory of the crime," Grandfather said.

"Bogus?"

"I can't imagine why anyone would have killed that Wright woman!" he exclaimed.

"Of course not," I said, in my most soothing tones. I was about to utter some noble platitudes about how utterly unthinkable murder was to any civilized being when he went on.

"Not with that Blanco fellow around and equally available to anyone who felt like improving the tone of

the neighborhood. Do you suppose whoever did it could
have made a mistake and knocked off the wrong professor?"

I eyed him suspiciously. My first thought was that Dad
had spilled the beans to Grandfather on his poison-in-
the-tea theory. After all, even a crazed killer would
probably notice whether the person he was coshing on
the head was a man or a woman. Poison, though, could
easily go astray and be given to the wrong person. So if
Grandfather was suggesting Dr. Wright had been killed
by mistake . . .

"Do you mean you think whoever hit her over the
head did it by mistake while trying to kill Dr. Blanco?"
I asked.

"Of course," he said. "Why not?"

"They don't look that much alike," I said. "Different
genders, to start with."

"I don't mean to imply that the killer couldn't tell
them apart." He frowned as if I were being deliberately
obtuse. "But what if the killer rushed in, hoping to get
the drop on Blanco, and realized, too late, that he was
about to slay the wrong person? He might just go ahead
with it. What else could he do if she'd already seen him
about to kill her?"

"I can think of plenty of things short of murder!"

"Such as?" My grandfather crossed his arms and
lowered his brows, as if he'd just issued an impossible
challenge.

"He could have shouted, 'Look out! It's right behind
you! Have you ever seen a rat that big?' Or stopped,
and laughed, and said, 'Haha! Fooled you!' Or if he
was a drama student, like ninety percent of the suspects, he could always stop in his tracks, look stern,

and say, 'No, no. That won't work for this scene. What's my motivation?' Or—"

"Yes, you can think of a lot of other things the killer *could* have done, but none of them sounds as logical as my theory," Grandfather said. He began trying to take off his coat. "He knew if he let Dr. Wright live she'd cast suspicion on him when he eventually succeeded in killing Blanco, so he said to himself, 'What the hell—in for a penny, in for a pound.'"

"All of which would be worth considering if Dr. Wright were such a pleasant, likable person that no one could imagine anyone wanting to kill her. But unfortunately for your theory, most of the people around here hate her a lot more than Blanco."

"How can that be?" he said. "Damn—help me off with this thing."

Apparently venting was doing the trick.

"Most of them haven't the faintest idea who Blanco is," I said as I held the coat for him.

"That could be, I suppose," he said. "But still—if my theory is right, Blanco's next. Should we warn him?"

"If you truly think he was the intended victim, maybe you should."

"You don't think it might be more interesting to give the killer a sporting chance?"

"No," I said. "I don't think killers deserve any kind of a chance. What do you have against Dr. Blanco, anyway?"

My grandfather frowned, and at first I didn't think he was going to answer. Then he harrumphed.

"Blasted busybody's the one standing between me and my building," he said finally.

"Your building?"

"Been trying to donate a new building to the biology department," he said.

"They probably don't want a new building," I said.

"Their facilities are completely antiquated, not to mention way too small for them. Why wouldn't they want a new building?"

"Because this is Virginia, remember?" I said. "Who wants convenience when they can have history? The biology building is the third oldest on campus and was used as a military hospital during the Civil War. Plus it's barely large enough for all the tenured professors to have tiny, cramped offices, which means all the rest of the faculty have to be farmed out to even more cramped offices in other, less convenient buildings, thus making everyone's rank in the hierarchy blatantly apparent. I could think of a few more reasons, but those should be enough."

"Hmph," my grandfather said. "Maybe that blasted Blanco is trying to lead me on, then."

"Lead you on how?"

"Well, according to him, the biology department would love to have a new building but there's some kind of complicated financial arrangement he wants me to go through to get it done, and it just doesn't make sense. Instead of just handing them a check, he wants me to put the money in some kind of trust fund that will disburse the money to the college in a different tax year. Sounds overly complicated. Makes me wonder if he's up to something."

I pondered this for a few moments.

"Have you tried talking to an accountant about it?" I said. "Or a tax attorney? The college has a whole lot of foundations and funds and things designed to make sure that they and their donors get maximum advantage from every dollar donated."

"My foundation's got a small army of accountants and tax lawyers," he said. "And they don't like it either. The way they read the documents, I'd have no guarantee of how the money is used—they could use it for general operating expenses or to fund some project that's an environmental menace. Hell, until we get some kind of proof that this Caerphilly Philanthropic Foundation really is affiliated with the college, we'd have no proof Blanco wasn't using it to fund a trip to the Caymans. So if you asked Blanco, he'd probably say it's my people holding up the transaction. Which is nonsense. No one's going to give the college that kind of money without appropriate due diligence. He's the roadblock."

"It might not be his fault," I said. "Did you read the editorial The Fa—the college president wrote in the last alumni bulletin?"

"I'm not a Caephilly alumnus, dammit!"

"Sorry," I said. "Anyway, it was all about what a pain it was when people gave money with so many restrictions that the college could in theory have millions in endowments and not have enough cash to pay the light bill. The Face is big on nonrestricted donations. Maybe Blanco's just trying to please his boss."

"Hmph!" my grandfather said. "Then he should grow a backbone."

With that he strode off. But toward the kitchen, not out the front door, so apparently venting to me had cooled his temper some.

"Come on out to the barn," he called over his shoulder. "Your mother's doing a buffet out there before the dress rehearsal."

A buffet in our barn? Trust Mother to treat a murder investigation as yet another social occasion. She probably knew exactly what wines went with forensics and interrogation. Or was the rehearsal the reason for the festivity?

If Grandfather had waited a few seconds I could have asked him to send someone back to the house with a plate for me.

I could always wait until someone came back to the house.

My stomach rumbled.

I rummaged through the racks until I found the loosely cut coat I'd been wearing this winter, and then through the baskets until I found a hat, scarf, and gloves that at least looked like mine. I caught sight of myself in the hall mirror. Did I look more like an arctic explorer or an overcoat-clad walrus?

I deferred the question and headed for the back door.

But I couldn't help thinking about Grandfather's diatribe. Was Blanco really trying to keep him from giving the college the money for a building? I doubted it. More likely, Blanco was trying to get Grandfather's money for the college with as few strings as possible attached.

Unless he was scrambling to cover up something worse. Like the college really not having enough money to pay its bills. Or its payroll. What if the whole problem with Randall Shiffley's check was not Blanco's inconsiderateness or inefficiency but his desperate attempts to juggle until he could find enough money to cover the check? If that was the case—

I didn't want to think about it right now. I shoved the door open and stepped onto the back stoop.

NINETEEN

Outside it was getting dark already. The sun hadn't quite set, but it was hidden behind thick clouds. The air was cold, but with no wind at least it was a bearable cold.

I picked my way carefully down the back steps and paused to look around. To my left, I could see the lighted windows of the library. Inside, Horace was methodically picking his way through a section of the students' belongings. Poor Horace was in for a long night.

The table where Dr. Wright had been killed wasn't visible from this angle, but much of the library was. Should I point this out to Chief Burke? Ask if he'd interrogated the students, particularly any smokers who'd used the backyard, to see if they'd seen anyone other than Dr. Wright in the library?

Probably not a good idea. He resented people interfering in his investigations. So far I'd managed not to set him off today. I decided to keep it that way.

I'd tell Horace and let him ask the chief.

For its first ten or fifteen feet, the path to the barn was lined on both sides with several dozen black plastic garbage bags, all tied at the top and neatly arranged. Someone had posted a "trash" sign to the left and a "recycling" sign to the right. Every week the students were here we had more bags of both kinds. Maybe we could just get our trash company to leave a Dumpster for the next few weeks.

And maybe anyone who had been on trash-removal duty would also be a good candidate for interrogation about whether they'd seen anything suspicious in the library.

Ahead, light spilled out of the barn windows. A slight breeze rustled the trash bags and picked up a few stray leaves in the yard. I pulled my coat tighter and hiked to the barn.

I slid open the door a little way and the light and noise hit me.

"Come in and shut the door!" half a dozen voices sang out in unison.

"It's Mrs. Waterston!" another voice called. "Open the door for her!"

The door flew aside so abruptly that it almost dragged me sideways with it.

"Meg!" Rose Noire was at my elbow, steering me inside. "What are you doing out here? I thought you were napping!"

"I was hungry," I said.

"You could have called me," she said. "I'd have brought you a plate."

"And miss the party?" I said. "I'm fine. Point me toward the food."

I let her take my hat, gloves, and scarf, but since the barn wasn't actually heated, I hung onto my coat.

Across the room I could see a flock of students under Mother's direction setting up several rows of folding chairs facing toward the far end, which I deduced was to be used as the stage for the dress rehearsal. In the stage area, other students were arranging stacks of zucchini and other articles that I recognized as props for Señor Mendoza's play. The stagehands looked a little flustered, though—Señor Mendoza and Bronwyn were standing on opposite ends of the stage, shouting what I deduced were contradictory sets of instructions. In the time it took me to reach the buffet tables, one poor young man carried a potted lemon tree back and forth between stage left and stage right four times before giving up, dropping the pot center stage and running over to clutch a couple of Mother's folding chairs as if his life depended on deploying them.

I was relieved to see that Mother hadn't actually called in caterers. The buffet was spread out on the four old picnic tables we used for outdoor family events during the summer. A mixed assortment of tablecloths covered them. Stacks of pizza boxes filled one entire table and the others held bowls of chips, salads, and other side dishes in quite an assortment of serving pieces. Back in our hometown of Yorktown, this would have meant that Mother had called upon her large extended family to contribute to the potluck event. But we were in Caerphilly, an hour away from the heartland of the Hollingsworth family. Had she dragged them all up here?

Some of them. I recognized the odd, handmade pottery dish in which Cousin Lacey always brought her corn pudding. I made sure to snag a couple of Aunt Bella's lighter-than-air crescent rolls from her familiar wicker breadbasket. I avoided the cut-glass dish in which Great-Aunt Louella brought her famous pickles. The dish was emptier than usual, probably because the students didn't yet know that Louella's pickle recipe contained enough jalapeno and habenero peppers to supply a Mexican restaurant for half a year. We'd be finding bitten-into pickles hidden in corners for weeks.

But some of the offerings looked more local. I spotted one of Mother's friends from the historical society arranging gingerbread men on an antique plate. I was almost certain that the duck-shaped lemon congealed salad came from one of Dad's bird-watching comrades. The tarts strewn with rose petals had to be from a garden-club member.

When I'd first moved to Caerphilly to be with Michael, I'd decided that one of its charms was that it was close enough to see my family whenever I wanted to, but far enough away that I didn't have to see them all the time. Now, Rob and Rose Noire had moved to town, Mother and Dad had bought what they referred to as their vacation cottage nearby, and before long—

"What's wrong?" Michael said, appearing at my other elbow.

"Nothing's wrong," I said. "I'm in awe. Look at all this food."

"Lovely spread," he said. "Here, let me carry your plate."

I was about to protest that I could do it myself, but why should I? Having Michael hold my plate would be a lot easier, and after the kids were born, who knew how often he'd have the time or energy to be chivalrous?

"I'll get you some hot chocolate," Rose Noire said, and flitted off.

"I see Mother has won over Caerphilly, too," I said as I speared a slice of Smithfield ham and deposited it on the plate.

"Won it over how?" Michael pointed to a platter. "Don't you want some corn bread?"

"Yes," I said. "I just don't know if I have room for it. By won them over, I mean she's got them all bringing her food."

"Bringing *us* food," Michael said. "I admit that your mother probably got the word out that with our kitchen off-limits we could use a potluck dinner. But most of this came from our friends, not your family. Minerva Burke brought the corn bread."

"That settles it." I added two chunks of corn bread to my platter. "If I don't have room now, I'll take it upstairs for later."

"And Randall's mother sent over the venison stew," Michael said, pointing. "The samosas from Professor Kumar disappeared a long time ago, but I saved you a few. Professor Ortiz brought some early Christmas tamales, and Abe's wife sent chicken soup and—"

"Meg, dear." Mother appeared at my other side. "We could have brought you a plate."

"I'll be fine." I was eyeing another table, set at a distance from the others. "What's over there?"

"Nothing you'd be interested in," Mother said. "Would you like some chicken soup?"

"How do you know I wouldn't be interested?" What were they trying to hide from me? I'd actually taken a few steps toward the mysterious table when Mother's voice stopped me.

"That's where we put the seafood, dear. Since you seem to find it so . . . unsettling."

I blinked in surprise. For years, Mother had treated my seafood allergy as if it were merely an inconvenient personal idiosyncrasy. She never tired of plying me with dainty morsels of substances that I knew perfectly well would give me a rash if I were foolish enough to eat them. Was she now giving up the battle? Conceding that if I was old enough to be a mother, I was old enough to know what was and wasn't good for my body?

"Thank you," I said, and surprised her with a brief but fierce hug.

"You're welcome, dear," Mother said. "Now let's find you a quiet, comfortable place to sit while you eat."

In a few minutes I was tucked up in an Adirondack chair with a blanket over my legs and a large box at my elbow to serve as a table.

Suddenly music blared out—a lively cheerful tune played by what sounded like a variety of flutes and trumpets accompanied by a small drum. In the open space between the chairs and the buffet, Señor Mendoza was chivvying a dozen or so people into joining hands to form a circle.

"What's he up to?" I asked Michael.

"Teaching them the sardana," he said. "The Catalan national dance. He thinks Ramon should add it to the play."

When Mendoza stood in the center of the circle and demonstrated, the dance steps seemed a simple sequence of steps forward and back, left and right. Occasionally one foot would cross over the other.

Of course, when Mendoza stepped back into the circle and set his troops in motion, the simple steps he demonstrated proved far more complex for them all to execute, in unison, in time to the music.

Still, they persevered, and people began deserting the buffets and the rehearsal preparations to hover at the periphery, watching the dancers, trying out the steps themselves, and eventually joining in. A second circle was forming.

"Go try it if you like," I said to Michael.

"Want to join me? It doesn't look that strenuous." He held out a hand to help me up.

"A month ago I would have," I said. "But now I think I'd better stay in the audience. You go ahead."

Michael seemed to get the hang of the sardana almost immediately and threw himself into it with the same enthusiasm as Señor Mendoza. Rose Noire's sardana matched their enthusiasm, but you could tell she was merely improvising on the footwork. Mrs. Fenniman was dancing with her ancient black umbrella clutched in one hand, to the peril of anyone nearby. I had no idea whether Mother's rendition was particularly accurate, but it was certainly elegant.

I found myself wishing Señor Mendoza would switch circles for a little while. The second circle looked a lot less authentic than the first, and whatever the ragtag third circle was doing certainly wasn't the sardana. It looked more like a crew of inebriated morris dancers trying to perform a group tango. But maybe I was being too picky. Maybe the important thing with the sardana was not accuracy but the emotion and camaraderie of the dancers.

Perhaps a good thing I'd stayed out, then. I suddenly realized that I felt rather out of step with all these happy, energetic people. Granted none of them had any particular fondness for Dr. Wright, but did they think that made it all right for someone to murder her? Maybe they felt no guilt or sadness, but didn't any of them feel anything? Not even a little shiver of mingled relief and melancholy at realizing that the Grim Reaper had struck so close by? Or the tiniest inkling of fear that we didn't yet know who'd been helping the Reaper out?

But everyone certainly seemed to be having a great

time, with the possible exception of Ramon, who was watching the dance with a baleful glare. Somehow I didn't think much of Señor Mendoza's chance of adding a sardana to the play. Or was Ramon glaring because Bronwyn had deserted him to dance with Mendoza to her left and the earnest and slightly clumsy Danny Oh on her right? Of course, Danny might not have been so clumsy if he could have taken his eyes off Bronwyn occasionally, to see where his feet were going.

And there was one other person not joining in the general gaiety: Dr. Blanco. He was sitting on one of the folding chairs, as far from the makeshift stage as possible. His elbows were on his knees, his shoulders were slumped, and he held his cell phone cradled in both hands. Now and then he glanced at it forlornly, as if waiting for a phone call that never came. Or perhaps he was using it as a clock and feeling dismayed at how slowly time was crawling by. Even though his overcoat was tightly buttoned, he looked as if he felt cold.

I strolled over to him. When he spotted me, he sat up with a look of mingled relief and anxiety. I probably looked much like that at my first school dance—terrified of being a wallflower and even more terrified that someone would invite me to dance and find out how awful I was at it.

"How are you doing?" I asked.

"Fine." He blinked in surprise. "Why shouldn't I be?"

"Well, you seem to be the only one here who really knew the late Dr. Wright very well."

"The only one who's not relieved at her death, you mean."

His bluntness was startling and almost refreshing. I couldn't immediately think what to say next. Luckily a small knot of dancers across the room burst into laughter, drawing our eyes and saving me from having to say anything. When I glanced back at Dr. Blanco, he was frowning, but then the frown dissolved back into a look of gloom.

"Not their fault," he said, nodding at the dancers. "I gather there is very strong opposition to some of the standards Dr. Wright was trying to enforce."

"Did you agree with her?" I asked.

He drew back slightly. Did I only imagine the brief gleam of panic in his eye before the bureaucrat in him rallied?

"I certainly supported her position as she explained it to me," he said. "Of course, since then I have come to appreciate that there were other points of view that had not been made available to me."

"Well weaseled," I wanted to say. But I didn't think it would help the drama curriculum's cause.

"Will you continue to advocate her position, then?" I asked aloud.

"No," he said. "The whole thing's really an internal English department issue and should be left to the faculty of that department, don't you think?"

I was tempted to point out that it had always been an internal issue and should have been left to the faculty members—all of them, not just one particularly fanatical one with a grudge against the theater. But if he'd decided to cede the field, who cared what words he used?

"It must be difficult for you here," I said, waving my hand to indicate the activity around us. "I suppose the chief wants you to stay around?"

"I imagine I could convince him to let me go home," Dr. Blanco said. "But the president indicated he'd like me to stick around. Keep my finger on the pulse, as it were."

Just then Rose Noire bustled up.

"You haven't eaten a thing," she said to Dr. Blanco. "Why don't you let me bring you a plate?"

"No, thanks," he said.

"Would you like something that isn't on the buffet?"

Something not on the buffet? I glanced over at the four overflowing tables. Was there any food not represented there?

"Really, I'm fine," he said. "I'm just not very hungry yet."

"But you need to—"

Blanco's phone rang. His eyes lit up.

"I beg your pardon, but I must take this. It's the president." He stood up as he flipped the phone open. "Just a moment," he said into the phone. "Let me find someplace quieter."

He scurried across the barn floor and out the door.

"Poor man," I said.

"He has a very forlorn aura," Rose Noire said. "Nothing like Dr. Wright's. I think the students are mistaken to dislike him so much."

"He's a pilot fish who's lost his shark," I said. "Weak, not evil. And probably not very dangerous. At least not until he finds another shark."

"He needs to open up and talk to someone about what he's experiencing," Rose Noire said. "But he's very resistant to the idea."

I sighed. Apparently Rose Noire was practicing therapy without a license again. Had Blanco's phone really rung or had he just been trying to escape Rose Noire?

"Well, I suppose we should give him some space for now," Rose Noire said. "I wanted to ask you—do you think I'm to blame for all this?"

"To blame? Why?"

"Well, I was the one who brought Tawaret into the house," she said.

"You didn't force anyone to pick her up and attempt homicide with her," I said.

"Yes," Rose Noire said. "But she's quite protective. Perhaps she sensed that Dr. Wright was a danger to you and the babies. And of course she comes from an age when people were a lot more direct about life and death. And less respectful of human life. Perhaps it was a mistake, bringing her into such a fraught situation. Of course, I didn't know at the time it was fraught, but still—"

"It's an interesting idea," I said. Actually, I thought it was a crazy idea. Was I going to follow in Mother's footsteps, and teach my children that when they couldn't say anything nice, they should fall back on the word "interesting?" I'd decide later. "But maybe you shouldn't spread your theory around too widely."

"Why not?"

"Imagine how Chief Burke will feel if whoever he arrests tries to use that as a defense," I said. " 'Tawaret made me do it.' "

"You're just humoring me," she said.

"I'm just trying to cheer you up," I said. Would she feel better if I told her Tawaret wasn't the actual murder weapon? Maybe, but maybe not. And I'd promised Chief Burke I wouldn't tell anyone. "Look," I said aloud. "I don't think Tawaret magically convinced anyone to kill Dr. Wright. The killer made his—or her—own decision."

"Thank you," she said. "But I'm still going to consider this an important lesson!"

She looked very determined. I wasn't sure quite what lesson she was learning from today's events. Never give presents large enough to become murder weapons?

Never trust pagan goddesses who might have their own agendas? Time would tell. I found a chair, closed my eyes and tried to wiggle into a comfortable position.

"Good news!"

I opened one eye to see Dr. Blanco standing in front of us looking much more cheerful than before.

"The president is coming!" Blanco said.

"You mean all the way from Washington?" Rose Noire asked.

I choked back my laughter. Yes, given the mingled awe and excitement in Blanco's voice, I could see how she might jump to the conclusion that we'd be meeting the occupant of the White House.

"No, the president of the college," Blanco said.

"Oh," Rose Noire said. "Well, that's nice." She hurried off. I gathered from her tone that either she'd met The Face before or she remembered some of our stories about him.

Her lack of enthusiasm seemed to take all the starch out of Blanco. His shoulders slumped and he seemed smaller and not nearly as imposing.

"He's coming out to see the rehearsal," Blanco said. "So he can judge for himself what action to take."

He sounded anxious. No wonder. He'd lost a staunch ally in Dr. Wright. He'd spent the day with people who obviously wouldn't mourn if he met the same fate. And now his boss was coming, no doubt to take personal charge of a matter that Blanco thought he was being allowed to handle. To my astonishment, I found myself feeling sorry for him.

"I've got to get things ready!" Blanco exclaimed, and dashed out.

"Meg, dear." Mother appeared in front of me. "What was Dr. Blanco so upset about?"

"I think he was excited, not upset," I said. "The Fa—the college president is coming to see the rehearsal. Damn. I should go back in to make sure he finds his way out here."

"Surely he'll see the lights coming from the backyard and realize that everyone is out here in the barn," Mother said.

"I doubt it," I said. "In fact, unless Dr. Blanco stations himself in the hallway awaiting his arrival, The Face will probably just stand there ringing the doorbell until someone hears him. Or until he gets tired, after an hour or so, and goes home puzzled and insulted. And possibly with frostbite in his fingers and toes."

Mother gave me a sharp look, realized I wasn't kidding, and closed her eyes. Counting to ten before saying anything, no doubt. I'd learned the habit from her. Though I doubted I'd ever master the air with which she did it, as if bearing up nobly in spite of almost overwhelming trials. When I counted to ten, I usually just looked cross.

"Then we must station someone to make sure he's let in promptly and brought back here where he can enjoy the buffet," she said.

"I suppose I can do it," I said. "Just let me finish this."

"Rose Noire can do it," Mother said. "It will be more restful for her."

I followed Mother's eyes. Yes, Rose Noire was probably overdoing it. Had probably been overdoing it ever since the students arrived, trying her best to see that our guests were well cared for. Now she seemed to be speeding around the barn on hyperdrive, darting into one of the sardana circles, then dashing out to wait on someone before dashing back and dancing frantically, as if to catch up.

I'd have been overdoing it myself if I hadn't had the twins to slow me down and remind me that the students weren't our guests, they were temporary fellow residents. And Rose Noire was probably driving herself even harder today out of guilt at bringing Tawaret into our lives.

I should have seen that. I put down my plate and began gathering myself to rise.

"Sit down," Mother said. "I'll tell her."

"I'm not going in to welcome The Face," I said. "It's getting near my bedtime. Don't let Rose Noire know you're doing it for her own good."

"I will convince her that making the president feel welcome is of the utmost importance." Mother strode off with her head held high.

"It very well might be," I muttered.

I put down my plate and made my way to the barn door. I had to go the long way around, skirting the edge of the dance floor. On my way past the buffet I snagged an empty Tupperware container and filled it with a few delicacies for later.

Then I donned my hat, gloves, and scarf and went to haul the barn door open far enough for me to slip out. And then a little farther, since I realized I hadn't allowed for how big Tom and Jerry had become.

It was fully dark now. I pulled out my cell phone and glanced at it. 5:30. Early for me to go to bed, but this had been a long day.

I stepped outside.

"Meg! Where are you going?"

Michael appeared in the doorway.

"I'll be fine," I said. "Close the door, quick. You're letting all the heat out."

"There's no real heat in here," Michael said. "It's just not quite as frigid as outdoors."

"You're letting out all the not-quite-frigid air, then," I said.

"I'll make sure you get safely back," he said. He pulled the door shut after him and held out his arm to steady me.

The air had grown much colder, or perhaps it was only the rising wind that made it seem that way. Halfway back to the kitchen steps we had to stop and turn our backs to the wind to ride out one particularly strong gust. I was relieved when we reached the garbage bag gauntlet, since it would partially shield us from the next gust.

And then I realized that the top of one bag was flapping open in the wind, sending bits of trash skittering across the frozen ground.

"Damn!" Michael gave chase to the flying garbage. "I'll have to tell everyone to be more careful."

I'd have said that everyone was already being rather careful. None of the other bags was flapping open, and I didn't remember this one doing so when I'd walked by it earlier. Perhaps someone had opened it to add more garbage and forgotten to tie it up again.

But why choose this one, which was already full and in the middle of the lineup to boot?

I stepped closer to the bag, peered in, and sneezed several times.

"Let me do that," Michael called from across the yard.

But I was already reaching into the bag. My hand slid through several squishy things that I tried not to think about. I burrowed a little deeper and my hand encountered the butter-soft texture of expensive leather. I grabbed the leather object and pried it out of the surrounding goop.

"What's that?" Michael strode up with his arms full of trash.

I held the object up so we could see it in the light from the kitchen windows. It was a rectangular black leather clutch purse. It was large for a clutch purse—perhaps six by eleven inches. Even considering its size it had a remarkable number of nonfunctional buckles, straps, zippers, and other bits of metal. And it was too flat to be very practical. It wouldn't even have held my wallet, much less all the gear I toted every day. The sort of purse you could afford to carry if you spent most of your day in your office and had a briefcase to carry any larger items when you left it.

"I think it's Dr. Wright's purse," I said. "We need to take this to the chief."

TWENTY

"Are you sure it's Dr. Wright's purse?" Chief Burke asked. He had set the purse on our kitchen table and he, Horace, and Dad were peering at it.

"Not a hundred percent sure," I said. I was sitting a few feet away, where I could see but not smell the purse. "I'm not much of a fashion expert. It's a pity Mother didn't see Dr. Wright arrive. She'd not only know whether it was Dr. Wright's purse or not, she could tell you the brand, the model, how much it cost, and whether you could possibly buy one like it in any of the local stores."

"Just knowing it's hers would be sufficient," the chief said.

"It's not mine, and I can't imagine any of the women students throwing away a perfectly good purse like that. See—it's a designer brand."

I pointed to the word "Coach" embossed onto a leather patch on one side—probably one of the few designer purse brands I'd have recognized.

"But what convinces me that it's hers is the smell," I went on.

"I assumed it picked up that rotten, garlicky smell in the garbage," Horace said.

"Never mind the garlic," I said. "The thing reeks of Dr. Wright's perfume. That damned scent made me sneeze every time I got near her, and it permeates that bag."

"Did you look inside?" the chief asked.

"I thought you'd rather do that," I said.

"Let's take it to my—to Dr. Waterston's office," the chief said. Horace picked up the purse in gloved hands and carried it out. Dad followed. The chief glanced out the kitchen windows briefly, as if puzzled how it had gotten dark so quickly. I realized he'd spent much of the day in Michael's office, where the heavy thermal curtains were tightly drawn to keep out drafts. Then he sighed and followed Dad and Horace.

"I should get back to the rehearsal," Michael said. "You should go up to rest soon."

"Soon," I said. "I just want to see this through."

I followed Horace, Dad, and the chief, bringing up the rear of the procession, keeping far enough back to prevent the chief from getting annoyed.

Back in Michael's office, Horace spread out a large sheet of paper on the desk and set the purse carefully on it. I sat down on a book box and tried to fade into the shadows.

No such luck.

"Did you touch the purse?" the chief asked me.

"Only with my gloves on," I said.

"Leave your wraps here," Horace said over his shoulder as he examined the bag. "I'll need to take samples of the fibers."

Presumably he needed to eliminate any threads I'd left on the purse from any the killer might have deposited. I struggled out of my wraps and left them on one of the book boxes.

I almost fell asleep while Horace was fingerprinting the purse's exterior. Or perhaps I did fall asleep. But I was jolted wide awake by the chief's voice.

"Let's have a look inside."

I watched from afar as Horace carefully began extracting the purse's contents.

A gold pen.

A small perfume vial—presumably the scent I found so annoying.

"When you get a chance, tell me what that vile stuff is," I said. "So I can write to the manufacturer and complain."

They ignored me.

A small leather-bound notepad. We all watched eagerly as Horace flipped it open, but we saw only blank pages. Horace shook his head and reached back into the purse.

"Uh-oh," Horace said.

He pulled out a small bottle.

"Is this what I think it is?" Horace handed the bottle to Dad.

"Yes," Dad said. "I'm not surprised."

"You did say to keep an eye out for it," Horace said.

"It could explain everything!" Dad exclaimed. "Of course there's no way to tell before the tox screen comes back."

"But I bet this is what poisoned her," Horace said. They were nodding happily at each other and didn't seem to notice the chief's growing irritation.

"It accounts for her condition and the timeline," Dad went on. "I was never happy with the notion of it being digitalis. Too slow."

"And she didn't drink enough of the tea," Horace said, nodding. "If they'd put enough digitalis in for that much to kill her, she'd have noticed the taste. And what's more—"

"Just what in blue blazes is that thing?" the chief asked.

"Insulin," Dad said. "Was there a syringe?"

Horace peered into the bag again, then carefully inserted his hand and pulled out a syringe. Dad shook his head as if sadly disappointed at the murderer's clumsiness in leaving such clues behind.

I leaned a little closer so I could see the vial. There was a tiny amount of clear liquid in the bottom.

"It's nearly empty," I said. "Is this a bad sign?"

"A very bad sign," Dad said. "That much insulin could easily have killed her."

"But you don't know that it was given all at once, do you?" I asked.

"We don't know, but the odds are it was," Horace said. "There's a date on the label. The prescription was refilled yesterday."

"So either she picked up her insulin yesterday and had to use it several times within twenty-four hours, which seems unlikely," Dad said. "Or it was given all at once."

"You're sure that much insulin would be fatal?" the chief asked.

"Oh yes," Dad said.

"How fast?"

"That would depend on how it was administered," Dad said. "IM—in the muscle—maybe four to five minutes. Could take more like ten to fifteen minutes sub-Q—under the skin."

"Would that require medical expertise?" the chief asked.

Dad shook his head.

"Just about anyone could have managed to do it subcutaneously," he said. "Especially if she was unconscious and unresisting. Of course, that does leave us with two interesting questions."

"I'm all ears," the chief said.

"First, who knew that she was an insulin-dependent diabetic?" Dad asked. "She didn't exactly advertise it—we didn't find a medic alert bracelet or tag of any kind."

"And it's definitely her prescription?" the chief asked. "Her name on the label?"

Horace nodded.

"So the killer had to be someone who knew her well," Horace said.

"Not necessarily," the chief said. "All someone had to do was see her injecting insulin at any time in the past and they could be reasonably certain she'd have it with her."

"True," I said. "But unless she did her injecting very publicly—like in the middle of a class—and a whole lot of people knew about it, I bet you're going to have a hard time finding anyone who'll admit to knowing it, since knowing it makes someone even more suspicious."

"Of course, right now, only the killer knows that insulin was what killed her," the chief said. He turned back to Dad. "You said two questions. What was the other?"

"Just how many attempted killers do we have here?" Dad asked. He sounded rather more gleeful than I would have been if I were asking that question. "It's almost like *Murder on the Orient Express*."

"Only they don't play well with others, these killers," I said. "Since we have three or four separate attempts to kill her instead of one coordinated effort."

"Can we reconstruct a sequence of events from this?" the chief asked.

"A hypothetical one," Dad said. "Either Ramon or Bronwyn or both doctored her tea with what they claim was sleeping medicine—probably Ramon's Valium. The order in which they did it doesn't matter, since she'd have ingested both at the same time. Sometime later, after she had ingested some tea and presumably fallen asleep due to the Valium, she was injected with insulin. And sometime after that, she was hit over the head with the statue—an attack that would have been fatal if she hadn't been already dead when it occurred."

"You're forgetting one possibility," the chief said. "We know these people claim to have put Valium in her tea, and we know there was Valium around for them to use, but what if one or both of them drugged her tea with something other than Valium? Señor Mendoza's heart medicine, for example. Maybe the insulin was unnecessary too. Maybe she was already dead or dying when they gave her the insulin. We won't be able to tell until the tox screen comes back."

"Not for sure," Dad said. "But I'll tell you what I bet we'll find. May I show you something?"

He had pulled out his iPhone and was waving it about.

I cringed. Dad's iPhone was a relatively new acquisition and he was still consumed with the zeal of the recent convert, always trying to find new ways to make use of his expensive little toy. But now was not the time to show it off to the chief.

"If it's relevant," the chief said. "I mean, if there's a reason I should not arrest Señor Mendoza for the murder of Professor Wright, I'd like to hear it."

"Are you serious?" Dad asked anxiously.

"Of course not," the chief said. "If I thought the old guy really had bludgeoned her with the statue, I'd have already arrested him, no matter how distinguished he is in Spain. Just because she wasn't alive when someone hit her doesn't mean it wasn't attempted murder. Or if I really believed he was the one who poisoned her, I'd bring him back and question him some more."

"Poison doesn't seem like his style," I said. "A sword, maybe, or pistols at dawn, but nothing subtle like poison."

"And he's probably the least likely of anyone here to have the inside knowledge that a potentially deadly vial of insulin was in her bag."

"He's the least likely suspect for any of what went on," the chief said.

"He was hanging around the kitchen during the time someone drugged Dr. Wright's tea," I said. "He could have done that. Or seen it done, or just suspected someone used his pills. Or maybe he confessed so implausibly to the bludgeoning because he put his heart pills in her tea and wanted to make himself look implausible as a suspect."

"Yes, but even if Señor Mendoza put his heart pills in her tea, that couldn't possibly have killed her," Dad said.

"And just how do you figure that?" the chief said.

"They're not digoxin."

"Not digoxin?" the chief said. "How do you know? And if they're not digoxin, what are they?"

"They're not any kind of heart medicine I've ever seen. Wrong size, shape, and color."

"Couldn't they be the Spanish versions?"

"Most common pharmaceuticals are pretty international these days," Dad said. "And I did some research to see if these could be a variant more common in Europe, but they weren't. So whether Señor Mendoza or anyone else put them in her tea is irrelevant. They're almost certainly not what killed her."

"How can you be sure?" the chief asked. "I mean, even if they're not digitalis, they could be something else toxic."

"Well, we won't know anything for sure until the autopsy," Dad said. "And until the analysis of those pills comes back. But I can hazard a guess. When I first went into medicine, it was pretty easy to tell what a pill was. Not that many meds and only a few manufacturers. These days, there are so many more drugs, plus all the generics—it can be impossible to tell for sure. That's why I have this nifty little application on my iPhone that's designed to help doctors identify meds in an emergency. Would you like to see?"

He held the iPhone up again and waved it around excitedly.

"I'll take your word for it," the chief said, stepping back slightly. Perhaps he shared my tepid enthusiasm for cell phones. "So if they're not digitalis, what do you and your iPhone think Señor Mendoza's pills are?"

"Probably a benzodiazepine," Dad said. "Could be more diazepam—Valium—or something similar. There's a European factory making a generic diazepam that looks just like this, so I suspect that's what it is."

"So even if someone tried to use Señor Mendoza's pills to kill her, all they did was give her more Valium?" I asked.

"Precisely," Dad said.

"Enough Valium to be dangerous?" the chief asked.

Dad thought for some moments.

"Probably not," he said. "Ramon's pills were two-milligram doses. That's also what a prudent doctor would probably prescribe for an elderly patient like Señor Mendoza—two milligrams two to four times a day. These look to be two-milligram pills. And the normal dosage can be up to ten milligrams four times a day for a healthy adult."

"So someone could throw eight or ten of these pills in the tea, assuming they'd just delivered a lethal dose of digitalis, and still be way short even of the maximum daily dosage of Valium?" I asked.

Dad nodded.

"What if they went in for overkill?" the chief said. "And gave her fifteen or twenty milligrams?"

"They could feed her Señor Mendoza's whole bottle and it would be extremely unlikely to prove fatal, particularly in the short time we're talking about," Dad said. "I'm not saying it's harmless; she might have side effects. But no matter how much Valium she swallowed, it wouldn't cause death so suddenly. Very few poisons could—digitalis wouldn't, for example; it would take hours. And most of the poisons that fast would cause some pretty dramatic symptoms that we'd be able to pick up on. But the condition of the body's consistent with insulin poisoning. That's why I told you earlier I didn't think testing the tea would get us anywhere."

The chief thought for a moment.

"I don't have to tell any of you to keep this to yourselves," he said. He was, of course, looking at me.

"Don't worry about me," I said. "I realize that we already have at least two self-confessed criminals in the house, and the total will probably rise to three or four when you figure out who shot her up with the insulin and who bludgeoned her with the statue. I might be a little careless with my own safety, but I have no intention of putting Chip and Dale in danger."

I patted the twins as I spoke. Chip responded by attempting to turn a somersault, causing Dale to begin his relentless, rhythmic kicking. I wasn't looking forward to refereeing when they got older.

"That's good," the chief said. "I appreciate you calling me when you found the purse instead of going off half-cocked and trying to solve the murder yourself. But it might be a good time to get a little rest and keep your distance from all those folks."

"At least until you figure out which ones are homicidally inclined and which ones just full of talk when it comes to Dr. Wright," I said. "Point taken. Actually, I'm heading up to bed. Though I was wondering if I could get my laptop while I'm here."

"Allow me," Horace said. He disappeared into the closet and emerged holding the familiar battered carrying case that held my laptop.

The chief was eyeing the laptop with disfavor. Surely he knew better than to think me capable of online sleuthing.

"Thanks," I said. "If anyone looks for me, I'll be upstairs, either doing a few last minute searches on those 'What to Name Your Baby' sites or taking a long overdue nap."

TWENTY-ONE

"Finally," I muttered, as I reached the top of the stairs. I stood there until my breathing slowed down a bit. These days, Hansel and Gretel didn't leave me much room to draw a deep breath. Then I headed toward our bedroom.

Of course, before I got there, I had to pass the door to the nursery. Since Mother hadn't gone home in a huff after talking to Michael, I assumed he had approved her plans. Surprising that she hadn't tried to tell me about them out in the barn. Perhaps she was too busy playing hostess and dancing.

Or maybe I should check on what she'd been doing.

The door was open and I heard a radio softly playing country music, interrupted occasionally by a gentle tapping noise. I took a deep breath, stepped inside, and looked around.

It wasn't as bad as I'd feared. Not yet, anyway. The walls had been painted a soft bluish-lavender, and Randall, on an eight-foot ladder, was applying a foot-deep wallpaper border with a twining leaf pattern along the top. One of Randall's cousins was assembling the second of two matching cribs. The first stood already assembled, its white painted wood gleaming, its mattress already covered with a lavender sheet. The lavender

walls matched the sheets so exactly that I knew Mother
had given someone down at the hardware store fits per-
fecting the paint color match.

"If you're looking for your mother, she just left,"
Randall said, from atop his ladder. "Brought us some
plates from the buffet."

"That's good," I said. "I was hoping to sneak a peek
without her around."

"Not too bad, is it?"

"No, it's lovely," I said. "Though unnecessary. Even
if either of the kids inherits Mother's decorating gene,
it'll be a few years before they're old enough to appreciate elegant nursery design."

"And by the time they are, they'll have knocked the
dickens out of it and it won't be quite so elegant," Randall said with a chuckle. "Hope you don't mind that we
took the job."

"You needed the money," I said. "That's the one
thing that keeps me from putting my foot down and
telling her to send all this expensive stuff back. We
don't need it, but Mother can afford it, and if it's helping keep local businesses going, I can live with it."

Randall nodded. He still looked troubled. He glanced
over at his cousin.

"Hobart," he said. "You mind if I talk to Mrs. Waterston in private for a moment?"

"Sure thing, Randall. I'll go get some more pie."
Hobart nodded to me and shuffled out the door.

Randall followed him to the door and shut it. I sighed
and looked around for someplace to sit, or at least something I could lean against. Randall seemed to guess my
intent and fetched a stool with soft green upholstery.

"Here," he said. "We haven't assembled the matching rocker yet, but this is better than nothing."

"Thanks," I said. "What's up, Randall?"

"Got something I want to run by you," he said.

"Okay," I said.

"It's about the library."

"I told you before, we're just not ready to do the library," I said. "Actually, we're ready, but our bank account isn't. When we can swing it, we'll definitely give you first crack at bidding on it."

"That's not what I meant," he said. "I know you're not ready to do the whole library yet, but I thought maybe I'd work up a plan for how you could do it in stages. Get a plan in place, and maybe I could start keeping my eyes out for good deals on the supplies. And yeah, I was hoping if I could come up with a good price, maybe you'd be willing to start the first stage. I could use the work. Work from a client who actually pays, that is."

"I can understand that," I said. "We probably won't be ready to go forward until we find out about Michael's tenure."

"Which isn't all that long, right?" Randall said. "That's what I was figuring. So anyway, while your mother was showing her plans to Michael earlier today, I slipped down to the library with my camera and my tape measure. Figured I'd take a few measurements, a few photos. Get what I needed to do some sketches and estimates. Only when I went into the library, she was there."

"She? You mean Dr. Wright?"

"The dead lady, whatever her name was."

"But she wasn't dead then, was she?"

"How should I know?" he said, with an exaggerated shrug. "She had her head down on the desk. I walked in, looked around, saw her, and said, 'Excuse me, ma'am, but do you mind if I take a few measurements of the room?' "

"And did she answer?"

Randall shook his head.

"I figured she must be fast asleep, so I said, 'Sorry to disturb you'—real soft like—and headed back for the door. I was almost out of the room when that other jerk showed up. Blanco."

I noticed that with Blanco gone, he didn't pretend to mispronounce the name.

"Dr. Blanco was in the library?" I asked. I winced at the eager sound of my own voice. Even though I'd mellowed toward him, I hadn't grown so fond that I would object to having him turn out to be a suspect.

"No, he was banging on one of the French doors to the sunroom and yelling, 'Jean! Jean! I need to talk to you!' I stood there, because I figured if he woke her up, maybe I could do my measuring after all. But she didn't move, and after he'd banged and shouted a couple of times, he said, 'We need to talk. Call my cell phone.' And then he went away. And I figured maybe I should too."

He paused. I waited. On the radio, the last few bars of a twangy, upbeat song gave way to the opening chords of Patsy Cline's "Crazy," and I realized he'd said all he was going to say.

"You should tell the chief," I said.

"I wasn't going to," he said, "because I knew anyone who'd been near the library would look suspicious. But then I realized that if anyone did see me going to the library, it would look even more suspicious if I didn't tell. And then I thought about that jerk Blanco."

"What about him?"

"He was trying to get in to talk to her, but he went away without succeeding," he said. "I can vouch for that. And a little while ago I overheard a couple of students talking. Sounded as if they were pretty relieved that the Wright woman was dead, and one of them said the only thing that would make it better would be if the chief arrested Blanco. They were joking about telling the chief they'd seen him sneaking into the library. At least I hope they were joking."

I winced. The chief was going to have a hard enough time sorting this one out without having to deal with a bunch of the students deliberately giving false evidence.

"They'd better be joking," I said. "Would you recognize them if you saw them?"

" 'Fraid not," he said. "They were coming in from the barn, all muffled up in coats and such. But the more I thought about it, the more I realized I can't let them frame the guy. Even if he's a jerk, that doesn't make him a murderer. Hell, even before I heard them, I was starting to feel bad about not telling the chief."

"Tell him what you saw, then," I said. "And what you heard. He needs to know. And it's safer for you, too. What if they find your fingerprints in the library?"

"As much work as we've done for you over the past few years, I wouldn't be surprised to find my fingerprints anywhere in the house," he said.

"What if you accidentally touched something that wasn't here last time you were?" I said. "Tell the chief."

"Yeah, I guess I should," he said. "Much as I'd like to see the jerk in trouble, I want it to be for something he deserves, like screwing up this whole heating plant thing for the past month. Not something he didn't do."

He turned away and did something with his tools for a few moments, then strode to the door and opened it.

"Thanks," he said. "Going to see the chief now. Hobart!"

In a second or two his cousin ambled back in holding a plate with a half-eaten slice of apple pie.

"You keep on with that," Randall said, pointing to the crib. "I'll be back in a while."

Hobart nodded amiably, still chewing, and returned to the crib. Randall strode out.

I followed him out into the hall. I peeled off at the bathroom, though, for another pit stop. As I was reaching for the doorknob, the door flew open and Kathy stepped out.

"You're out of toilet paper in the bathroom," she said.

"The students never replace the rolls," I said. "There should be some under the sink."

She shook her head.

"Then check the linen closet." I led the way, and pulled open the door. "There should be plenty of—oh!"

Our linen closet was larger than usual, but still a tight fit for the body curled up on its floor. Batman and Robin began wriggling, apparently reacting to my shock. Then the body shook slightly, and I realized it—she—was sobbing.

"Alice?" Kathy said. "Is that you?"

The body made a strangled noise that I couldn't decipher. Apparently Kathy could.

"What are you doing in there, anyway?" Kathy said. "Come out this instant!"

The body uncurled and crawled out of the closet, revealing the redheaded Alice.

"I'm sorry," Alice said. "It's just that I need to be alone when I'm upset, and there's just nowhere else to be alone in this house."

"You're telling me," I said. "Why are you so upset?"

She sniffled slightly for a few moments, as if trying

to decide whether to confide in us or not. Then she burst into tears again.

"They're going to arrest me," she said. As well as crying, she was quite literally wringing her hands. I stared at them in fascination, since I couldn't recall ever seeing anyone actually do that in real life before.

"Why should they?" I asked as I stared at her writhing fingers. "What did you do?"

"Nothing!" she exclaimed. "But they're going to find my fingerprints on the statue. The one of the lady hippo goddess."

"Tawaret," I said.

"You mean the murder weapon?" Kathy asked.

Alice nodded. I suppressed the urge to tell her to relax, that Tawaret wasn't the murder weapon after all.

"Why will your fingerprints be on it?" I asked instead.

"I took it to the library," she said. "Remember? You came downstairs carrying it and handed to me and told me to put it on a shelf in the library. You do remember, don't you?"

She'd stopped wringing her hands and was now torturing one long, trailing lock of her red hair. If she kept on like that she'd be bald by morning.

"That's right," I said. "I remember." Actually, I didn't specifically remember her—I'd been relieved that Kathy had used her name so I didn't have to think of it. But I did remember handing off Tawaret to a student. I had a vague recollection of the hippo goddess floating off beneath a cloud of red hair, so it probably was her. "Okay, your fingerprints will be on it, but so will mine, and Rose Noire's, and who knows how many other curious people who picked it up to look at it."

"I can't imagine why anyone would want to pick it up," she said, with a shudder. "And—"

She broke off and jammed the end of the hair lock in her mouth.

"Stop that," I said, slapping her hand slightly. She looked startled and pulled the hair out.

"Yeah, ease off on the hair, Alice," Kathy said. "Bronwyn doesn't need a bald understudy."

"Oh, you're Bronwyn's understudy?" I asked.

"That's right," she said. "Of course, you wouldn't know that since Bron hasn't missed a single damned rehearsal yet. If she broke a leg, she'd talk Ramon into letting her do the play in a wheelchair."

"You never know," I said. If Bronwyn turned out to be the killer, Ramon would need Alice. Then again, if Ramon also got arrested . . .

"So your fingerprints are on the statue," I said aloud. "That's easily explained. Why would the chief jump to the conclusion that you killed her?"

"Because everyone knew how much I hated her," the girl said, burying her face in her hands. "I got the part of Ophelia in the studio production of *Hamlet* last fall, and she took it away from me."

"Took it away from you? I didn't realize she had any influence over casting department shows."

"She doesn't," Kathy said. "But you can't appear in a show if you're on academic probation."

"And she flunked me," Alice said. "The witch. Claimed I didn't turn in a paper on time, and it's a lie. She lost it—maybe deliberately. But of course, I can't prove that."

"How sure are you that you turned in the paper?" I asked.

"Positive," she said. "I even turned it in a week early. As soon as the cast list went up on Friday and I knew

I'd be doing Ophelia, I wanted to clear out everything else so I could just concentrate on the play."

"Very commendable," I said. I suspected the not unearned reputation drama students had for disorganization stemmed at least partly from the long hours they put in on shows. That and their belief that organization was boring and uncreative.

"So I spent the whole weekend in the library working on my paper for Dr. Wright." Her hands were still now, clasped in front of her, and she held her head high. She was acting, I realized. Of course, that didn't necessarily mean she was lying, only that she'd probably told this story many times.

"Monday morning, as soon as I finished typing it, I went down to Dunsany Hall to put it in her box," she went on. "And I ran into her there. It was before six, but she was already there, drinking tea and staring at something on the bulletin board. She said, 'You're up uncharacteristically early'—I guess she noticed I didn't always get there by nine, when the class started."

"Nine's early for drama department people," I said. I'd come to hate the semesters when Michael's schedule called for him to teach a morning class.

"I told her I wasn't up early, I'd stayed up late finishing my paper, and she smirked and said, 'You pulled an all-nighter for nothing, then—it's not due till next week.' So I told her I knew that, but that I was about to be very busy with rehearsals for *Hamlet*, and I wanted to get it done before that happened. You'd think she'd be glad someone was being responsible."

"She wasn't?"

"No," the girl said. She had gone back to hand-wringing. "She just stood there holding my paper with her thumb and forefinger, like she thought it might have cooties or something. And she didn't say anything—not 'Thank you' or 'Good morning' or even 'Go away and leave me alone.' It was kind of awkward. So I offered her a chocolate macaroon—I'd stopped by Geraldine's on the way to get some for my breakfast—and she acted as if I'd tried to hand her a chocolate-covered worm. She snapped, 'No!' and reared back like she was going to lecture me. I wasn't sure what I'd done wrong, so I just said 'Sorry!' and ran away as fast as I could. I still don't know what I did to upset her. You'd think I'd tried to poison her or something."

"Actually, you did try to poison her," Kathy said. "Though she should have known it was quite unintentional. She was diabetic."

TWENTY-TWO

Luckily Kathy was so focused on comforting Alice that she didn't see my jaw drop when she revealed her knowledge of Dr. Wright's medical history.

"Diabetic?" Alice said. "Oh no, I had no idea."

"Yes," Kathy said. "And much as I adore Geraldine's cookies, they're definitely not something a diabetic should be eating."

"Did a lot of people know this?" I asked Kathy.

"Hardly anyone," she said. "I only know because I caught her shooting up in her office one time. I knocked before I went in, but apparently she didn't hear me so I went on in to leave some papers in her in-basket, and she was sitting there with her skirt hiked up, injecting herself in the thigh."

There would be a needle mark on the body, I realized. Had Dad spotted it? Was that why he'd told Horace to be on the lookout for insulin? And would there be some way of telling the fatal needle mark from any Dr. Wright had recently made herself?

"What did she do when you interrupted her?" I asked.

"Chewed me out something wicked for trespassing," Kathy said. "And I did knock. Then she showed me the insulin bottle—as if I'd really think she was doing smack or something—and told me that her medical history was her own business and if this got out in the department, she'd know who was responsible."

"So you never told anyone?" I asked.

"Not till now," Kathy said. "And I was living in fear that someone else would find out and leak it and she'd blame me. But I guess she's beyond caring about her privacy now, and beyond retaliating against me for spilling the beans."

I nodded. I ached to tell poor Alice that she could relax, that her fingerprints on Tawaret weren't going to be as incriminating as she thought—but the chief wouldn't like it if I spilled the real story of Dr. Wright's death.

And the chief would probably want to know that one of his suspects was aware of Dr. Wright's diabetes.

"Wow," Alice said. "I didn't realize. No wonder she snapped at me."

"But she didn't have to be so rude," I said. "She could have just said 'No, thank you.'"

"Yeah, but what if she loves cookies and can't eat them, and there I was, waving them under her nose," Alice said. "When you come down to it, I was torturing her."

"That may be," I said. "But you can't just go around losing people's papers when they annoy you."

"Except she did, all the time," Kathy said. "That's one of the reasons she hated me so much. She was doing this to students all the time—to drama students, that is. That's why we started this thing where people who were afraid she'd do it to them would give their papers to her in front of me. So they'd have a witness."

"Stupid me," Alice said. "I should have done that. I thought turning it in a week early would be safe."

"You need to tell the chief about all of this," I said.

"All right," Alice said. "If you'll go with me."

"We'll all go together," I said. "Right, Kathy?"

Kathy turned pale. Then she nodded and began burrowing in her cavernous black tote bag.

"Before we do," she said. "Here."

She handed me a thick file folder.

I opened it. The first page was a typed table of contents for the documents in the file. It was her evidence against Dr. Wright.

"We should take this to the chief, too," I said.

"That was my idea," she said. "I brought two copies. One for Dr. Wright, so I could try to talk some sense into her, and one for Abe, that I was going to give him if I failed, so he wouldn't be totally blindsided. The chief doesn't need both. Give that copy to Abe. He and Art and Michael might be able to use it."

"Don't they already know about it?" I asked.

She hesitated.

"Not really," she said. "I told Abe I had some information about her treatment of students that might be useful. I don't suppose he had any idea how much information."

I glanced down at the file, which was over an inch thick.

"We should make sure it's okay with the chief," I said, tucking the folder under my arm. "Let's go."

We marched downstairs, making a strange procession. Alice went first, holding her head high, looking like a defeated queen marching to her execution. Kathy just looked anxious, scurrying along with the tote bag containing her file clutched to her chest. I brought up the rear, keeping an eye out to make sure neither of them suddenly changed her mind.

As we reached the bottom of the stairs, I felt a familiar

slight twinge of pain in my abdomen. But it didn't
repeat during the whole long way down the hall to
Michael's office, so apparently it was just another
Braxton-Hicks contraction. I couldn't decide whether
to be relieved or disappointed.

As we turned into the hallway to the library, the
doorbell rang. I looked over my shoulder and saw Rose
Noire scurrying to answer it.

"Is this the residence of Professor Waterston?"
boomed a resonant voice. The Face had arrived. I
breathed a sigh of relief that Rose Noire would be dealing with him. I'd once had to make conversation with
him for ten minutes at a faculty party, and it had seemed
the longest ten years of my life. I hurried after Kathy
and Alice.

The chief and Sammy were standing at the end of the
hallway.

"More witnesses for you," I called, as our procession
approached.

I found myself remembering a long-ago fall when
mice moved into the basement of our family house. The
chief's face wore the same look of truly mixed feelings
that Mother's had each time our cat caught a mouse and
proudly deposited it at her feet.

We all filed into Michael's office and, being old hands,
took seats on whichever boxes and stools we thought
would be preferable to the awful chairs. The chief, who
followed us in, frowned slightly. I suspected he was
about to ask to speak to his witnesses alone.

"Kathy and I convinced Alice that she should come
and talk to you," I said. I made the mistake of patting
Alice's hand in a comforting manner, and she seized
mine with a death grip.

"Don't be afraid, Alice," Kathy said. Having seen

what had happened to me, she patted Alice on the shoulder and managing to avoid being grabbed herself.

With much encouragement from Kathy and me, Alice sobbed out her story of Dr. Wright's persecution and her fears that having touched the statue would make her the chief's prime suspect. It took rather longer than necessary, but probably less time than it would have taken him to extract it from Alice by himself.

"Thank you," the chief said, finally. "Let this be a lesson to you not to withhold information in the future."

"You're not going to arrest me?" Alice asked, sniffling slightly.

"Not unless some other more compelling evidence of your guilt comes up," the chief said. He stood up to usher her to the door.

"Wash your face in cold water," Kathy called after Alice. "And go lie down for a while. They might need you for rehearsal."

"Fat chance," Alice said as she closed the door behind her.

The chief sat down again. He glanced at me and then fixed his gaze back on Kathy.

"So, Ms. Borgstrom. Do you also want to confess having handled the statue?"

"No," Kathy said. "I wanted to give you this."

She handed him the file folder. The chief opened it, leafed through the first few pages, than glanced up as if asking for an explanation.

"I've been keeping a dossier of things Dr. Wright has done to various drama students," Kathy said. "Actions that might be illegal and certainly were unethical. Losing their papers, grading them more harshly, refusing them extensions and other accommodations that she routinely granted to other students."

"For what purpose?" the chief asked.

"Who knows?" Kathy said. "The woman had a pathological hatred of the theater."

"I meant why were you keeping this file?" the chief said.

"In the hope that we could use it against her," Kathy said. "Even a tenured professor shouldn't be allowed to get away with some of this stuff."

"So you were hoping to get her disciplined?" the chief asked.

"I was hoping Abe could use her misconduct in his campaign to liberate drama from the English department," Kathy said. "It needs to be an independent department. So I started documenting everything. I figured one or two incidents she could easily explain away, but not a pattern documented over several years' time. And when I heard about what she was pulling now, trying to ruin Ramon's career, I thought maybe it was time to confront her."

"So you brought this file out here to give it to Dr. Sass?" the chief asked.

"Actually, I planned to confront Dr. Wright with it," she said. "And maybe put her on the defensive before the meeting with Abe, Art, and Michael. It sounded as if they were going to bring up the idea of secession."

"She gave me the copy she brought for Abe," I said, holding it up. "Is it okay if I give it to him?"

"Let me see it first," the chief said, holding out his hand.

Kathy and I watched as he flipped page by page through both files. At some point I realized I was holding my breath, so I stopped and took a few deep, calming breaths. The chief took out his notebook, glanced at it from time to time, and made a few new notations.

No doubt he was seeing which of the people in Kathy's evidence were already on his suspect list and which he'd have to hunt down. And, of course, making sure my copy didn't contain anything extra.

Eventually, though, he handed one of the files back to me.

"Oh, one more thing," I said. "It may not be relevant, but Kathy, you should tell the chief what you told Alice and me. About Dr. Wright's health."

"Her health?" Kathy repeated. "Oh, you mean that she was a diabetic?"

The chief froze, just for a split second, and stared intently at Kathy. But she was looking at me, waiting for an answer, and missed it.

"Yes," I said. "Any medical detail could be relevant. Dad was telling me the other day about a crime that wasn't solved until they figured out that the victim was a hemophiliac. Without knowing that, their time of death calculations were all off. So the chief—and Dad—might need to know about Dr. Wright's diabetes."

Kathy shrugged, and repeated her tale of interrupting Dr. Wright in the act of injecting herself with insulin. The chief continued to scribble for several minutes after she finished.

"Anything else?" he asked.

Kathy shook her head, and stood up to go.

"I have just a couple of questions," he said. "Sit down, please," he added when Kathy continued to stand as if poised for flight.

Kathy sat and composed her face into a friendly, helpful expression. Was she really that unworried or was she just a good actress? I felt a pang of anxiety and I wasn't guilty of anything except barging in on the chief's interrogation.

"What time did you learn of the proposed meeting about Mr. Soto's dissertation?" the chief asked.

"When Meg and Michael called me," she said. "I don't remember the time."

"Michael can tell you from his cell phone," I said. "But I can tell you approximately. Right after Michael called Kathy, I called my brother for some help." I pulled out my cell phone, scrolled down the list of calls I'd made that day, and showed the chief the one to Rob at 11:55 a.m. He nodded and jotted the time down in his notebook.

"Thank you," he said, nodding to me. "And what time did you arrive here at the house, Ms. Borgstrom?"

"I don't know exactly," Kathy said.

"Approximately, then."

Kathy frowned in concentration.

"About 1:30?" she said. "I guess. Do you remember, Meg?"

My turn to concentrate.

"I don't really know what time it was when she came to the door," I said to the chief. "But it was shortly after you finished questioning me. Just before I took my nap. About the time you had your officers take the witnesses out to the barn so Horace could examine the kitchen. Although—"

"Yes, that's right!" Kathy beamed as if I'd passed a difficult test. "I remember I went out to the barn to see Abe and everyone was just settling down there."

I glanced at the chief, wondering if I should bring up the curious gap between when Michael and I had talked to Kathy and when she actually arrived at the house. Probably not. Maybe he'd already noticed, and if he hadn't, he'd probably rather I not bring it up in front of Kathy.

"I see," the chief said. "Then would you mind explaining how you managed to park your car so it's blocked in by Mrs. Langslow's?"

"Mrs. Langslow?" Kathy shot a puzzled look at me.

"My mother," I said. "She came out to decorate the nursery."

"And entered the house at 12:15, some time before Meg discovered the body," the chief said. "We know the precise time because Mrs. Langslow noted it in her Day-Timer to keep track of the hours her contractor worked on the decorating project. According to Mrs. Langslow, she has been either in the nursery supervising the decorations or in the barn helping with the refreshments all day and did not move the car at any time. Given the position of your car, right up against the barn with a tree on one side and shrubbery on the other, you couldn't have driven it in or out any other way. So, Ms. Borgstrom, if you arrived at 1:30 would you care to tell me how you happened to be blocked in by a car that had been here since 12:15?"

TWENTY-THREE

Kathy stared openmouthed at the chief for a few seconds, then burst into tears. Without taking his eyes off her, Chief Burke reached behind him, took a tissue from the box at the back of the desk, and handed it to her. Kathy swiped at her eyes and blew her nose.

"I knew you'd suspect me," she said. She was still sobbing intermittently. "She was so awful to me and she was trying to get me fired, and when I heard what she was trying to do to Ramon, I decided to confront her. Just as I told you."

"With the contents of this folder?" the chief said.

"Yes," Kathy said. "Before the meeting with Abe, and Art, and Michael. I told you that."

"And what happened when you attempted to blackmail her?" the chief asked.

"It wasn't blackmail," she said. "And nothing happened. I didn't get to talk to her."

"And if I said that you were seen entering the sunporch?" the chief said. "The students who smoke spent quite a lot of time in the backyard, with a good view of the sunporch." I noticed that he didn't actually say any of them had seen her.

"Yes, I went into the sunporch and I looked into the library through the French doors," Kathy said. "But I could see it was no use going in."

"Why not?" the chief said.

Kathy closed her eyes and scrunched up her mouth as if making an effort to get words out. Or keep them in; I wasn't sure which.

"Because there's no use talking to a dead woman!" she said finally.

"How did you know she was dead?" the chief asked, glancing at me. "Meg assumed she was merely sleeping."

"Meg didn't see that man hit her over the head with the rhinoceros statue," Kathy exclaimed.

"Hippopotamus," I muttered.

"What man?" the chief asked.

"I don't know," she said. "Not one of our drama students. He was Asian, tall, wearing glasses and jeans and a black T-shirt."

I winced. We had several other Asian students in the house, but the only one who wasn't a drama student was Danny Oh.

"And you didn't report this because . . ." the chief asked.

"Because it would be my word against his, and everyone knew how much I hated her. And then I realized that the longer I didn't report it the more suspicious I would be, and I figured you'd catch him somehow."

"Was he wearing gloves?" the chief asked.

"No," she said. "Mittens. Fluffy pink mittens."

"Oh my God," I said, causing them both to turn in my direction. "They're probably my mittens. I keep them in the front hall."

"Did you notice them missing?" the chief asked.

"No, but I wouldn't," I said. "I never wear them. They were a present from an aunt who must think I'm still in grade school. When the students arrived, I left them in one of the baskets in the front hall in the hopes that someone who didn't have gloves would borrow them and forget to bring them back. I wasn't expecting the borrower to be a murderer."

"Attempted murderer, I think," the chief said, almost absently. "After all, we know that the blow to her head was not what killed Dr. Wright."

"We do?" Kathy said.

"Yes," the chief said. "The wound made by the statue didn't bleed, indicating that Dr. Wright was already dead when it was made."

"But who would hit a dead woman over the head like that?" Kathy asked.

"Someone who didn't realize she was dead," I said. "Someone who thought she was just asleep, the way I did when I first found the body."

"Then if the man who hit her didn't kill her, who did?" Kathy said. "And how?"

"We have reason to believe that she was injected with a fatal overdose of her own insulin," the chief said.

"Oh." I could see Kathy digesting this. She glanced up at me, but to my relief, it wasn't a reproachful glance. "I can see why you're arresting me, then," she said finally.

The chief sighed.

"I'm not arresting anyone yet," he said, "since we don't technically know the cause of death. Dr. Langslow's pretty sure it's insulin overdose, and I have every confidence that he's right. But a judge is going to want to see a toxicology report, and we don't have that tonight. So for now, you're free to go. Don't leave town, though."

"And you might want to find a defense attorney, just in case," I said, reaching for my notebook. "I can give you some names."

"Thanks," Kathy said. She accepted the slip of paper I offered, tucked it into her purse, and stood up.

"You're absolutely sure you didn't tell anyone else about Dr. Wright's diabetes?" the chief asked.

"I wish," Kathy said. "I wish I could tell you that I announced it at the last cast party and posted it on the department Facebook page, but I didn't."

"If you find anything that indicates someone else does know, let me know immediately," the chief said.

Kathy nodded and left.

The chief and I sat in silence as her footsteps disappeared down the hall.

"Seems like a nice lady," he said at last.

"She is," I said.

"I notice you're not hurrying to assure me that she couldn't possibly have done it."

I sighed.

"She cares so much about the department," I said. "About her boss and the rest of the faculty and all the students."

"I don't go into a murder investigation looking for a villain," the chief said. "All too often, the killer is someone who cares a little too much about something and gets carried away when that something is threatened. So you think she's the killer."

"I don't know," I said. "I certainly hope not. And I can't tell you how glad I am that it's your job, not mine, to figure that out."

"Though you have been rather busy sending me suspects and witnesses." Was that a hint of a chuckle in his voice?

"Can I help it if people keep confessing things to me, or to each other when I'm within earshot?"

"No," he said. Yes, there was definitely amusement in his voice. "I appreciate your promptness in bringing all these bits of information to me instead of running wild trying to solve the case yourself. Which reminds me." He stood up, walked over to the door, and stuck his head out into the hall. "Sammy!"

A few seconds later, Sammy entered, accompanied by Horace.

"Sammy, could you go and get—what's wrong?"

I glanced up. Sammy looked so morose that I immediately wondered if Hawkeye had taken a turn for the worse. Rocky and Bullwinkle, apparently already animal lovers in the womb, squirmed with anxiety.

"Sammy?" The chief's voice was suddenly gentler. "What's wrong?"

"We're never going to catch the jerk who hit Hawkeye, are we?" Sammy said. "He's going to get away with it."

"We'll catch him," the chief said. "Debbie Anne's got that list of possible vehicles down at the station. There's only about thirty of them. I know you're disappointed that we haven't already caught him, but you understand the murder investigation has to take priority."

Sammy nodded. I knew exactly how he felt. What a rotten break that the hit-and-run—which normally would have been the biggest case the Caerphilly police saw for weeks—had to happen on the same day as a murder. I felt a brief, irrational pang of resentment—

against Dr. Wright or her killer, I wasn't sure which. Maybe both.

"But in a day or so, we'll be able to get to that list," the chief went on. I noticed that he was reaching down to scratch behind Scout's ear as he talked. "And I promise you, we will do everything we can to find the culprit."

"Longer we wait, the harder the forensics will be," Sammy said. "There could be—you know, trace evidence on the car right now. But what if he takes it to a car wash?"

"There's no car wash on this planet that can get it so clean I can't find something," Horace said. "If there's anything to be found, I'll find it, if I have to go over the whole front end of every single suspect SUV with tweezers and cotton swabs."

"You might find some DNA," Sammy said. "But then what? The department doesn't have money for DNA testing. Not on a dog."

"We'll find it somewhere," the chief said.

"I could hit up my grandfather for a donation," I said.

"You think he'd be interested?" Sammy asked.

"It's an animal-welfare issue," I said. "I'll make him interested. He'd probably want to get some PR out of it. Issue a press release and have his picture taken with Hawkeye for the newspapers."

"He'd be welcome to all the PR he can get if he helps us catch the hit-and-run driver," the chief said.

"Thanks," Sammy said. His voice sounded a little funny and he had to clear his throat before he could go on. "I really appreciate it. Everything."

"Cheer up," the chief said. "Now I'd like you to go and fetch me some witnesses. If it's any comfort, thanks to some information Meg just brought me, we're a lot closer to wrapping this up. And when we get the forensic results back, I think that will clinch it. I just need to talk to a couple of people again."

"Yes, sir," Sammy said. "Who do you need?"

"Mr. Soto, Mr. Oh, and the lovely Ms. Jones."

"I'm on my way," Sammy said, and vanished.

"Can you really use dog DNA to solve the hit-and-run?" the chief asked Horace.

"Sure," Horace said. "They're starting to do a lot of DNA on animals, for a lot of the same reasons they do on humans—to find out if they're at risk for hereditary diseases, to verify paternity, and of course for legal cases, like figuring out which dog bit someone. Cost's coming down, too, so it might not break the bank."

"Still not something that would be easy to explain to the town council," the chief said, glancing down at Scout.

"Understandable," Horace said. "But if Dr. Blake won't spring for it, we can pass the hat down at the station and take care of it."

"Good," the chief said. "Count me in for a double share. Speaking of forensic testing—"

"I'm on it," Horace said, and vanished.

"And you'd probably like me to leave you alone with your witnesses," I said. I straightened up, rubbed my aching back, and prepared for the effort of standing—challenging even though I was sitting on the ottoman instead of the dangerous comfy chairs.

The chief cleared his throat.

"Normally I would ask you to leave," he said. "But under the circumstances, it would be helpful if you could stay. I'd like you to hear what they say when I confront them—see if it differs materially from what you overheard."

"Right," I said.

"But don't you say anything," he cautioned. He handed me a legal pad and a pen. "We'll pretend I need you to take notes. If there's anything you need to tell me during my interview with these three, write it down, then cough, and I'll find a way to look at what you've written."

"Got it," I said. "You're going to talk to them all together?"

"I've already talked to them individually," he said. "And got nothing but lies, apparently. Let's see what I can pry out by using your information and playing them against each other."

I took the pad and pen and pulled my seat as far into the corner as possible.

"Sammy!" the chief called. "You can send them in."

I watched silently as Ramon, Bronwyn, and Danny filed in.

"You can have a seat if you like," the chief said.

All three students glanced quickly at the evil guest chairs. Clearly they'd been in Michael's office before and knew the danger.

"No, thanks," Ramon said.

"I sit too much anyway," Danny said.

Bronwyn just folded her arms and leaned against the wall. Danny and Ramon, on either side of her, followed suit.

"Suit yourself," the chief said. "Ms. Langslow, you can start taking notes now. Arthritis," he added, turning back to the students. He flexed the fingers on his right hand a couple of times, as if stretching out a cramp. "Ms. Langslow is being kind enough to give my hand a rest."

They all gave me a perfunctory glance and then focused back on the chief.

"Now," he said. "Any of y'all got anything you want to add to your previous statements? Here or in private?"

They stared at him.

"I thought not," he said. "So I wanted to notify all three of you that you might want to find yourselves attorneys."

TWENTY-FOUR

Danny's and Ramon's mouths fell open. Bronwyn's tightened.

"I'm probably not going to arrest anyone till after I get the preliminary tox-screen results," the chief went on. "But all of you already have a lot of explaining to do. First, Mr. Soto. You want to tell me why you slipped some of your sleeping pills into Dr. Wright's tea?"

Ramon's face drained of blood, and after standing frozen for a couple of seconds, he whirled to face Browyn and took several steps away from her.

"You said you wouldn't tell anyone!" he shouted.

"I didn't, you idiot," she said. She didn't look at all shaken, either by the chief's revelation or Ramon's anger.

"No, she didn't," the chief said. "We learned that through another source." I was grateful that he didn't even glance in my direction as he said that. "Though since we're tying down every loose end, I'd appreciate it if you would make a statement about what *you* observed, Ms. Jones."

"And why should I?" she said. "You'll only use it to frame Ramon for the murder."

"At the moment, we're not charging Mr. Soto with

murder," the chief said. "I expect the DA will go for reckless endangerment."

"Reckless endangerment!" Ramon exclaimed. "I wasn't trying to hurt her! I just wanted to put off the damned meeting that was going to kill my hopes of ever getting my doctorate."

"It doesn't matter what you were trying to do or why," the chief said. "You gave Dr. Wright a dose of your Valium."

"No, it was my sleeping medicine," Ramon said.

"Your sleeping medicine *is* Valium," the chief said. "Or, more accurately, diazepam, the generic for Valium."

Ramon blinked. Another person who hadn't done a bit of research on the drugs he was so happily chucking down this throat.

"Even if that's so, Valium's just a mild sedative, right?" Ramon said when he found his voice again.

"To most people," the chief said. "We have no way of knowing if she had any medical conditions that would make it dangerous to her. And even if your medicine didn't harm her, you knocked her out and made her vulnerable when someone else came along who did want to kill her. I'll let the DA decide whether that justifies a charge of accessory to murder."

"But I had no idea anyone was trying to kill her!" Ramon spluttered.

"Doesn't matter," the chief said. "You contributed to her death. Then there's Ms. Jones, who also added something to Dr. Wright's tea. Just what was it?"

Bronwyn looked a little shaken now.

"I didn't," she said. "You're just making that up to threaten me."

"I have very reliable evidence to indicate otherwise," the chief said. He turned toward Danny. "Mr. Oh—"

Danny started as if the chief had fired a gun.

"You idiot!" Bron snapped at Danny.

"It wasn't me!" he said. "You have to believe me, Bron!"

"As I was about to say—" the chief said.

"I'd never do anything to—" Danny began.

"Oh, shut up," Bronwyn snarled. "It was just more of Ramon's sleeping medicine," she said, turning to the chief. "It was his idea, and I thought he wanted me to do it. I didn't realize he'd already done it, or that it could hurt her."

"I did not!" Ramon exclaimed. "She's lying!"

"And it was only two tablets," Bronwyn said. "I told Ramon that would be enough, but he didn't agree. He argued with me. I bet he gave her more than he's admitting."

"Bron—" Danny began.

"Shut up," she snapped at him.

Danny blinked. His face wore a look of hurt surprise, like a puppy who'd been kicked.

"She's lying," Danny said finally. "She put at least four in there."

Bronwyn looked from Danny to Ramon. Ramon was glaring at her. I'd have found Danny's look of painful disillusionment harder to bear, but Bron probably didn't care.

"Maybe I lost count, but they were just Valium," Bronwyn said. "What's the harm?"

"Are you sure about that?" the chief said. "Remember, when the tox reports come back, it may tell us an interesting tale. Were all of those pills you people put in her tea from Ramon's pill bottle, or are we going to find out that Dr. Wright also ingested some of Señor Mendoza's pills?"

I had to admire the way he avoided lying about what was in Señor Mendoza's pill bottle.

Ramon looked puzzled. Bron looked paler but put on an air of offended dignity.

"The pills I used were from Ramon's bottle," she said. "I don't know about Ramon. He was awfully interested in helping pick up Señor Mendoza's pills."

"You lying b—" Ramon spluttered. The chief rapped sharply on the desk, and we all jumped.

"None of that language, young man," he said, with a sharp look at Ramon. "As I said, we'll see what we find when the tox reports come back. Meanwhile, on to another subject. Mr. Oh?"

Danny, who had been staring at Bronwyn with a look of utter misery on his face, turned slowly to face the chief.

"She put the pills in the tea," Danny said. "At least four of them. Could have been more."

"Pills that may have poisoned Dr. Wright," the chief said. "Or at the very least, immobilized her sufficiently to give the real killer a chance to strike. Would you like to tell me what happened when you went into the library, Mr. Oh?"

Danny's mouth fell open and then his shoulders slumped and he looked down at his feet.

"I don't know why I did it," he said. "Actually, I do—I did it because Bron kept going on about how Dr. Wright was doing this to hurt her career—"

"Her career!" Ramon snorted. "That's rich."

"And when I saw her just lying there with her head on the desk and that horrible statue was right there. . . ."

He began shaking his head, slowly and repetitively, as if doing it enough might shake off the memory of what he'd done.

"You hit her on the head with the statue?" the chief asked.

Danny nodded.

"You did that for me?" Bron asked.

Danny's head shot up.

"Yeah," he said. "Pretty stupid, right? Committing murder for a bi—a worthless harpy like you. I must have been crazy."

Bronwyn looked more shaken at the defection of her conquests than she had at the chief's veiled threats. The chief looked as if he felt a little sorry for Danny.

"Actually, we don't yet know that you did commit murder, Mr. Oh," the chief said. "The wound you made bled very little. Dr. Langslow tells me that she was probably already dead when you bludgeoned her."

"I didn't kill her?" Danny asked. "What a relief!"

"Don't be too relieved," the chief said. "I think the DA will go for attempted murder. After all, you were trying to kill her. Even if she was already dead when you made your attempt, that doesn't change your intent. And even if you get off, which is always possible, you'll have to live for the rest of your time on this Earth with the knowledge that you're capable of taking a human life."

"Yeah, but at least I didn't actually do it," Danny said. He sounded almost tearful with relief.

"So if she wasn't killed with the statue, how was she killed?" Ramon asked.

"We believe she was poisoned," the chief said. "We'll know for sure when the tox screen comes back."

Bronwyn frowned. You could almost see the wheels turning in her head.

"You realize, don't you, that you'll never prove who put what in the tea," she said with a smug smile.

"I don't think we'll have too much trouble figuring out who poisoned her," the chief said. He was wearing what I thought of as his Cheshire Cat smile. "And all three of y'all are in for some legal trouble. Murder, attempted murder, accessory to murder, reckless endangerment—they all carry hard time. I'll let the DA sort out what he thinks he can convict you people of. If any of you think you have information that might help you make a deal, I'd cough it up soon. The DA's not a patient man. Now, unless you have something to say, make yourselves scarce. But don't leave the county."

The three of them looked at each other. Ramon and Danny looked properly stricken, as if they had at least begun to realize how badly they'd screwed up their lives. Bronwyn was glaring at the two of them as if she thought they were to blame for her predicament. She was the first to move.

"I think you're bluffing," she said, and sailed out with her head held high.

Danny and Ramon both watched her go, then turned and looked at each other.

"Man," Ramon said, shaking his head.

"Yeah," Danny said.

The two of them stumbled out shoulder to shoulder.

"I think this is the beginning of a beautiful friendship," I said.

"Good," the chief said. "Then they probably won't mind if they have to share a cell in a day or two. Our jail's pretty small."

"And now I understand why you wanted to interview them together. Seeing Bronwyn in action really hit Ramon and Danny hard."

"Yes," the chief said. "I suspected that they would continue to protect her unless confronted with the reality of her self-centered behavior. Nice to know my plan worked."

He frowned and shook his head slightly.

"What's wrong?" I asked.

"Good thing none of them is a lawyer," the chief said. "I got carried away. Reckless endangerment is only a misdemeanor. You don't do hard time for a misdemeanor."

"Any criminal record is the kiss of death to the college," I said. "To say nothing of the job market, which all three of them may find themselves facing sooner than planned, and without their degrees. Unless, of course, they end up getting room and board courtesy of the state."

"Sad," the chief said. "I have a hard time feeling sorry for Ms. Jones, but I can't help but feel a little sorry for both of those young men. Particularly Mr. Soto, considering the pressure he was under."

"But is that any excuse?" I said.

He sighed and took off his glasses to rub his eyes.

"Speaking as an officer of the law, no," he said. "But if I were that young man's attorney, I think I'd try to make the jury understand what a toxic atmosphere that woman had created for the students under her power."

He leaned back in the chair, pulled out his pocket handkerchief, and polished his glasses as he spoke.

"Just one student and you could say he's a wacko," he said. "But we have three of 'em hating Dr. Wright enough to take some dire action against her. And at least a dozen others who hated her so much—and were so vocal about it—that they're petrified I'm going to arrest them on motive alone. What kind of a person inspires that much hate?"

"A very bad one," I said. "But unfortunately the

Commonwealth of Virginia hasn't yet declared an open season on bad people."

"No," he said. "Thank goodness, because sometimes it takes us longer than we'd like to get to the bottom of a case like this. Did you notice any discrepancies between what they said to me—the men, anyway—and what you overheard?"

I thought about it for a few moments.

"No," I said. "I think Bronwyn's lying."

He nodded.

"What about Ms. Borgstrom?" he asked.

"You're asking me if my friend is a murderer?"

"I suppose I am," he said.

I thought about that even longer.

"I don't know," I said. "If she did it, it was because of the same pressure Ramon was under. Only in Kathy's case, she wasn't only worried about herself, but about all students and faculty in the department. Especially Abe. He and his wife have been like second parents to her."

It wasn't the ringing declaration of Kathy's innocence that I wished I could make, but it was honest. The chief nodded.

"One more thing," he said. "I hope not to be occupying your husband's office much longer, but while I am, could I ask you a favor?"

"Of course," I said. I braced myself. Was he going to berate me for interrupting him too much, or chew me out for interfering in his investigation?

"May I get rid of these blasted things?" he said, pointing to one of the guest chairs. "I don't mean to insult your taste or Michael's—they're certainly attractive chairs to look at—"

"No they're not," I said. "At least I'm not particularly fond of them, nor is Michael."

"Bargain at the furniture store?" he asked.

"No, a present from Mother, and undoubtedly an expensive one, which makes it all the more ironic that they're the most miserably uncomfortable chairs I've ever had the misfortune to sit in. They look as if they'd be comfortable, but after five minutes you realize your back and shoulders and legs are all scrunched in odd positions. And as for getting out of them—forget it!"

"Then for the duration, may I swap them for a few of those nice, straight-back chairs I saw in your front hall?"

"Be my guest," I said.

"Sammy!" the chief bellowed.

Sammy poked his head through the door.

"Swap these chairs out for some of those in the front hall," the chief said, shoving one of the desk chairs at Sammy.

"Yes, sir."

"And you go and rest," he said, turning to me. "You look exhausted, and if you don't watch out you'll overdo it and go into labor early."

"Not that early," I said. "Thirty-eight weeks. Only fifteen percent of women last this long with twins. In fact, some doctors would consider that full term for twins and would probably start pressuring us to induce."

"Is that why you're running around the house bringing me suspects and evidence?" he asked. "Hoping to bring on labor?"

"No, I'm bringing you suspects and evidence because I keep stumbling over them, usually while on my way to a nap or the bathroom," I said. "Just saying that you don't really need to worry about me. If my running around brings on labor, it's not a disaster."

"And maybe a good thing?" he said, with a chuckle.

"Still, take care of yourself. It's—my goodness, nearly seven-thirty."

No wonder I was so tired. Most nights I was in bed by eight, following my doctor's advice that if sleep eluded me I could at least rest. And most days I didn't do nearly as much running around as I had today.

"Not much more to do here today," the chief was saying. "Though I'd like to keep this office available in case we need to work out here tomorrow."

"That's fine," I said. I waited to see if he had anything else to say. He did.

"Get some rest, Meg," he said. "You look all in."

"I will."

He nodded, turned back to some papers on his—well, actually Michael's—desk, and picked up the phone. I left and waddled through the long corridors to our front hallway.

There, I ran into my grandfather.

TWENTY-FIVE

"So, rumor has it you've solved the murder," he said.

"Rumor has it wrong, as usual," I said. "The chief is a lot closer to solving it, thanks in part to some witnesses I nagged into talking to him. That's all."

"Right, right," he said. "If that's the way you want it. Mustn't hurt anyone's feelings."

No use trying to straighten him out. I was planning to go upstairs—in fact, I was lifting my foot to the bottom step—when it occurred to me that I had something to talk to him about. Two somethings. I wasn't sure I had the energy to do it now, but I wanted to get it over with. I turned back and sat down in one of the dining room chairs Sammy hadn't taken.

"So, are you still interested in giving the college a building?" I asked.

My grandfather sighed.

"Probably not," he said. "I'm beginning to think it's not such a good idea."

"Why?"

"I don't like to cast aspersions on Caerphilly College," he said. "After all, your husband teaches there; I know you must feel some loyalty to the institution."

"My loyalty to the college is directly proportional to how well they treat Michael, and right now, I'm not exactly feeling the love." I was tempted to share Kathy's revelations, but I still felt enough loyalty—to Michael, if not to Caerphilly—that I didn't want to broadcast them to a potential donor. "So cast as many aspersions as you want, and I'll throw in a few of my own. What's your beef with them?"

"Well . . . Caerphilly's biology department is not really in tune with the most current scientific thinking in their own field," he said. "No real environmental consciousness. No apparent awareness of issues such as global warming or the need to maintain biodiversity. From what I can tell, they and the agriculture department have both been completely co-opted by big agribusiness."

"Big agribusiness can afford big donations. You only just found this out?"

"No." His shoulders slumped and he suddenly looked every one of his ninety-some years. "I knew it all along. I was hoping that through philanthropy, I could effect a positive change in their attitudes."

"In other words, you were hoping to buy their loyalty to your causes."

"If you want to put it that way, yes," he said. "But if I can't even get them to pay any attention to me when I'm trying to give them a building, it'd be unreasonable to expect them to do so after they'd already got their hands on the building. So no building for Caerphilly College."

"Don't be so hasty," I said. "The biology department isn't the whole college. No building for biology—but what about drama?"

"The drama department needs a building?"

"You've been to a couple of plays in the Pruitt Theater—what do you think?"

"I thought it was a charming little theater."

"Yes," I said. "The operative word is 'little.' It's a converted lecture hall. Nearly every show is sold out, but there are so few seats to sell that it's rare for a show to break even, and the college bean counters are always complaining and trying to cut back on the number of productions. And talk about not being in tune with the current developments in their professions—the drama faculty would like to be, but they don't have the facilities. The theater-technology students need to have a fully equipped modern theater if they're going to learn the skills they need to be competitive in the job market they hope to enter. Instead, they're back in the nineteenth century. What's more, the lion's share of the work out there is in television and film, not live stage. Just ask Michael how he feels about trying to teach film with no equipment other than a few Betacams one of the Richmond TV stations donated ten years ago, when they upgraded their own equipment."

"Hmm." It sounded like a "How do I say no gracefully?" kind of "hmm," but at least he wasn't rejecting the idea outright. Probably a measure of how eager he was to put his name on a building—and how frustrated he was by his quest's failure to date. "A theater's a nice idea, but I'm not sure I see how this fits in with the Blake Foundation's environmental mission."

"It could be a state-of-the-art green theater," I said. "Constructed with environmentally sensitive materials and designed for minimal energy use. You could put solar panels on the roof so it doesn't just generate enough energy to power itself, it could actually give back to the grid."

"Hmm," he said again. I'd been hoping for a "Yes!" but at least this was a more thoughtful, positive-sounding "hmm."

"And I'm sure you can find a way to encourage synergy between the drama curriculum and environmental issues."

"The hell with synergy. If I built them a nice professional film-production facility, you think I could get the college to let me use it whenever I needed to do some studio work on one of my nature programs?"

"You could probably even have a lot of the work done by student interns," I said. "Get someone on your staff to develop plans for a student internship program, and it's a win-win. You get affordable service and they get solid experience for their resumes."

"Hmm." Now Grandfather looked thoughtful. "The Blake Drama Building. The Montgomery Blake Theater. Yes, it has a nice ring to it. Who do I talk to?"

"Let me find out." I heaved myself out of the chair. "Don't say anything to anyone—especially not the annoying Dr. Blanco—until I can find some more information about how to get this done efficiently."

"Excellent," he said. "Nothing would please me more than doing an end run around that annoying twerp. Keep me posted."

"Oh, one more thing," I said. "Did you hear about Sammy Wendell's dog being run over?"

"Yes," he said, looking thunderous again. "Hell of a thing, someone running over a dog and not even stopping to see if the poor beast was hurt."

"We're collecting donations," I said.

"To pay the vet's bill?" He reached into his coat pocket. "Sure. How much do you need?"

"And the cost of a DNA test to help convict the perpetrator when we catch him," I added.

"Just tell me how much you need," he said. "Better yet, just have them send a bill to my office. So, you coming to the show?"

Show? It took me a few minutes to realize he meant Ramon's rehearsal.

"I've seen it," I said. "I want to see the inside of my eyelids for a while."

"I'm going to snag a good seat before things get too crowded," he said, and strode off toward the kitchen.

I followed, planning to retrieve the doggie bag I'd made myself in the barn, which I'd left on the counter in all the excitement over the purse. By the time I reached the kitchen, the back door was already slamming behind him.

The kitchen was still a mess, but not nearly as bad as it had been the last time I'd seen it. In fact, it hadn't looked this good in weeks. There were still about a million dirty dishes, but they'd been stacked neatly on the right side of the sink, and someone had actually scraped and rinsed enough of them to load and start the dishwasher. I could see clutter everywhere, but no half-eaten food, and there were two black plastic garbage bags, neatly tied, beside the nearly full garbage can. The air smelled floral, more so than the half-dozen little dishes of potpourri scattered around on the counters could possibly account for. Rose Noire had probably been spritzing essential oils to supplement the potpourri. A welcome change from the fish odor, whatever it was, and not annoying to my hypersensitive nose.

"Hey, Mrs. Waterston!" A couple of students were passing through the kitchen. "Can we save you a seat?"

"No thanks," I said. "Going to bed."

"Good night!" they called as they galloped out the back door and slammed it behind them.

I glanced out the back window. Occasionally, when the barn door opened, I could catch a burst of talk and laughter, so the noise level inside must have been very loud indeed.

"Ms. Langslow?"

I turned to find the chief standing in the doorway.

"What's up?" I asked.

"I've just talked to the DA," the chief said. "He's asked me to put Mr. Oh and Ms. Borgstrom under arrest now. Mr. Oh asked if he could talk to you for a couple of minutes before he leaves."

"No problem," I said. "As long as this doesn't take the place of a phone call to his lawyer."

"His lawyer will be meeting him down at the station," the chief said.

He stepped aside, and Danny entered the kitchen. He was holding a sheaf of papers under one arm. The chief took up a position by the back door, and I could see a tall deputy standing just outside the doorway.

"I'm sorry," Danny said. "I was supposed to be helping you and instead I ruined everything."

I didn't see any reason to disagree with him. If he was expecting me to pat his shoulder and tell him everything would be all right, he was doomed to disappointment.

"Helping you with what?" the chief asked, stepping forward.

"Investigating Dr. Wright and Dr. Blanco," I said. "Before the murder happened, when we thought our only problem was keeping them from canceling the play and shooting down Ramon's dissertation. I figured the more we knew about them, the better able we'd be to find a way to fight them. So I asked my brother to recommend someone to do the computer search. He steered me to Danny."

The chief nodded and stepped back to his place by the door.

"I didn't totally blow off your request," Danny went on. "I started looking for information on Dr. Wright and Dr. Blanco. Mostly about Dr. Wright, of course, because I knew Bronwyn was so down on her. And I admit, I was thinking more about Bronwyn than Ramon."

And perhaps he'd also instinctively realized that Dr. Wright was the real threat.

"And did you find anything of use?" I asked aloud.

"I think she and Blanco are—were . . . you know," he went on. "An item."

I glanced at the chief, who was listening intently and frowning.

"What makes you think that?" I asked Danny.

"Wright was always bonkers, hating drama students and giving them a hard time, but it wasn't till about two years ago that she started pulling the really awful stuff. It's like suddenly she knew she could get away with it."

"Didn't people complain?" I asked.

"At first," he said. "But they figured out pretty quickly that complaining about Dr. Wright was not such a good idea."

"Their complaints were ignored," I said, nodding.

"Worse than that. Bad things happened. Their dorm room assignments got lost, their cafeteria access disappeared, their log-in to the campus computer system stopped working, they couldn't get into the classes they wanted, their student-loan applications got lost in the system until after the deadline. Evil stuff like that."

"And you think Blanco was responsible?"

"I can't speak for the other departments," Danny said. "But with the computer stuff, I know some of the guys who had to deal with cleaning it up, so I got the inside scoop. All the problems came from edits to the student data system made by various accounts in administrative services. Admin services unchecks the field that says you paid your dorm bill and bingo! Someone else shows up with all their stuff, expecting to move into your room. And no one much argues when it comes from admin services because you never get a straight answer—they blame it on the system. Even when they're talking to the people who design and run the system; they don't care, because if you push them too hard, they can make the same bad stuff happen to you."

"And since Blanco's from admin services, he must be to blame?"

"Well, that plus it all started happening a few months after he came. I figured he and Dr. Wright . . . you know."

"You could be right," I said. Not about the romantic relationship—I'd seen the two of them together and hadn't noticed the slightest spark of chemistry between them. If they were romantically involved, Michael should have recruited both of them to teach acting classes. The besotted Danny clearly had romance on the brain.

But as allies in university politics—yes, that made a lot of sense. It explained how Dr. Wright could get away with her abuse of drama students. Any of them who tried to protest would fall victim to the dirty-tricks campaign.

And why was Blanco helping Dr. Wright? If he shared her irrational hatred of the drama curriculum, the persecution would probably continue. But it was looking increasingly likely that his actions were just part of his campaign to ingratiate himself with as many powerful people as possible. He probably played golf with The Face, tennis with the dean of the business school, and bridge with the chair of the math department. And in between singing madrigals with the chair of the history department and hymns with the dean of the religious studies program, he helped Dr. Wright persecute drama students. If that was the case, his opposition to Ramon's play and degree would probably evaporate overnight. Or at a minimum, he'd scramble to stay neutral on all theater issues until the dust settled and he knew how Dr. Wright's eventual replacement felt about the subject.

Which gave us—Abe, Art, and Michael, that is—a priceless opportunity to convince Blanco that it was in his self-interest to support the concept of an independent drama department.

Of course, how could we do that without stooping to his level?

"Anyway, I have this," Danny said, bringing me back to the present. A small sheaf of papers. "I can work on it some more when I get a chance. That kind of depends on whether they put me in jail or not."

If that was a plea for help, at least it was subtle enough that I could ignore it.

"May I see that?" the chief said, stepping forward and holding out his hand for the papers.

"Sure," Danny said. "I made two copies, 'cause I figured you'd want one. It would be great if someone would look into what they did. Maybe clean up some people's lives."

The chief took the papers and did a rapid but thorough comparison between the two sets. Apparently both contained the same things and neither had any secret messages for me. He handed me one copy and tucked the other under his arm.

"Thanks," I said to the chief. "And to you, too," I added, to Danny.

Danny mumbled something that might have been "You're welcome," and slouched out. I could see the tall deputy escorting him down the hall.

The chief stood scribbling in his notebook.

"You said you were arresting Kathy Borgstrom, too," I said. "What about her?"

He sighed and closed his eyes. I waited him out.

TWENTY-SIX

"The DA wants me to hold Ms. Borgstrom as a material witness in Mr. Oh's case," he said finally.

"Not murder?" I asked.

"He's probably going to want me to arrest her for the murder once the tox results come back. This way we can make sure she doesn't disappear before then."

"If you think she's a flight risk, you must think she did it."

"Your daddy would quote Sherlock Holmes at you," he said with a faint smile. "And tell you it was a capital mistake to theorize before you have data."

"But you have some data," I said.

"Yes, and what I have doesn't look good for your friend," he said. "We found some belongings of hers in your library, near the desk."

"She's been out here before," I said. "She must have seen two or three rehearsals this week alone."

"And did you know she was once a graduate drama student?" he asked. "Gave up in the middle of her doctoral program, about ten years ago."

"Here at Caerphilly?"

He nodded.

I hadn't known. I'd heard a rumor that Kathy was

ABD—all but dissertation—but I'd never asked her about it. And ten years ago would have been before Michael was there.

"Was Dr. Wright at the college back then, pulling the same kind of stunts?"

He nodded.

"I suppose that gives Kathy a motive," I said.

He frowned.

"I suppose it does," he said. "Especially since her academic career ended due to an accusation of plagiarism on a paper she wrote for one of Dr. Wright's classes."

"Plagiarism? Kathy?"

He nodded.

"You were unaware of the incident?" he asked.

"Completely," I said. "And it was before Michael's time, but Art and Abe were here ten years ago. If they thought she had committed plagiarism, I doubt they'd let her work in the department."

"I suspected as much," the chief said. "I'll be asking them about it. I wondered if it was generally known."

"No," I said. "And I'll bet anything it was a frame. And I don't believe she was the killer either."

"I'm not happy about it myself," he said. "Blessed if I can explain why. Maybe because I see it's going to be a long haul proving for sure she did it and an even longer one getting a conviction, with all these people running around confusing the case. Or maybe because she seems like a nice lady."

"A nice lady who just happened to commit a murder?"

"A nice lady who should have known murder wouldn't solve anyone's problems."

Except in this case maybe it had. There were probably other English professors who hated the drama department, but none who'd dared to persecute them as blatantly. Even Ramon's and Bronwyn's problems might have been solved by Dr. Wright's death if they hadn't tried to kill her themselves.

"You heading down to interrogate Kathy and Danny?" I asked.

The chief shook his head.

"Their attorneys will probably want us to wait till morning," he said. "And that's fine with me. Been a long day. Though I am going to stick around long enough to watch this rehearsal everyone's so fired up about."

"Are you really interested in watching the rehearsal or do you just want to keep an eye on the rest of your suspects?" I asked.

"A little of both," he said. "I'm curious to see the play that's caused such problems. And did I hear correctly that the college president is here to watch the rehearsal and make a decision about whether the show opens tomorrow night?"

"That's the plan," I said.

"Figure I'd better stick around, then," he said. "I suspect neither Mr. Soto nor Ms. Jones will try to flee the jurisdiction with their play coming up, but if the president cancels it, I wouldn't be surprised if one or both of them tried to pull a bunk. I think I should be here to see what he decides."

"He won't necessarily announce his decision tonight," I said. "He'll probably take the night to think it over. Or to consult with whoever actually makes decisions for him."

"If they're still in suspense, that's fine," he said. "Although I'm probably going to leave at least one deputy here to keep an eye on things, if you don't mind."

"Fine with me," I said. "We still don't know for sure one of them isn't the killer, so the more deputies the better as far as I'm concerned."

"See you at the rehearsal, then."

"Actually, no," I said. "I'm going to bed. This time for real. It's been way too long a day for me already."

"Smart decision," he said. "Good night."

He strolled out the back door.

I sat down and browsed through Danny's finds. I started with Dr. Blanco's information, since it consisted of only half a dozen sheets of paper. No surprises there. According to his CV, he'd graduated from a small Midwestern college that I'd never heard of. Apparently Danny hadn't either—he included a page about it from a college ranking site. A small but respectable liberal arts college in a small town. Did Blanco grow up in the area? And if not, why had he gone so far from home to such a small college? It didn't seem like a place where you'd find a lot of ethnic diversity, so in either case, maybe I was looking at the reason for Blanco's lack of enthusiasm for Latino culture.

The packet wasn't very informative, though. Neither was the larger wad about Dr. Wright. She, too, went to smaller schools, though in her case they were institutions I'd actually heard of. After a few years in an associate professor position at a large state institution, she'd come to Caerphilly twenty years ago, achieved tenure thirteen years ago, and made dean five years after that. None of which shed any kind of light on why she was murdered and who did it. I found myself yawning several times as I leafed through the file and was very close to giving up on the whole thing. Or perhaps saving it for some evening when I was suffering from acute insomnia.

And then the last few pages made the whole effort worthwhile. At first I was puzzled when I found a review of a college production of *The Importance of Being Earnest*. Not, according to the reviewer, a very able production. Of course he sounded like one of those reviewers who adored reviewing flawed shows, the better to show off his own wit and erudition.

I'd have given up after the first snide, gloating paragraph if I hadn't been curious to find out why this was in Danny's file of information on Dr. Wright.

Aha! "Possibly the worst performance came from Jean Wright, woefully miscast as Cecily Cardew." The reviewer went on to eviscerate her performance for another lengthy paragraph. I found myself wondering if the reviewer was perhaps a jilted boyfriend.

The next six pages contained more reviews, each of a play in which Dr. Wright had a part. The best of her reviews was lukewarm, and several other times she was singled out for particularly harsh treatment. And not always by the same person—two other reviewers also panned her performances. The reviews covered a three-year period corresponding to her freshman, sophomore, and junior years in college. In her senior year, she'd either given up acting or stopped being cast. I scanned the reviews again. In the earlier ones, she'd had fairly large roles; in the later ones, she'd sometimes had roles so small that she had to have been pretty awful to be noticed at all, much less singled out for criticism.

"So now we know why she was so down on the drama students," I murmured aloud. "She was jealous."

A pity Kathy hadn't uncovered these reviews. I suspected they might have worked far better for intimidating Dr. Wright than any of the material Kathy had collected about harsh treatment of Caerphilly students.

I tucked the papers under my arm. I'd show them to Michael later. Tomorrow, most probably. Time for me to get to sleep.

"You should be in bed, dear," came a voice from behind me.

"That's just where I'm heading, Mother," I said.

"Good." I turned to see that she was wearing a heavy but elegant coat and hat and pulling on her gloves.

"Going to see the show?" I asked.

"Yes," she said. "After all, 'The play's the thing/ wherein we'll catch the conscience of the king.' "

"Are you implying that the play has something to do with the murder?" I asked. "Or will have something to do with solving it?"

"Half the suspects are in it, aren't they?" she said. "And the other half will be watching. If Chief Burke or your father leaps up in the middle of the second act and announces that he's just solved the murder, I don't want to miss it. What happened in here, anyway?"

She was indicating, with a sweeping arm gesture, the whole cluttered, untidy kitchen. I had my failings as a housekeeper, although keeping a messy kitchen wasn't normally one of them. But under the circumstances . . .

"We've got several dozen extra people living here," I said. "Puts a strain on the kitchen facilities, even if half of the students survive on pizza and Snickers bars. Pretty depressing, isn't it?"

"I could organize those students to come in and clean up," she said. I had to smile. Yes, she probably could. The students wouldn't know what had hit them.

"That's okay," I said. "They're busy, and this is actually better than usual."

Mother took a long, slow look around the room and shuddered.

"You mean it's usually worse?" she asked.

"Yes, but usually it doesn't really bother me," I said. "For some reason, today it does. For the last day or two, actually."

"You're probably getting close to having the babies," Mother said, nodding.

"Well, we knew that," I said, glancing down at the inescapable evidence.

"Very close," she said. "The nesting instinct has kicked in. You should have seen me the three days before you were born. I couldn't live unless I cleaned the house from top to bottom."

"All by yourself?" I asked. Mother's contribution to household cleaning was usually supervisory.

"Of course not," she said. "I had a sudden surge of energy, and you'd be amazed at how much I did, but I couldn't possibly have done it all by myself. Some of the cousins helped."

"Ah." I nodded. That sounded more in character. Mother had always had a curious ability to enlist the members of her large extended family to carry out projects for her. I could envision several dozen aunts and cousins swarming over the house until it was ready for a white-glove inspection while Mother performed the truly challenging tasks like doing the floral arrangements for the dining room and choosing the objets d'art on the coffee table.

"We should probably do the same for your house," she said. "If you don't think the students would be cooperative, I'm sure the family can help out. Let me make a few calls."

She was reaching into her pocket for her cell phone.

"Not tonight," I said. "Just the thought of having more people in the house exhausts me, even if they would be helping out. And even tomorrow would be too soon. Chief Burke would probably rather we wait until his investigation is over before we turn the house upside down."

"But wouldn't it be nice to bring the babies home to a beautifully clean house?" she asked, still holding her cell phone at the ready.

"Yes, just as it would be nice to bring them home to a house that contained nothing but family," I said. "But I'm not going to throw the students out on their ears, so that's not going to happen, either. Rose Noire promised that as soon as I leave for the hospital, she'll get the master bedroom, the master bath, and the nursery in perfect shape. It's not as if I'll be spending much time anywhere else for the first few weeks. If you think some cousins would like to help, you and she can call them when I head off to the hospital. Or recruit them for a grand cleanup once the students finally leave."

"Or both." Mother kissed me on the cheek and turned toward the back door. "I'll talk to Rose Noire, dear. You get some rest."

"That's my plan," I said, as she left.

I picked up my Tupperware doggie container and turned out the light as I left the kitchen.

I found Sammy sitting in one of the dining room chairs in the front hall, with his chin in his hands.

"Good news," I said. "Grandfather's happy to fund the canine DNA tests."

"Good," he said. "Of course, we have to catch the guy first. And the way it's going, I won't even be able to start till tomorrow. The chief wants me to stay around and keep an eye on things here."

"So you're on duty?"

He nodded.

I had a brainstorm. I pulled out my cell phone and dialed the police station. Debbie Anne, the dispatcher, answered as usual.

"Hey, Meg," she said. "How's things there?"

"You waiting around to help process the suspects the chief's sending down?" I asked.

"You guessed it," she said.

"Can you do something for Sammy while you're waiting?"

"Sure thing," she said.

"You know that list of vehicles the chief had you get from the DMV? Could you send it to our fax number?"

Sammy sat up with an eager look on his face.

"I can't exactly share that with a civilian, Meg."

"I know that," I said. "But in about five minutes, Sammy will be calling you from Michael's office to confirm that he and only he is standing there, ready to pull the pages out of the machine."

"I get it," she said. "Give me the number."

I did, thanked her, and hung up.

"Meg, thanks," Sammy said as he headed for the hallway to the office. "I can start studying the list and planning how to tackle them."

"Just don't get so caught up in the list that you let any of our suspects escape," I said to his back.

I continued on up the stairs.

In our bedroom, I found Abe, Art, and Michael.

"You're going to miss the play," I said as I poked my head in.

"We just wanted to have a quick powwow before the rehearsal begins," Abe said.

"Sorry to interrupt," I said.

"I would object if you didn't interrupt," Art said. He stood up, and the others followed suit. "You need rest."

"Finish your conference," I said.

"And you'll want to get dressed for bed," Abe said.

"I can do that later," I said. "I'm going to read for a while first."

Michael hurried to take the leftovers out of my hands and help me onto the bed.

"We're just having a quick conference on how to handle The Face," he said. "We figure now's the time to strike."

"Yes," I said. "From what I can see, Blanco doesn't really have it in for the drama students. He was just trying to please Dr. Wright. So he might be lying low and staying neutral until he sees which way the wind is blowing."

"That's what we think," Abe said. "And we need to do as much as possible to see that it's blowing in our direction."

"You might want to use this," I said. I handed him the wad of papers I'd received from Danny Oh, the thick file folder Kathy had given me, and finally, on top, the paper Josh had given me. Michael and Art came to peek over his shoulders.

"You see!" Michael said, snatching up the copy of Dr. Wright's e-mail. "He did get permission."

"Think what a lot of bother it would have saved if the young fool had kept that e-mail handy," Abe said, shaking his head.

"What's the rest of this?" Art asked.

"Some documents Kathy gave me," I said. "And some stuff from Danny Oh."

I leaned back and uttered a sigh of contentment.

"You're tired," Art said. "You want us to leave? We could find someplace else to do this."

"There isn't anyplace else, and I'm fine," I said. "As

long as I'm awake, you're good company, and when I'm
ready to sleep, you could clog dance on the dresser and it
wouldn't bother me. Just poke me if I snore loud enough
to drown out your discussion."

I picked up my bedside book as if I were planning to
read, to reassure them that they weren't keeping me up.
Michael came over, pulled an afghan over me, and gave
me a quick kiss before returning to join Art and Abe.

After a few moments, I let the book fall on my chest.
I did the yoga breathing exercises Rose Noire had
taught me. I wondered what time it was, but I couldn't
muster the energy to turn my head toward the alarm
clock. Hansel and Gretel were squirming enough to
keep me from falling asleep, but with luck they'd settle
down eventually. And in the meantime, it was peaceful, lying there on our nice, warm bed, listening to the
faint rustle as Michael and his colleagues turned pages.

Eventually, though, the rustle of pages began to be
accompanied by muffled exclamations and sharp in-
takes of breath.

"Good God," Abe said finally, in a low tone. "We
knew we had a problem, with some of our best perform-
ers not wanting to become drama majors."

"And the fact that not a single graduate student has
actually completed a degree in the last three years," Michael added.

"I thought we could get around it by helping them
select English classes with teachers who weren't in on
it," Art said.

"It's gone past that," Abe said.

"We knew it was bad," Art said.

"But not this bad," Abe added.

"Why didn't the students come to us?" Michael said.

"Because you'd have tried to do something," I said

without opening my eyes. "And they know that, and they were afraid you'd all try to do something and end up getting hurt."

A few moments of silence.

"They were trying to protect us?" Michael said.

"And we should have been protecting them," Abe put in.

Something that had been bothering me all day popped back in my mind and I sat up.

"Answer me one question," I said. "If everyone knows Dr. Wright hated drama students so much and did everything she could to torpedo their academic careers, why didn't they just avoid taking her classes?"

"They did, as far as possible," Abe said. "At least after we all realized what she was doing and began steering them away from her classes. But last year she managed to have one of her classes made a degree requirement."

" 'Literature and Popular Culture,' " Art said. "A semester's worth of listening to Dr. Wright rant about everything she hated about the modern world."

"She got Blanco to do it for her," Michael said.

"For years, she and a couple of other English professors have been doing what they could to make life miserable for the drama students," Abe said. "But it wasn't till Blanco started helping them that things got really bad."

"And now we'll never know just why she hated the theater so much," Art said, shaking his head.

"Yes we will," I said. "She was a frustrated actress."

"No way," Michael said.

"Way," I said. "Check the stuff Danny found. Bottom of the stack."

The three of them bent their heads over the photocopies. I settled back under the afghan and listened again to the rustling paper and their muted exclamations.

"Fascinating," Michael said at last. "And while normally I feel sorry for anyone who's been bashed that badly by a reviewer, I can make an exception in Dr. Wright's case."

"Yes," Abe said. "Just because life spoiled her dream of an acting career doesn't excuse her torturing drama students for the rest of her life."

"Inexcusable," Michael said. "But at least now we understand why."

"By the way," I said. "What's the scoop on Kathy Borgstrom? The chief heard that she was expelled from the graduate drama program for plagiarism."

"She was," Abe said. "The charges turned out to be unsubstantiated."

"The charges were phony," Art put in. "It was a frame."

"We have always suspected it was," Abe said. "And we might have been able to prove it if Dr. Wright had been willing to cooperate."

"We did cast enough doubt to allow her to work for the department," Art said.

"So she's got even more reason to hate Dr. Wright," I said.

None of them said anything, so I gathered they agreed with me. And maybe they were wondering, just a little, if Kathy were guilty.

"Should we be going?" Art said, after a while. "It's 7:55."

"No wonder I'm so tired," I muttered. I usually began the night's tossing and turning at eight, and I couldn't remember the last time I'd spent so much of the day not only out of bed, but on my feet.

"Yes," Abe said. "The rehearsal starts in five minutes."

"We need to get seats near The Face," Abe said.

"Ramon's saving us three at the front," Michael said.

"Go get 'em," I murmured.

I heard footsteps. I felt Michael kiss the top of my head and twitch the covers up a little. Then I faded into sleep.

TWENTY-SEVEN

I was dreaming that an army of people was crawling over the house, some of them cleaning it while others messed it up again so the cleaners wouldn't run out of things to do, and all of them keeping me from sleeping. And just when I finally managed to lock myself in the hall bathroom, the doorbell began ringing over and over again.

I woke up and answered the phone.

"Meg?" It was Clarence Rutledge, Spike's vet. "Did I wake you?"

"What's wrong?" I asked, sitting upright. "Is Spike all right?"

"Spike's fine," he said. "You can send someone to bring him home again tomorrow."

"Damn," I said. "I was hoping he'd require at least a week of hospitalization. What about Hawkeye?"

"He isn't fine yet, but he will be eventually," Clarence said. "He's a lucky dog. If Sammy and Horace hadn't gotten him in so fast, and if your father hadn't been around to help—well, all's well that ends well."

"I just hope they catch the bastard who did it," I said.

"That's why I was calling. Is the chief still there?

I've taken the DNA swab from Hawkeye and wanted to find out what to do with it."

"He's out in the barn, watching the play," I said. "You could leave a voice mail on his cell phone."

"Do you have the number?"

I fished out my cell phone, looked up the chief's number, gave it to Clarence, wished him a good night, and turned out the light again.

Unfortunately, by this time I was wide awake.

I tossed and turned for a while, worrying about Kathy, Danny, Ramon, and even the unlikable Bronwyn. And about the play. What was The Face thinking? Were Michael and his colleagues making any progress in the quest for secession?

I finally decided that as long as I was up, I might as well go to the bathroom. I reached over to the bedside table for the flashlight I kept there. I'd gotten in the habit of using the flashlight to keep from waking up Michael every time I had to go to the bathroom in the night.

It wasn't on the bedside table. I turned the light on and looked again. No flashlight anywhere.

Of course, now that I had the light on, I could just as easily have gone to the bathroom without the flashlight. Michael was still down at the rehearsal—probably wouldn't come to bed for hours. But the lack of the flashlight bothered me. I could always just use the light and wake Michael. Or ask him to get me one when he came up to bed. We kept several downstairs in the hall closet.

Or I could go down to the hall closet and fetch one for myself. The self-sufficiency of that pleased me.

I got up, stuck my cell phone in the pocket of my robe, and made my pit stop before heading for the stairs. And then turned back to grab my keys. I remembered that for once I'd actually locked the closet, as we'd been trying to do, so the flashlights and other useful items it contained would still be there when Michael and I went looking for them.

As I climbed down the stairs, I realized that I didn't feel all that bad. In fact, considering how long and exhausting a day I was having, I was feeling remarkably energetic. My back felt better than usual. Perhaps all the exercise was good for me.

Or perhaps I was still revved up from too much excitement.

The front hall was quiet. Apparently Ramon had a full house for the dress rehearsal. I unlocked the hall closet and rummaged through the shelves until I found a flashlight on one of the higher shelves. I tested it— working fine. And then I stuck it in my pocket and turned to go.

Something fluttered to the floor in front of me. I stooped to pick it up and saw that it was a worn envelope in the characteristic pale blue used for all official Caerphilly College papers. And there was something typed on the outside: "Dr. Enrique Blanco—confidential."

I turned it over. It was folded in half, so I unfolded it and saw that although the gummed flap had been sealed at some point, someone had opened it. A good thing, since it saved me from the moral dilemma of whether to unseal it. All I had to do was pop the flap open to sneak a peek at the contents.

I pulled out several folded pieces of paper and opened them up. The top one was a photocopy of a yearbook page. The top half of the page showed a dozen teenagers lined up in two rows under the headline "Business Club." The bottom showed the chess club gathered picturesquely around a table. Two of their number were glaring at each other over a chess board, while the rest assumed eloquent attitudes of fear, triumph, scorn, or indifference. Who'd have expected such a flair for the dramatic from a group normally dismissed as the school geeks? Were any of these hams now treading the boards in our barn? I pored over the photo and studied the names beneath, but none were familiar.

I went back to the top photo. Business club? Was this some kind of organization for high schoolers who had already figured out where they were getting their MBAs and which corporation would be the target of their first hostile takeover? Not my idea of a fun way to spend your after-school hours, and from the looks on the faces of the four girls and eight boys, probably not theirs either. The business club members had "pad your extracurricular activity list for that college application" written all over their faces.

Most were staring awkwardly at the camera, wearing the sort of fixed smiles that always result when the photographer says, "Hold that smile. . . . Just one more shot." And to make it worse, they were all sporting fashions from the late '70s and early '80s, including some truly memorable examples of why big hair had been such a hideous trend. Was it quite fair to shudder at fashion crimes you'd once committed yourself? Surely most of these earnest-looking young future businesspeople had sworn off mullets and Farrah 'dos and grown up to regret what they were wearing here?

At the far right side of the back row I spotted Enrique Blanco. Apart from the slight suggestion of a mullet, his hair wasn't too bad, and his clothes were pretty bland compared to the rest of the crew. Only his air of superiority remained unchanged. He stared out with a faint frown on his face, as if preparing to chide the photographer for taking too much of his valuable time.

I turned my head aside to sneeze. The old papers must be dustier than they looked.

I turned back to the photocopy and read the caption. Just a list of the names, but I studied them anyway.

Odd. Enrique Blanco wasn't listed. Yet there was his face, radiating juvenile pruniness.

I counted the names till I got to the seventh one, corresponding to his place in the group shot. The face I knew as Enrique Blanco was listed as belonging to a Henry White.

Henry White?

Blanco was Spanish for white, and if I wasn't mistaken, Enrique was the Spanish equivalent of Henry. Had Blanco gone through a period of juvenile rejection of his ethnic heritage? Bronwyn wouldn't be surprised.

I flipped the paper over and looked at the next sheet. It was a bad photocopy of what appeared to be a court document of some sort.

After peering at it for a few moments, I suddenly realized what I was seeing. A copy of a twenty-year-old court document granting Henry S. White a change of name to Enrique Blanco.

No wonder Blanco had been so unsympathetic to Ramon's cause and so reluctant to address Señor Mendoza in Spanish. He probably wasn't Latino at all.

The other papers in the envelope were a medley of little Henry's greatest hits since changing his name. Enrique Blanco accepting a scholarship from the Spanish Culture Association. Enrique Blanco awarded a certificate for outstanding Hispanic student at his business school. Enrique Blanco being honored as the Latino administrator of the year by some other organization.

Why had someone hidden an envelope in our closet containing evidence that would do serious damage to Dr. Blanco's career if it were made public?

My nose was tickling again. I turned my head again and sneezed several times.

It wasn't dust. I lifted the envelope to my nose, took a hesitant sniff, and then had to turn aside to sneeze six times in a row. The envelope was permeated with the faintly acrid and completely annoying smell of Dr. Wright's perfume.

Had this envelope come out of Dr. Wright's purse?

Most probably. When she'd looked in her purse for her PDA—was it only this morning?—she'd taken out her wallet and a folded envelope. I was willing to bet this was the same envelope—and also the reason for Blanco's curious willingness to connive in Dr. Wright's persecution of the drama students. If she had proof of his underhanded behavior and threatened him with exposure, he'd probably have done anything she asked. Until he got a chance to eliminate her.

And he had probably taken these papers from her and then hidden them in our closet in case the chief searched him, either individually or as part of a general search of all the suspects. Rotten luck for him that I'd decided to lock the closet after he'd stowed the papers there.

I needed to tell the chief about this. It gave Blanco the strongest possible motive for murdering Dr. Wright. And if he was, by his own admission, her closest friend at the college, who more likely to know about her diabetes?

And from his retreat in my office, out in the barn, he could easily sneak across the yard and in through the sunporch to the library. What if he'd been in the library when Randall Shiffley entered the library? He could have shouted and waved outside the window not because he was trying to get in, but because he was trying to disguise the fact that he'd already entered, killed her, and fled when he heard Randall's approach.

I stuffed the papers back in the envelope and reached for my cell phone as I backed out of the closet.

I bumped into someone on my way out.

"Sorry," I said. "I didn't see you."

Suddenly I felt something cold and hard poking into the middle of my back.

"Don't move."

TWENTY-EIGHT

"Very funny, Dr. Blanco," I said, forcing a laugh and projecting my voice as much as possible. "But I'm a little tired for practical jokes. Why don't—"

"Shut up and give me the envelope," he said, emphasizing his words with a jab from the gun. At least I assumed it was a gun. I didn't think Blanco had enough imagination to fool me with a pencil or an umbrella. "And stop shouting. It won't do you any good. Everybody's out in the barn watching that wretched farce."

"Does that mean you're hoping The Fa—the president will cancel Ramon's show?"

"I couldn't care less whether it's canceled or not," he said. "That was Jean Wright's particular obsession."

"Great," I said. "Then we have no quarrel. Here."

I held the envelope over my left shoulder. After a second, I felt it snatched away.

"Now if you'll just let me go back to sleep—" I began.

"Oh, do shut up," he said, jabbing the gun in my back. "And drop the cell phone."

I complied.

"There's no need to—"

"Shut up!" He jabbed me again. "You're annoying me, and you're going to make me late for my plane."

"Plane?" I echoed.

"Yes, I'm leaving," he said. "And no, I'm not going to tell you where I'm going. Let's just say there's no extradition and my money will be waiting there to meet me."

A sudden thought hit me.

"Your money?" I echoed. "Strictly speaking, aren't we talking about the college's money?"

"Mine now," he said. "And it's all Jean Wright's fault."

"It was her idea to embezzle from the college?"

"No!" His voice was scornful. "She has enough family money to have no financial worries, and she's not interested in anything except her stupid little department. But if she hadn't been blackmailing me to help her with all her dirty tricks, I wouldn't have needed the money. I could have just stayed here and built up my resumé until I finally got a well-paid administrative job at an important college. But then she came along. And I knew sooner or later she'd spill the beans."

"That you'd cheated your way into your position, taking scholarships and awards that were intended for deserving Latino students."

"I was deserving, too," he said. "I was tired of seeing people whose grades weren't any better than mine getting all the breaks just because they belonged to some minority, while I had to work and take out thousands of dollars of loans to get what was being handed to them."

I was tempted to echo Ramon and point out that he didn't know what those other students had gone through to get those grades and what kind of prejudice they'd experienced. But I got a feeling that starting a debate over affirmative action wasn't in my best interest at the moment. Not with my opponent holding a gun at my back.

Suddenly I realized that my legs and feet were wet. Had I peed myself out of fright? Not my normal reaction to danger. I usually coped well as long as a crisis lasted, and then got the shakes afterward. But who knew what the hormones were doing to my normal reactions.

Wait—the hormones . . .

"Oh my God!" Blanco exclaimed. "You just peed on my foot!"

"No, I didn't," I snapped. "My water just broke!"

"Your what?" He stepped away from me, and I'd have breathed a sigh of relief, but when I turned around, the gun was still pointed at me.

"My water," I said. "Amniotic fluid. What the babies are floating in."

"Yuck!" His tone was a curious mixture of disgust and puzzlement, as if he were trying to figure out if this was less gross than being peed on, or more. For that matter, I wasn't sure myself whether my water had broken or whether the stress had made my bladder give way.

"Wait!" he said. "Does this mean—?"

"That I'm going into labor?" I said. "Probably. I have no idea how soon, though. Could be anytime, though since—*aaaaahhhhh!*"

I faked a contraction, clutching the twins and doubling over as if in pain. I wasn't sure how long a first contraction was supposed to last. Probably best if I make it relatively short, though long enough to rattle him. I relaxed my tensed body and glanced back at Blanco.

He was still pointing the gun at me and looked annoyed, not rattled.

"Stop that," he said. "We don't have time for that now."

"I can't very well stop it," I said. "It's labor. It happens when it happens, and you can't—AAAAHHHH!"

This time the contraction was all too real, as if my body wanted to say, "You think that was what labor's like? You have no idea. Watch this!" I vaguely remembered that there was something I was supposed to be doing to get me through this. But what?

Patterned breathing! That was it! If only I could remember how it went. I'd thought the father's role as a Lamaze coach was designed to make him feel like an integral part of the birth process rather than the anxious, useless bystander he'd have been a few decades ago. Now I realized how critical it was going to be to have Michael beside me, shouting instructions about whatever the hell it was I was supposed to do to get through this horrible pain.

"I said stop that!"

It had to be several centuries later, and for all I knew, Blanco had been uselessly nagging at me to stop the whole time.

As the pain finally eased, I heard a burst of laughter in the distance. From the rehearsal in the barn. They had to be pretty loud for us to hear them all the way in here. No way they'd have heard me over that, especially since everyone thought I was upstairs in bed. I was on my own.

"Get up!" Blanco snapped.

I found myself staring up at him from the floor, where I had crouched to ride out the pain. The gun was still pointed at me. I stood up, more than a little shaky. The gun lifted, but only to the level of my belly.

A wave of rage surged through me and I suddenly knew the answer to one of those philosophical questions the students were so fond of debating. Was I capable of killing another human being? Yes, in a heartbeat. At least this particular excuse for a human being. Maybe I wouldn't have felt that way if he'd kept that gun aimed at my head. But there it was, pointing at my twins, and if the sheer force of my anger had any power to touch him, he'd already be lying in small bloody pieces on the ground.

Just wishing him dead wasn't going to work, though. I'd have to figure out a way to make it happen.

"Move!" he said.

"Move where?"

"None of your business. You'll find out when you drive me there."

Like hell was I driving him anywhere. I looked around for a weapon. Nothing but the chair farm and the forest of coatracks and coat trees, all of them draped with wraps. Could I throw a coat over him and smother him to death? Or at least immobilize him long enough to get my hands around his throat?

"My coat's upstairs," I said. "I should—"

"Just borrow someone's," he said.

"If I can find one to fit me," I said, grumbling. I pretended to consider and discard a couple of coats on one of the racks. "Maybe Rose Noire's cape."

I moved on to a large, ornate Victorian coat tree, as if expecting to find the cape there. As my hand touched the sturdy oak upright portion of the tree, I faked another contraction. I figured I knew what the real thing was like now and could do a better job of faking. I grabbed the coat tree as if for support, and as I pretended to hunch over in agony, I turned so I was facing Blanco. I could see through my not-quite-closed eyes that he was flinching a bit. Maybe he was reconsidering the wisdom of taking a hostage who was about to turn into three hostages.

Another wave of laughter from the barn. His eyes flicked toward it, distracted for just a second.

I grabbed the coat tree by the shaft, heaved its base into the air, and lunged at Blanco, holding it under one arm like a lance.

"Take that!" I shouted, as it slammed into his solar plexus.

He doubled over and fell back, landing so hard in one of Michael's exiled office chairs that it skidded across the polished floor and hit the wall with a thud. No use trying to run away, as slow as I was, so I charged after him, dropping the coat tree on the way.

He tried to stand up and failed, of course. No one had yet succeeded in escaping the comfy chairs without a strong push with both arms, and he was still holding the gun in one hand and his precious envelope in the other.

By the time he fell back in surprise, I had grabbed his gun arm and was twisting it, as hard as I could, trying to take the gun away. I slipped, landing hard on his lap, knocking the breath out of him.

"No!" he wheezed. He began pulling the trigger over and over, but I had a good grip on his arm, and the shots fired harmlessly away from us.

Well, not quite harmlessly. A couple of the students' coats would probably have holes in them, and one bullet knocked down a big chunk of the plaster we'd recently paid good money for the Shiffleys to repair and paint.

As soon as I heard the gun click empty, I heaved myself up again.

Blanco was still struggling to rise, and having trouble because he was still holding the gun. If he dropped it and used both arms, or worse, reloaded, I could be in trouble. Surely someone would have heard the shots by now.

I fumbled in my pocket. Aha! My flashlight. I grabbed his hand with one of mine and beat on it with the flashlight until his fingers opened and the gun fell out.

I snagged the gun and stood up, holding it in my right hand and the flashlight in my left. I began backing away, trying to decide if I should run for it. Probably better to find a way to keep him in the chair, since in my current condition I'd have trouble outrunning an elderly snail.

"Meg? Are you all right?"

Help was on the way. Deputy Sammy. I could hear his footsteps running up the front walk.

I pointed the gun at Blanco.

"That's stupid," he said, still a little breathless. "I emptied it while you were attacking me."

"Are you sure?" I said.

I pulled the trigger.

He flinched as the gun clicked uselessly.

"Ah, well," I said.

Just then the front door burst open, and Sammy strode in, holding his gun at the ready.

"Stand back, Meg," he said. "I've got this covered."

I dropped the now-useless weapon and put a well-stocked coatrack between me and the comfy chair Blanco was still trying to get out of.

"Are you Dr. Enrique Blanco?" Sammy asked.

"Yes," Blanco wheezed. "How dare you point that gun at me?"

"Are you the owner of a dark blue Escalade?" Sammy asked, and he rattled off a license number and a VIN number.

Blanco blinked in surprise. Clearly this wasn't what he was expecting to hear.

"Yes," he said.

It wasn't what I was expecting to hear either.

"Arrest him, Sammy," I said. "He's the one who killed Dr. Wright, and he tried to kidnap me."

"And ran over my puppy with his horrible SUV," Sammy said. "Horace is out there taking forensic samples. You'll do time for this, you jerk!"

I heard voices and footsteps coming from the kitchen.

"Meg! Are you all right?" Michael.

"Ms. Langslow?" The chief.

"I'm fine," I called. "And Sammy has your murderer."

TWENTY-NINE

Michael and the chief burst into the hallway in a dead heat. The chief skidded to a stop to draw his weapon and back Sammy up. Michael hurried to my side. Behind the chief, Art, Abe, The Face, Dad, and an assorted crowd of students were jostling in the hallway, trying to see.

"Are you okay?" Michael asked.

"I'm fine," I said. "We need to—"

"She hit me with a piece of furniture," Blanco said.

"That's because he was attempting to kidnap me," I said.

"I can't believe the SUV that hit Hawkeye was parked right outside all day," Sammy said. "If only I'd had a chance to patrol the grounds earlier."

"Sammy!" Horace burst through the front door. "He's got suitcases in his car! He was about to flee the jurisdiction."

"You might want to search the suitcases for wads of cash, or bearer bonds, or whatever absconding embezzlers like to pack these days," I said.

"No, he's probably just taking clothes." Josh pushed through the crowd, carrying a laptop under one arm. "I just figured out a little while ago that he sent a whole bunch of wire transfers this morning to his offshore banking accounts. The college would have been fifty million dollars poorer if he'd gotten away with it."

"Fifty million dollars!" The Face yelped.

"Would have been?" the chief echoed.

"I fixed it," Josh said, punching the air with his fingers as if imitating their rapid flight over the keys of his computer. "The money's all back in his U.S. accounts now. Easier to reclaim."

"No wonder he wasn't paying the damned bills." Randall Shiffley's voice came from the crowd behind the chief.

"His real name's Henry White," I said. "Dr. Wright found out he was pretending to be Hispanic and she was blackmailing him into helping her persecute drama students. He killed her."

"You'll never prove it!" Blanco said.

"We'll see about that," the chief said. "Now, Ms. Langslow, if you could tell me just what—"

"Later," I shouted as another cramp hit me. "Call Dr. Waldron. Take me to the hospital!"

"Breathe," Michael ordered, and he began doing the hee-hee-hee-hoo breathing.

It wasn't just him. I looked up to see not only Michael, but also Art, Abe, and Rose Noire, all hovered over me, going hee-hee-hee-hoo. Dad was checking my pulse. The chief was looking anxiously from me to the coaching squad, as if not sure whether to hee-hoo or not.

"Enough already," I said. "Save it for the next contraction. I need to talk to him."

I pointed to The Face, who started, making his normally handsome features look just a little like those of an anxious sheep. Everyone else turned to stare at him, visibly puzzled.

"Now!" I said. "And give us some privacy," I added. "Everybody out but Michael, Art, and Abe!"

"And me," the chief said.

"I'm staying," Dad said.

"Whatever," I said. "But I need air. Get the rest of these people out of here."

"Everybody out!" the chief said. "Right now!"

People streamed out of the hall in every direction.

"Aren't you going to read me my rights?" Blanco asked.

"You hush up a moment," the chief said. "Your time will come. This could be important."

The Face shuffled cautiously nearer. Just as he reached my side, another contraction hit. I hee-hee-hee-HOO'd though it and when I turned my attention back to The Face, he was wide-eyed with terror.

"Sorry about that," I said. "I'll make this quick. When the chief and his men finish sorting through Dr. Blanco's and Dr. Wright's offices, I think they'll find that in addition to Blanco's fiscal misdeeds, the two of them have been up to a great many things that you don't approve of." At least I hoped Blanco had been pulling the wool over his boss's eyes, not carrying out his policies. If The Face was in on it, Caerphilly was in more trouble than I wanted to imagine.

"Oh, yes, definitely!" The Face said. He was almost babbling. "I can't tell you how dismayed I am. He seemed quite reliable, of course. Unfortunately that led to his being given a great deal of independence. I'm afraid most of his recent actions and decisions will have to be very carefully reviewed by the appropriate administrative entities. There may need to be changes."

"Yes," I said. "For example, you may want to rethink his attempt to cancel the performance of a play by one of Spain's most distinguished living dramatists." Michael coughed slightly at that, but I pressed on. "Think of the international incident that would occur if the play isn't performed. And if the press found out that it was canceled at the behest of a cold-blooded murderer . . ."

"Oh, I'm sure there's no problem with the play going on," The Face said. "It's a little risqué, of course, but then so is Shakespeare at times. I've been quite enjoying the rehearsal. The play can definitely proceed. Is that all?"

"Not quite," I said. "Did you know that my grandfather has been trying to give the college a building?" I asked.

"A building?" The Face liked the sound of that. He assumed the unctuous look he usually reserved for large donors. "What building?"

"A new state-of-the art theater," I said. "Unfortunately, it looks as if Dr. Blanco was trying to get his hands on the money Grandfather was planning to donate and abscond with it."

The Face frowned—a rare expression, and one that could only have been evoked by the idea of someone extracting money from the college coffers rather than adding to them.

"Fortunately, the chief has foiled his plot," I said. "And the donation can go forward. Of course, it comes with a few strings."

The Face sighed. He was probably all too familiar with the kind of strings donors thought up.

"He's taken a dislike to the English department," I said. "Doesn't want to give them a building. Can't blame him, given all the revelations we've had about Dr. Wright's dirty tricks. But if there were an independent drama department to take charge of it . . ."

"Is that possible?" The Face asked.

I glanced at Art and Abe.

"I think you'll find we've already worked out a feasible structure for the change," Abe said. He took The Face by one elbow. Art closed in on the other side, ready to steer him away and close the deal. Abe gave me a thumbs-up sign behind The Face's back.

"Good work," Michael said.

"Once the department's independent, I think you should talk Kathy Borgstrom into reapplying for the Ph.D. program," I said.

"That's a great idea," he said. "But right now we need to head for the hospital."

"One more thing," I said. "Where's Grandfather?"

"Right here!" He stumped in from the living room. "I overheard you talking to that bureaucrat. You think I'll get my building?"

"Odds are good," I said. "Meanwhile, I'd really like to come home to a house empty of students."

"I hear you," he said. "I'd like to move back to the Caerphilly Inn, but fat chance of that, either. No offense, but your guest room doesn't quite match a five-star hotel. Still, it'll have to do till they fix the heating plant."

"Randall!"

Randall Shiffley loped into the room.

"Thanks," he said. "Looks like we've solved the mystery of why that jerk wasn't paying me. Maybe I won't go broke after all."

"If someone were willing to front you the money to buy that part for the heating plant, how fast could you get the damned thing working?" I asked.

Randall and my grandfather looked at each other.

"I'm not sure we could have it done by the time you get home," Randall said. "They kick new mothers out of the hospital awfully soon these days. But I'll do my damnedest."

"How much money do you need?" my grandfather said.

"Go talk about it somewhere else," Michael said as he helped me to my feet. "We have a rendezvous with an obstetrician."

"Meg, can I have the gun now?" Horace asked.

"Okay, Dr. Blanco," the chief said. "You're under arrest. Sammy, read him his rights."

"You have the right to remain silent," Sammy began.

"I'll give my statement later," I said as Michael opened the door.

"Hey," Randall called. "You still haven't told us what you're having. Boys, girls, or a mixed set?"

"Wait and see," Michael and I said in unison.

Read on for an excerpt from

THE REAL MACAW

—the next Meg Langslow novel from
Donna Andrews and St. Martin's Paperbacks:

"Stop!" I hissed. "Bad dog! Don't you dare bite me!"

Spike, aka the Small Evil One, froze with his tiny, sharp teeth a few inches from my ankle. He looked up and growled slightly.

From one of the cribs across the room I heard another of the faint, cranky whimpers I'd detected over the baby monitor. Jamie always woke up slowly and fussed softly for a few minutes, which gave us a fighting chance of getting to the nursery to feed him before he revved up to cry so loudly that he woke his twin brother. Josh never bothered with any kind of warning, going from fast asleep to wailing like a banshee in two seconds or less.

"I mean it," I said to Spike. "No more treats. No more sleeping in your basket here in the nursery. If you bite me again, you're out of here. Back to the barn."

Do animals understand our words, or do they just pick up meaning from our tone of voice? Either way, Spike got the message.

He sniffed at my ankle. Pretending to recognize my scent, he wagged his tail perfunctorily. Then he trotted back to his basket, turned around the regulation three times, curled up, and appeared to fall asleep.

I tiptoed over to Jamie's crib in time to pick him up and shove the bottle in his mouth a split second before he began shrieking.

I settled down in the recliner and leaned back slightly. Not for the first time, I felt a surge of gratitude to my grandfather, who had given us the recliner and helped me fight off all Mother's attempts to banish it as an eyesore from the nursery she had decorated so elegantly in soft tones of lavender and moss green.

Eventually, Jamie finished his milk and fell asleep. I gazed down at him with maternal affection—and maybe just a guilty hint of gratitude that he and his noisier brother were, for the moment, both fast asleep and not demanding anything of me.

I pondered whether to get up, put him in his crib, and go back to bed, or whether it would be just as efficient to doze here until Josh woke up for his next bottle. If I dozed here, I could turn off the baby monitor and make sure Michael got a full night's sleep, so he'd be well rested for teaching his Friday classes.

Or should I rouse myself to pump some milk for the boys' next meal? I glanced at the clock—a little after 2:00 A.M. Dozing was winning when an unfamiliar noise woke me up.

It was a dog barking. And not Spike's bark, either. At eight and a half pounds, Spike tried his best, but could never have produced the deep basso "woof!" I'd just heard.

Or had I just imagined it? I wriggled upright and stared over at Spike.

He was sitting up and looking at me.

"Did you hear anything?" I whispered.

He cocked his head, almost as if he understood.

We both listened in silence for a moment. Well, almost silence. I could still hear the faint, almost restful sounds of the white noise machine we ran at night to minimize the chances of some stray sound waking up the boys.

Just as I was about to relax back into the recliner, I heard another noise. This time, it sounded more like a cat meowing.

Spike lifted his head and growled slightly.

"Shush," I said.

There was a time when shushing Spike would have egged him on. But almost as soon as we'd brought the twins home, he had appointed himself their watchdog and guardian. His self-assigned duties—barking whenever he thought they needed anything, and then biting anyone who showed up to take care of their needs— were made all the more strenuous by the fact that in spite of our efforts, the boys maintained completely opposite sleep schedules, so there was nearly always at least one twin awake and requiring Spike's attention. After four months, like Michael and me, he'd learned to grab every second of sleep he could.

He curled back up on the lavender and moss-green cushion in his bed and appeared to doze off. He looked so innocent when asleep. An adorable eight-and-a-half-pound furball. What would happen when the boys started crawling, and mistook him for a stuffed animal?

I'd worry about that later.

I sat up carefully to avoid waking Jamie, and managed to deposit him, still sleeping, on the soft, lavender flannel sheet in his crib. I glanced over to make sure Josh was still snoozing in his own little moss-green nest. Then I tiptoed over to the nursery door, opened it, and listened.

I could hear rustling sounds that weren't coming from the white noise machine. Soft whines. An occasional bark. Meows. Cat hisses.

Probably only someone in the living room watching Animal Planet on the big-screen TV and being inconsiderate about the volume. Most likely my brother Rob, and it was just that sort of behavior that had inspired us to get the white noise machine.

But white noise wouldn't keep the growing commotion downstairs from waking Michael, who had to work tomorrow. Or five-year-old Timmy, our newly acquired long-term houseguest, who needed to be up early for kindergarten.

Unless of course Timmy was downstairs with Rob, watching television on a school night again.

"Woof!"

Definitely a dog, and not Spike, and it sounded a little too immediate to be coming from the television. Had Rob, miffed that Spike had deserted him for the twins, acquired a new four-legged friend? Or perhaps the local burglars were celebrating Bring Your Dog to Work Day.

I turned the monitor back on, slipped out of the nursery, and closed the door behind me. Now that I didn't have the white noise machine to mask it, I could hear rather a lot of animal noises. A few barks and yelps. And an occasional howl that sounded more like a cat. Definitely not burglars, unless they'd stopped in midcrime to watch Animal Planet. Time to go downstairs and see what was up. I didn't exactly tiptoe, but I moved as quietly as possible. If someone had smuggled in a contraband menagerie, I wanted to catch them red-handed.

I stopped long enough to peek into the guest room that had become, for the time being, Timmy's room. He was fast asleep with his stuffed black cat clutched under one chubby arm. Under any other circumstances, I'd have been tempted to fetch the digital camera and take a photo I could e-mail to his mother to prove that yes, he'd settled in fine and was enjoying his stay. And maybe ask again if she knew just how long that stay would be. But that could wait. I shut his door to keep out the increasing din and crept downstairs to track the din to its source.

No dogs festooning the tall oak staircase or lurking in the front hall. I even glanced up at the double-height ceiling, because my first martial arts teacher had railed about how most people never looked up and were thus remarkably easy to ambush from above. No dogs or cats perched on the exposed beams, and no bats or ninjas hanging from the chandelier.

I stopped outside the wide archway to the living room, reached inside to flip on the light switch, and stepped into the room.

"Oh, my God!" I exclaimed.

The room was entirely filled with animals.

A dozen or so dogs, ranging in size from terriers to something not much smaller than a horse, were in the middle of the floor, lapping up water from several serving dishes from my best china set. Bevies of cats were perched on the oak mantel and on the tops of the bookshelves, some gobbling cat food from antique china dishes while others spit and hissed at the dogs and uttered unearthly howling noises. One irritable-faced

Persian was hawking strenuously, apparently trying to launch a hairball at our wedding photo.

Several rows of crates and animal carriers were ranged up and down both sides of the room, some empty, while in others I could see eyes and noses of dogs and cats peering out at their liberated brethren and perhaps wondering when their turn for the food and drink would come.

A tiny black kitten was licking the oriental rug— had we spilled milk there, or did he just like the taste of rug?

A Siamese cat had ventured down from the mantel and sat atop a leather photo album on our coffee table, fixedly eyeing a cage in which a small brown hamster was running frantically in his wheel, as if hoping that he could propel the cage away from the cat with enough effort. Several less anxious hamsters and guinea pigs gazed down from cages perched on other bits of furniture.

On our new sofa, an Afghan hound sprawled with careless elegance, like a model artfully posing for a photographer, its white fur vivid against the deep turquoise fabric.

"Hiya, babe! How's about it?"

A bright blue parrot was fluttering in a cage just inside the door. I eyed him sternly, and he responded with a wolf whistle.

"Meg! Uh . . . what are you doing awake at this hour?"

My father had popped up from behind the sofa. He was holding a small beagle puppy in each hand. The two puppies were struggling to get at each other, and from the soprano growling that erupted from behind the sofa, I suspected there were other juvenile beagles still on the floor, tussling.

"I was feeding the boys," I said. "What the hell are you and all these animals doing here?"

Dad looked uncomfortable. His eyes scanned the room as if seeking a safe place to set down the beagles, though I suspected he was merely avoiding meeting my eyes.

"We won't be here long," said a voice behind me.

The tall, lanky form of my grandfather appeared in the hall. He was carrying two Limoges soup tureens full of water.

"If you were thinking of giving those to the dogs, think again," I said. "They belong to Mother, who will eviscerate you if you break them."

"Oh," he said. "They were just stuck on a high shelf in the pantry—I thought they were things you didn't use much."

"We don't use them much, mainly because they're expensive antiques that Mother lent us for that big christening party we threw last weekend," I said. "And they were on a high shelf in the pantry to keep them as safe as possible until we got a chance to return them. I can show you some crockery you can use, but first I want to know what all these animals are doing here."

"It's no use," came another voice. "The window's too small."

I turned to see the enormous leather-clad form of Clarence Rutledge, the local veterinarian. Since Grandfather was an avid animal welfare activist and Dad a sucker for anything on four legs, the menagerie in our living room was beginning to make a little more sense. But only a little.

"You were trying to break into the barn, I suppose." They all looked a little startled at what I assumed was a correct guess. "We keep it locked, since all my expensive blacksmithing equipment is out there. But I might be persuaded to unlock it, if somebody could just tell me what the hell is going on."

They all exchanged looks. One of the beagles Dad was still holding began peeing on him. He rushed to deposit both puppies on a nest of newspapers in a corner.

I fixed my gaze on Grandfather.

"It's all Parker's fault," he said. "If he'd showed up on time, we never would have come here. I'm going to call him again."

As if that had explained everything, he stumped over to our living room phone.

"Want to use this?" My father held out his beloved iPhone.

"No, I want a real phone," Grandfather said. He began dialing a number from memory.

I looked at Clarence.

"It's a matter of life or death!" he exclaimed. He clasped his hands as if pleading for mercy, clenching them so hard that the tattooed ferrets on his burly forearms writhed.

I looked at Dad. The weather was mild, not warm, and yet his bald head glistened. Nerves, probably. A trickle of sweat began running down his face, and he dabbed at it absentmindedly with one of the puppies.

"Just why is our living room filled with dogs, cats, puppies, kittens, hamsters, guinea pigs, and parrots?"

"Only the one parrot," he said. "A macaw, actually—very interesting species."

"Hiya, babe!" the macaw said.

"Whatever," I said. "Why are they here?"

"It's because of that new county manager," Dad said.

"Horrible man," Clarence muttered.

"You mean Terence Mann?" I asked.

"Dammit, Parker, answer your bloody phone!" Grandfather snarled into the receiver.

"Hey, Clarence!" My brother, Rob, bounced into the room. "There's a window open on the second story of the barn! So if you can help me haul the ladder over, we can— Oh. Hi, Meg."

"Hi," I said. "What's your version?"

"My version?" Rob looked guilty for a moment. He fiddled with the black knit cap that concealed his shaggy blond hair, then his face cleared. "I was helping Dad and Granddad."

"Helping them do what?"

"Foil the new county manager," Dad repeated. "That Mann fellow. He's cutting the budget right and left."

"Probably because the town of Caerphilly will go bankrupt if he doesn't," I said.

"And most of his cuts we can understand, no matter how much we hate them," Clarence said. "Cutting back on the library hours."

"And the free clinic hours," Dad added.

"Postponing the teachers' raises," Rob said.

"But then he decided that the town animal shelter was too expensive," Grandfather said. "So he said the town could no longer afford for it to be a no-kill shelter."

"Can he do that?" I asked.

"Well, in the long run, probably not," Clarence said. "Public opinion is against it, about four to one. But we were afraid that some of the animals might be harmed before we could convince him to reverse his policy."

"So you adopted all of the animals from the shelter?" I asked.

"No, actually we burgled the place and stole them," Rob said.

"Wonderful," I said. "Our living room isn't just filled with animals. It's filled with stolen animals."

"Rescued animals," Grandfather said.

A burglary. Well, at least that explained why all four of them were dressed completely in black. Individually, none of them looked particularly odd, but anyone who saw the four of them skulking about together in their inky garb would be instantly suspicious.

"Did you really think you could get away with it?" I asked aloud.

"We don't care if we get away with it," Grandfather said, striking his noblest pose.

"Once the animals are safely out of his clutches, we don't care what happens to us," Dad said, following suit.

"And we knew Mann would quickly figure out that prosecuting us wouldn't do him much good in the eyes of the public," the more practical Clarence added.

I looked around. Okay, the animals were refugees. They might have been saved from an untimely death. Of course, that didn't make it any less annoying to see them lying on, shedding on, and in a few cases, chewing or peeing on our rugs and furniture. At least, thanks to the child gates we'd recently put up in all the doorways in case the boys started crawling early, the livestock weren't free to roam the whole house.

"The problem is that they're not safely out of his clutches," I said. "What now? Were you planning on hiding them in our barn until you change the county manager's mind?"

"We weren't going to bring them here at all." Dad plopped down on the sofa with a sigh. The Afghan hound scrambled over to put its head in his lap. The patch of upholstery it had vacated was covered with so much shed fur that it looked like tweed. "We'd arranged to have them taken to new permanent or foster homes outside the county," Dad went on.

"Outside the state, in fact," Grandfather said. "Parker Blair made the arrangements."

"He has that big truck he uses to make deliveries from his furniture store," Dad explained.

"We were going to meet Parker at midnight down by the haunted graveyard, load all the animals on his truck, and there you have it!" Rob exclaimed. "Like *The Great Escape,* with poodles."

"Unfortunately, Parker hasn't shown up," Grandfather said. "I've been leaving messages for nearly two hours now. Not sure what the holdup is, but as soon as he gets here, we can load the animals and have them out of your hair. But in the meantime—"

"Shhh!" Clarence hissed. He was peering out one of our front windows. "It's the cops!"

Everyone froze—even the animals, who seemed to sense danger.

I strolled over to the window and looked out.

"It's only Chief Burke," I said.

"Oh, no!" Dad wailed.

"We're lost," Clarence muttered.

"Get rid of him," my grandfather said.

The chief was getting out of his car. I hadn't heard a siren, but I could see that he had the little portable flashing light stuck on his dashboard.

"If he were just calling to see the babies, maybe I could." I glanced at my watch. "But the chief doesn't usually make social calls at two thirty in the morning."

"Then stall him while we move the animals," Dad said.

"Move them how?" Clarence asked. "All the pick-ups are out front where he's probably already seen them."

"Put the animals in the barn till Parker gets here," my grandfather said. "I'll call him again."

He grabbed our phone and began dialing. Dad leaped off the sofa, picked up a puppy in one hand, and grabbed the macaw's cage with the other.

"All gone!" the bird trilled.

"I wish," Clarence muttered.

The windows were cracked slightly, to let in a little of the mild April air—or possibly to prevent the smell of the animals from becoming overwhelming. I could hear the staccato sounds the chief's shoes made on our front walk.

"There is no way in the world I can stall the chief while you move all these animals to the barn," I said. "And even if I could, do you think they'd go quietly?"

As it to prove my point, one of the dogs uttered a mournful howl, and several others whimpered in sympathy. I even heard a faint bark from the porch.

"Besides," I added, "the chief has probably already spotted the dog you left outside."

"What dog?" Dad asked.

"I thought they were all accounted for." Clarence was fishing in his pockets for something. "We have an inventory."

"Dammit, Parker, pick up!" Grandfather muttered.

The dog on the porch barked again.

"Just let me handle it," I said. "The chief's an animal

lover. He probably won't approve of your methods, but I'm sure he shares your concerns. Let me assess what kind of a mood he's in. Maybe we can work something out."

Clarence and my father looked at each other, then back at me.

"What else can we do?" Dad said.

The dog outside barked.

The doorbell rang.

Upstairs, Josh erupted into howls.

"Damn," I said, pausing halfway to the door. "I was trying to let Michael sleep."

"I'll take care of the baby," Clarence said, bolting for the stairs. "You deal with the chief."

"Why doesn't the bastard answer his phone?" Grandfather growled.

"Hiya, babe!" the macaw said.

"Put a lid on him," I said to Dad, as I turned back to the door.

He scrambled to pull a tarp over the cage.

Upstairs, Jamie joined the concert.

"I've got it," Michael called from upstairs.

"I'm almost there," Clarence called, from halfway up the stairs.

I opened the door. The dog outside barked again, but I pretended not to hear him and didn't look around to see where he was.

"Good morning, Chief," I said. "What are you doing up at this hour, and more important, what can we do for you?"

The chief held up a cell phone. I looked at it for a moment.

The cell phone barked. Clearly it belonged to a dog

lover. No one else would choose such an annoying custom ring tone.

"I'm investigating a murder," Chief Burke said. "And I came over to ask why for the last couple of hours, you've been trying to call the dead guy's cell phone."